PEDRO'S THEORY

PEDRO'S THEORY

REIMAGINING THE PROMISED LAND

MARCOS GONSALEZ

MELVILLE HOUSE
BROOKLYN • LONDON

Pedro's Theory: Reimagining the Promised Land

First published in January 2021 by Melville House

First Melville House Printing: January 2021

"Grow Up, Pedro" was previously published in *carte blanche* 33, Summer 2018

A previous version of "Cousin of a Cousin Named Pedro" was published on *Catapult* on November 16, 2017

"Pedro Full of Grace" was previously published in *Black Warrior Review*, Winter 2018

"A Brief and Uneventful History of Burlap" was previously published in *Ploughshares*, Spring 2019

"Border Theories" was previously published in the *New Inquiry* on November 13, 2017

Melville House Publishing
46 John Street
Brooklyn, NY 11201

and

Suite 2000
16/18 Woodford Road
London E7 0HA

mhpbooks.com
@melvillehouse

ISBN: 978-1-61219-862-0
ISBN: 978-1-61219-863-7 (eBook)

Library of Congress Control Number: 2020945253

Designed by Beste M. Doğan

Printed in the United States of America
1 3 5 7 9 10 8 6 4 2

A catalog record for this book is available from the Library of Congress

To write the body.
Neither the skin, nor the muscles, nor the bones,
nor the nerves, but the rest: an awkward, fibrous,
shaggy, raveled thing, a clown's coat.

—Roland Barthes,
Roland Barthes by Roland Barthes

Return is as much about the world to which
you no longer belong as it is about the one in which you
have yet to make a home.

—Saidiya Hartman,
Lose Your Mother

We live by recouping mournful images, whose
number we can never guess.

—Edmond Jabès,
The Little Book of Unsuspected Subversion

CONTENTS

PROLOGUE

TO A FATHER AND SON

The world will come between you.

But for now, for this photographic moment, you are father and son. Embraced. Two together there in the early nineties. The soft eyes looking forward, what looks to be soft skin, what is difference of skin. Father's hands clasp the son's, man holding child, loving tenderly. Both are seated on the couch belonging to the son's grandmother. This is not the father's mother but a woman through time he will come to know well. He, like her, a far-flung soul, a weary body, she from the beaches and waters of the Caribbean and he from the mountains and lakes of Mesoamerica. Hundreds of years of history, conquest, migration, and survival coming together to form a point of convergence in a small town in New Jersey. One photograph can tell so much.

Who takes the photo? No one seems to know, and no one can remember. All there is of a time and place and moment is a photograph. Two bodies in a photograph who I don't even know, strumming my fingers twenty years or so later across an image of my father and my younger self hoping to recall the moment, for memory to activate. But from this still life all

I get are fantasies. Imagining moments on that couch, held, napping away summer afternoons. Laughing on his back as he does push-ups on wintry morning days. Contemplative stares into brown eyes during cool spring nights.

I think of all this past that is and is not mine as so ordinary. Just life, just living. Because if I do not, if I do not stretch a photograph beyond its frame, into language, into story, into feelings, then you two are lost to me forever. If I do not push to remember again, remember anew, then I relegate you to the dustbins of history, to the narrative of pain and disconnection perpetrated by the world outside. I know how the world will tell me how to think about the father and son. How the world will tell me how to think about the father, of his skin, his place of origin, his condition of being in these Americas. How the world will tell me how to think about the son, of his body and mind, to hate and despise all that he is, all that he comes from. I know how shame and internalized hatred will define how I think of you two for so long. I know how your story will unfold, which is why looking at this photograph is that much harder to do.

I don't know you two anymore. Maybe I never really knew you to begin with. So this is a letter addressed to two people who reside in an image, which is to say, this is a letter to no one, and a letter to no one is a letter to anyone. To all the anyones we never got to be, all the anyones denied us, to all the anyones who need to live again. What I know I take from the photographs of those early years of the boy's life. Each in their context, in their place, bearing their particularities. I look through them, glide fingertips across their surface, hoping to know some concrete story, wanting epiphanies and revelations, but instead I am met with daydreams and musings, mourning and loss. In these photographs I wander in the fulfilling nothingness of the what could have been.

The writing in these pages will take many shapes. Reminiscences, speculations, and reckonings. They will be letters like this one, addressed to you and to others. They will be displacements in the third person of my childhood self. They will be monologues and ruminations from this person who I am today. They will be present tense wanderings. Above all, these are words reaching out to the two in this photograph, to their many selves across time and space, where past becomes present becomes future all at once, reaching out to the many lives they are connected to, known and unknown, words reaching out across the vastness of time and space.

The world will come between you. Father and son. Boy and man. Kin and kind. But for now, for this photographic moment, you are father and son, smiling and embraced, telling a different story from the one you both carry the burden of having to know.

PART I

PEDRO ON MAIN STREET USA

I

GROW UP, PEDRO

1

Sunlight. Treetops garlanded by a cotton candy–like mass of white, the sagging pouches of it skimming the heads of passersby. Little bodies wriggle in the white-webbed splendor, trying to break free, trying to plummet to the ground in order to feed. It's the season when a great migration settles in a backyard. A mass metamorphosis on the horizon.

A boy contemplates down below. A thought on the butterfly-to-be, then another on the voyage south, the journey through the Americas, these thoughts strung together concerned over the brief life of the butterfly. A net is in his hand. He wants to catch one to look closely at the features of it. Then, as quickly as he captures it, he will let it be free.

In the distance a woman's voice. Familiar to him. *"Marcos, ven a comer! Marcosssss!"* She is calling him home to eat. He walks and he will pass through his neighborhood. There down the street are his sister and brother playing basketball with their high school friends. There on the corner of the block is the old Puerto Rican couple who breed rabbits. There is his mother on the other road gossiping with the neighbor. There down the street men outside on lawn chairs drinking beers, mariachi music playing, men with field dust all over their clothes and hair crooning off-key. There's his father in his brown truck driving a friend to his house in the trailer park nearby.

The boy gets home within a few minutes. His grandmother is at the front gate. *"Que andariego tu eres . . ."* she says to him, playful and stern. She thinks he wanders the street too much, thinking this boy is too bold, too in the world. She will say this to the boy even into the days when he becomes a man, andariego

andariego

andariego

andariego,

saying this word to him as he travels across the Americas, the Americas she has traveled herself, saying this word until the end of her days, until he must be an andariego all alone.

The setting sun shines upon her thick-lensed glasses. She smiles. A wrinkle there, a wrinkle here, she wears her age upon her face with resplendence. They go into the house together, and the screen door closes behind them.

THERE'S NO BETTER storyteller than a child. Broke one of the fancy plates in the kitchen? Cousin Juan did that when he was running through the house dribbling a basketball and blah blah blah. What did you do at school today? I made a book and wrote a whole story about a mermaid princess who blah blah blah. Any situation becomes an opportunity to prove one's skills at imagining a world a bit larger, a bit more magical.

I don't know how to tell such stories as a kid. I am blamed for something and I just say no I didn't do it, the waterworks ensuing. I come home from school and tell no one of my day. As a child, I don't feel myself as having a language in which to tell these stories. Speaking both Spanish and English, I live in a dual world, a world divided, a dizzying world. Spanish is spoken with my grandmother and father, with my siblings it is English, with my mother English and Spanish, and in school it is only English. Words zigzag in my brain with no pattern to their movement. I speak and I don't know exactly how these words are forming, how the meaning is coming across, if I am articulating myself at all.

As an adult I struggle to tell stories, to know what language I can tell these stories in. Who is the boy there in the photo smiling in front of his birthday cake? How can he smile with so much strife behind those brown eyes? I struggle to articulate childhood Marcos, the matter of his history, his being in a small town in the United States. His 1990s self is and is not a presence in this second decade of the twenty-first century. Awaiting the day his story, his many stories, can find a language in which to be told, in which to be communicated. Waiting . . . and waiting . . . waiting as he has been doing for a lifetime . . .

2

COLORED BLOCKS on the floor, the grind of the pencil sharpener, alphabet posters on the walls. Children's voices rising and falling. The boy is stimulated by all this newness. These are not the children of his neighborhood. He marvels at a Rebecca's platinum blonde hair, the blue of a David's eyes, the pigmentation of an Abigail's skin. They are foreigners to him.

He contemplates but soon enough there is an interruption. The teacher looks at him from the chalkboard. Her face is pinched, her teeth gritted, her eyes blue and sinister. The teacher descends upon him, a bony colossus. Everyone is watching. *"Do not speak that language here. Am I making myself clear?"* That language? *Lang-uage. Lan-g-uage.* He tries to say the word but trips over the syllables. He does not know what she means by that word. All he knows are the eyes upon his body, a shame and a guilt he cannot find the source of, the difference he feels himself to be.

He does not speak again until sometime in the first grade.

NEW EGYPT, NEW JERSEY, is the small place on the map I have the privilege of calling my hometown. Mostly a farming town, which is why my family came here to begin with, but now it's a middle-class haven of housing developments. There are four schools, a primary, an elementary, a middle, and a high school, which are where I spend most of my time from the ages of five to eighteen. The center of the town is Main Street. The road well-paved, the mom and pop stores, the potted plants hanging from the lampposts. There's a grocery store where the local people can buy their goods without having to leave the parameters of the town. There's one Chinese restaurant, a little Mexican grocery store, and that's about as far as cultural diversity goes. This town is its own self-contained universe because that's what the people who live there want for themselves. Towns like this one all across the United States wanting something secure, something quaint, something all their own without the threat of difference entering. Why would you ever want to leave?

On the outskirts of the town is the neighborhood I grow up in. I am raised here by my parents, my grandmother, and my older brother and sister. My grandmother has her own house, which is where I spend most of my time, and my mother is the renter of various homes a minute's walking distance away throughout the years. My father and mother argue frequently, which culminates in my father getting kicked out. Sometimes he's gone for days, sometimes weeks, and other times months. My brother and sister are ten years older than me, where I'm the youngest, and they have a different father than mine. Their father was my mother's first love, a Puerto Rican chulo from Florida. My brother is the jokester of the family, six-foot-something, charming, and the very definition of masculinity. He always has a big smile on his face, an affectionate smile, which does a great job of masking the hurt he carries with him over his father leaving him when he was little. My sister is the bossy oldest sibling, always wanting to be in charge.

The little boys and girls who are my classmates growing up call this neighborhood "the Mexican ghetto." They call this place a ghetto because my neighborhood houses the new wave of Mexican, Guatemalan, and Honduran immigrants who are working the fields in the area. According to them, this ghetto is a place of lawlessness. Where children run the streets naked and dirty. Where we hang our wet laundry to dry because we cannot afford dryers. Where the people don't take showers. Where drugs are sold and drunks spill out on the street. Where music-playing rancheras and mariachis blare out at all hours of the day. Where women give birth to children when and how they want. Where immigration authorities and cops stake out our houses on the regular and conduct violent raids every other week. A no-man's-land of savages, the townsfolk say.

My father is one among this new population that lives here. Before his migration in the late eighties, there is another. Through the late sixties, seventies, and early eighties the neighborhood is a Puerto Rican neighborhood. This is the migration that includes my mother. My grandparents move into this neighborhood all the way from Brooklyn after having been told by another Puerto Rican friend how quiet and quaint this little area is. The houses small but cheap. The land spacious and not cramped like a New York City tenement. Opportunity for field work and domestic work. There is possibility here whereas in Puerto Rico and New York City they do not see much possibility. In this small town, in this neighborhood tucked away on the edge of it, they think they have a better chance of attaining the American dream. My grandparents are gone now, the house they lived in condemned and overtaken by the flora and fauna of the adjacent woods, nature taking what is hers to take. I still wonder if my grandparents found what they were looking for all those years ago when they decided to come to this small town. I wonder if they ever found their American dream.

This neighborhood where my parents meet, where I am born and raised, is a spot of brown amongst a surrounding mass of white. We are a fascinating anomaly for the white population of the town. A place to gawk at, to joke about, to conduct violent fantasies in when they dare even step foot in our boundaries. A place where the border between the United States and Mexico materializes. A place where the ocean between the mainland United States and the island of Puerto Rico opens up. A place where all the nobodies of the Americas come to congregate in order to debauch and terrorize and infest the United States, according to them. I live for nearly twenty years in this place constructed by the white imagination. And through this white imagining is how I conceive an image of myself and my family for the decades to come. An image of myself I have had to fight against day in and day out.

My parents no longer live in this town but they live nearby. Fifteen minutes away or so. Anytime I return to visit them, I like to drive over to New Egypt and cut directly through Main Street. I go to see what's new. A barbecue wing joint and a bagel shop are the newest additions. The video rental store long gone, the barbershop my grandmother's uncle worked at no more, the gas station bulldozed over. I ride through to feel nostalgic over a place I called home. But was it ever really home? Can you really call a site of cruelty and violence your home? Can you call a place of fantasy your home?

Each time I drive through Main Street I feel a welled-up rage build inside of me. A rage at how surfaces can lie to you. At how easily white America can hide its cruelty behind a veneer of innocence that is really just blatant ignorance. A rage at wishing others could see through the façade of what I had to endure.

Each time I drive through Main Street and feel this welled-up rage, this chest tightening and loss of breath, I know it's the little boy, the little Marcos, coming out, begging to be heard, begging to be seen, begging to get another chance at life, a life that does not have to be the one he had to live through for all those years.

THE SMALL ROOM encloses him. The boy cannot focus. The objects in the room steer him from Mr. S—, the man who takes the boy every day from his kindergarten classroom, the man who has many tools with which to quiz the boy. He is quizzed on words, on syllables, on pronunciations, on language. A card with an image is raised and the boy states what it is.

"No, it is not. What is this, Marcos?"

The yellow fruit shaped like a crescent moon is what he said it is.

"Guineo, it's a—"

"No, Marcos, tell me what this really is."

The boy thinks on this question but he is not sure he is doing it right, he thinks and he thi—

"Look at the picture and think hard about what it is."

The answer to the question is how the boy's grandmother or father would answer, how those in his family and neighborhood would answer. After all, he is of them, their ways of speaking, their kin and kind. This man, though, is not like them. The answer the man is demanding, then, if the correct answer is to be given, is one of Mr. S—'s making, somewhere in this room, in the likeness of his being.

The difference between the man and the boy's family is the answer.

"A banana. It's a banana."

"Yes it is, Marcos. Very good. What about this? What do you call this?"

3

AS A kid, I am such a crybaby. I cry *a lot.* Grow up, my siblings say, as I sit in a corner huffing and puffing, hoping someone will come over to console me. I don't want to grow up and that's that. I want to be able to just cry, crying as much as I want to, crying over the littlest things. Crying feels like a kind of relief for little Marcos, and for the Marcos of today. More than anything I want attention and want to be noticed. Tantrums are opportunities. My skills as a kid at pouting on cue are Oscar-worthy.

There is no guarantee I will be met with the response I crave. My mother, a woman who thinks with her hands before she thinks with her mouth, always moves in swiftly, correcting whatever wrong she thinks my body is doing by force, by her right to my body because she is my mother. I think for this reason I want her more than anyone to comfort me. To show me her love when all I get her is her irritation and anger. I want her to prove me wrong though this happens infrequently; she rarely gives in to being that kind of mother. Whenever I am upset over something, or feel hurt, I still to this day, as an adult, yearn for her comfort. Some kind of instinct in me kicks in, some primal maternal link I want to fulfill. I call her feeling emotional, she asks me how I am doing, and I pause. Do I tell her I am hurting? Do I tell her I want her comfort? Will she respond how I need her to respond? Each time, without a doubt, I pretend I am fine. I fail to tell her I am calling her because I need her.

Always working and away from home, my father rarely sees

my childhood pouting. When he does, he offers only his most striking indifference, no eyes or face or shoulders turned my way. Pay no mind to this child behaving as a child, it seems like he is saying with his back turned toward me, he will tire soon enough.

The only one who gives in to my childish demands is my grandmother. I can cry and complain and throw a tantrum every single day and she will always be there to coddle me, to rub my hair until I find peace. My grandmother goes so far as to scold my mother about her treatment of my crying time and time again but my mother pays no mind to such things. The audacity of it, she seems to say beneath the surety of her ironclad voice, how can this woman who was so cruel to me growing up, so forceful with her words and her hands, dare to talk of kindness? She treats you so good, my mother says to me all the time, jealousy transparent in the voice.

I am a point of tension between my mother and grandmother. My mother hates when she indulges in my crying. The way my grandmother treats me forces my mother to confront why she is the way she is with her. I try to defend my grandmother by saying she is a woman from an island—they do things differently. My mother takes this explanation with a grain of salt. She does not care how that island in the Caribbean shapes my grandmother, she does not want a five-hundred-year history to make excuses for her. My mother does not want to believe what I am saying because to believe it is to take a step toward forgiveness. My mother wants none of it. My mother wants childhood given to her, a childhood where she can be but a child, a childhood neither she, nor my grandmother, nor my father, nor I, can ever know.

I think of my crying childhood self a lot. Crying for attention, crying for sympathy, crying for love. I cry as a kid because I don't have a language to tell what is going on with me. I don't really understand what is happening in my young life. I go to school and words are said about me, my family, my neighborhood. I am tucked away in a separate classroom because I am some sort of problem. My parents argue right in front of me, my mother threatening to kick my dad out, my dad threatening to leave, and I don't know why this is happening. I pull out the hair from my scalp and eyebrows, mind distressed and hearing voices, and I am hit across the face, told to stop doing that.

Why, little Marcos, are you crying? What is it you need? I am still searching for those answers.

DURING THESE MIDDLE school and high school years, all these years mastering English, having no choice but to master English, the boy finds himself in precarious positions where his English skills are *too* good. He interprets, thinks, and overthinks on the meanings of their language, their syntax and their pronunciations and their words and their intonations all a part of a system the boy knows well. He is better at their language than they are themselves.

A David laughs at the idea. This David always begins his ideas with a rapturous smile, white teeth brimming, the whites of his eyes contrasted against the blue iris, the pompousness of white hands in gesture, "*Like, just imagine it, right, one of them is* ________________."

There are several options as to how this sentence can finish:

A. ". . . *riding their bike and you scream from the car. I did it one time and Pedro fell straight on his ass. I was cracking up so hard I almost swerved off the road.*"

B. " . . . *delivering the pizza late, and just waits at the door for a tip. A tip? Get the fuck outtaaaaaa here, Pedro. Don't expect nothing delivering my pizza pie late.*"

C. ". . . *in your house, cleaning and shit. They shower like once a week so this Maria was bombing up my house. I couldn't wait till she was gone.*"

THIS DAVID, OR Timothy, or Shane, or John, or whatever other name boys like him may have, ends their scenario with a hearty, and innocent, "*Dude, I love Mexicans.*"

ON OCCASION, MY father and mother like to lecture me on how bad my Spanish has become. I shrug my shoulders, feigning indifference, though their words do hurt me. They do not know the history of why my Spanish is as bad as it is. Of the many years in speech pathology I endure, the many hours I am forced to work on erasing the Spanish my family teaches me, the many times I am told Spanish is a poor people's language. Neither know this is happening when it does. No one signs off on the speech pathologist's "therapy." No one knows I am told not to speak Spanish in class. It's just procedure for little brown kids to be treated as a problem. For our ways of speaking to be policed at every turn. For us to be corrected by a world that would rather we not exist.

My father only speaks to me in Spanish, and my mother speaks to me in a mixture of both. The language of their love is Spanish. Their meeting in the neighborhood I grow up in happens through Spanish. He lives next door to her and she decides to talk to him one day as he's sitting on his porch. My mother, ever so bold, so willing to go after what she wants. I admire this about her. She says what she wants to say however she wants to say it. She doesn't care for consequences or who it offends whereas I am so in control, so moderated, so careful what people will think of me. I know language is a powerful thing, as she does too. She knows language can let her express exactly how she feels when she feels it, and I know language is something to manipulate, to use when you need it in order to get by. I, on one end of the spectrum, she, on another.

My mother sees my father from down the street and she wants him. His long hair, she tells me, all the way down to his butt, was so sexy. My father Moctezuma there on the porch, an Aztec warrior muscled and youthful. My mother won't deny herself this newcomer.

And both witness as a Caribbean kind of Spanish is replaced by a more Mesoamerican one as the demographics of the neighborhood change in the eighties. A few years after knowing one another, of speaking their different kinds of Spanish, comes me. My father's only child, and my mother's third, a pleasant surprise to them both.

To this day, my ability to speak Spanish is hampered by the speech pathology I am put into as a kid. Each time I speak to my parents in my broken Spanish and I think they understand me. Though I still get the occasional lecture about how my Spanish keeps getting worse, they accept the way I speak. Both are sympathetic to the fact I am a second-generation kid, dwelling in a primarily English-speaking world. When I speak Spanish I have to think hard about what I am going to say, translating in real time from English into Spanish. Each time I do this, I remember those afternoons with the speech pathologist and the teachers who tell me not to speak Spanish. The days upon days of confusion. How inadequate I feel as I am forced to speak and think differently. I don't even know yet who I am but I am being forced to change. Who am I? Where do belong? I, little Marcos, am a problem but I don't know why. Years later, as I read writers like Toni Morrison, Audre Lorde, Jamaica Kincaid, and José Muñoz in undergrad, writers analyzing how race and white supremacy operate in the United States and beyond, operating as something we aspire after and dream of and die for, I come to learn something. These little places, these Main Street, U.S.A.s, quiet and quaint as they are, aren't all that nice, are little more than a nice dream white America dreams up for itself. And time will tell how much longer the dreamer can keep on dreaming.

MY FIRST MEMORY might have been a dream. I am sitting between my mother and father in their bed. They are asleep and I am watching TV. *Barney*, my favorite show, is playing and the song "John Jacob Jingleheimer Schmidt" is being sung. Why am I here at this hour watching *Barney*? Does *Barney* even play at these hours?

The lines between fact and fiction are hard to discern for the child. Like a dream, moments are fragmentary and elliptical, a this or that happening to your body, snatches of memories drifting in and out on the tide, down and down the stream until they are no more. I ask my grandmother what she remembers from her childhood and she just smiles, turning away from the TV for a second, then returning to it without having spoken. Is this what happens when you have lived on the planet for eighty years? I want to believe my grandmother knows more than she is telling. I want to believe she is hiding these childhood memories because they are too intense, too hard to relive again, rather than the grim fact she may have simply forgotten them, that she can no longer relive their joy and their pain.

I want to be on my deathbed remembering my first memory—the one that might or might not be real. The darkness of the room, the TV's light upon my face, the heavy breathing of my parents. I want those details, all the ordinariness, at the final hour.

AN ABIGAIL LAUGHS at David's theory. It is a rapturous laugh. She believes what he is saying even more than he believes it himself. He has proof, he has evidence, he has the credentials giving legitimacy to what he is saying. It explains so much. She does not doubt him, nor contest his theory. She affirms it, builds onto it, advances it. His theory gives her the pleasure of reminding her she is Abigail, who resides in a cluster of houses upscale and secluded, whose dad will purchase her a spanking new car when she gets her permit to drive, whose life is a life best lived as a quarantine, a keeping out of all that is contrary to her and her being Abigail Baker.

His theory creates her laughter, her joy, her being Abigail in its fullness.

To sum up or simplify David's complex theory that he tells Abigail, while, unfortunately, in the process diminishing his rigorously thought-out theorizing, it would be this: Mexican people do not take showers because water was a scarcity for them in Mexico so they have evolved a natural aversion to it. As a substitute for this lack of hygiene, their solution, as he identifies it, is to take "Mexican showers." These showers are the dousing of the body in excessive amounts of fragrance. The odor of the Mexican is one so overbearing, so distinct, so swarming, it must be masked by those who have it. Those who have the scent do not want to be identified as a campesino nobody, some Pedro Schmo or Average Guillermo or Plain Maria. They want to be a knockoff Gucci, a counterfeit Chanel, a bogus Armani. They want to compensate for some lack, some not-being-something enough.

David's theory is as simple as that.

Overhearing his theory brings anxiety to the boy. He turns to his body. Does it smell like David's theory? Does it prove David's theory in any way? Too much fragrance suggests the boy is performing this ritual known as a "Mexican shower," and too little of it might mean risking potentially exposing himself as having the scent. David does not list any specificities of his theory so the boy is not sure how best to defend himself from it. How does it smell? Is the smell itself something unique to Mexican people? How does the scent come about? Does some genetic code live in the blood causing the sweat glands to secrete a particular pheromone? How does David know it so well? The boy wants to ask him particulars but he is afraid David will turn the question against him—*"Why do you want to know? Scared you smell like one of yours?"*

This hypothetical *yours* halts him from questioning David's theory. The imposed ownership, this being in a group against his will, this belonging exclusively to this *yours* he cannot really name but he knows is not of David's kind, it is distinct from him and inferior to him. The *yours* functions to make a distance out of him. He wants belonging in the *ours*—*"Why you want to know? Ours is a smell nothing like theirs"*—and the belonging in not belonging to *theirs*.

4

YOU CAN count how many students of color are in the New Egypt school system on two hands when I'm growing up there. Three or so Black students, one Asian, one Puerto Rican, three or so Mexicans, and one MexiRican. Our difference is stark, very visible amongst all the white. From the day I enter elementary school to the moment I finish twelfth grade on my way out to New York City for college, these white boys and girls make me feel my difference. They poke fun at my fat body, and touch me in ways I most definitely do not like. They make jokes about immigrants and Mexicans. They question my sexuality and mock my femmeness. They make it well known being poor isn't cool. When I am not the victim of their direct assault, they say things amongst themselves. About Mexican people, disabled people, Black people, Asian people, queer people, Muslim people, trans people, all kinds of people who do not fit into their little world. I always sit by quietly. Not wanting to expose myself to more harm, to their public cruelty, to the physical violence they are capable of.

This goes on for more than a decade of my life. None of my family know this is happening, no one asks. My mother knows what white people are capable of but for some reason she doesn't inquire. My father has never even gone to a day of school so he has no idea of what to expect within those walls. I don't have many friends to tell what happens to me. Who, after all, wants this queer and fat and poor and brown boy who comes from the "Mexican ghetto" in their house? Who wants to be seen with someone like me? I am terribly alone as a child and teenager. An unfathomable kind of loneliness that, looking back now as an adult, I can't even imagine it, write it into existence. It seems foggy, the loneliness, almost unreal. All I know is every day, between the ages of ten and eighteen, I think of taking my life. I want it over. I want this nightmare to end. I want total and definitive peace.

Those hallways with the brightly colored lockers, the artwork on the brick walls, the well-mowed lawns, are haunted. My childhood self lives there. That boy, that ghost, that yesterday, that Marcos. He wanders them now as I write this. Dazed and confused, afraid and ashamed, an anger building in him he will never be able to let go of. An anger and a pain he will hold onto that will make him question whether he is worthy of being loved, whether he is beautiful, whether he should even keep on living. Somehow, someway, something in him wants to live. Some small kernel of hope. A hope that one day, Marcos, older Marcos, another Marcos in a different timeline, will be happy, will be free of this. He does keep on living but another self died there in those hallways. Or maybe he never even got to live in the first place.

A WEEK BEFORE I head off to Mexico, my first time out of the country, I ask my father for permission. You're twenty-five, he says, you don't need my permission. But I do, I want to tell him, because I want to feel like a child again, feeling like an argument will ensue because he does not want me going, feeling like he is the authority on my life. Being an adult is overrated as I sit there next to my father wanting him to discipline me for my insolence, to be my father disgruntled and outraged and maddened.

But my father has never been that kind of father to begin with. Working day in and day out in the fields, arriving to our home with fatigue on his body, my father's parenting happens through distance. A *stop that* here, a *come over here* there. He never really has to discipline me much anyways because I do everything by the book. I get As in school. I never get detention. I rarely misbehave. I don't get mixed up in the "wrong crowd." Now that he is older, more worn down by time, by his thousands upon thousands of hours toiling in the fields across the Americas, he even less wants to parent. He does occasionally reprimand me for not wearing socks around the house though.

For the first time, I notice the crow's feet near my father's eyes. The jowl forming under the chin, the droop of the cheeks, the lines near the mouth. Age settles on his skin with such grace. My father, a man who has walked across a continent in search of life, a better one, a more hospitable one, now must reckon with old age.

My father in his youth is gorgeous. If there were photographs of Moctezuma, that emperor who with a firm solemnity watched as his empire burned to the ground at the hands of those Spanish conquistadors, as he stared up at the ashes of a new age dawning, my father would be him. The skin a lustrous brown, the hard lines of the body with its muscles, the black hair cascading down to around his torso. He's a presence divine in each photo.

There is only one photo I know of that might be depicting my father as a small child. He can't recall if it is him or a brother, he might not even be born yet. If it is my father, then the picture is of him on his mother's lap with his father standing next to them. A baby staring forward with interest toward the camera, a black-and-white eternity. There are more children around the mother. The mother stares forward with indifference, the indifference of the brown eyes my father gives so well. The father is smiling, a jokester no doubt. This one family portrait of my lineage on my father's side, my America.

I try to know more about my father's childhood but he reveals so little. His upbringing in Mexico he keeps stored within the caverns of his psyche, his life but a grand mystery to me. In a novel I write when I am around twenty-two years old, I recreate the scenes from his time in Mexico. I try to write how he and his siblings and his mother might have felt when his father passed away in a brutal bar fight, or when his sister died from a scorpion sting. I try to render those moments my father will give no details of off the bits and pieces he tells me, the facial expressions and the voice modulations and the body postures that accompany his recounting, the tears welling up in his eyes or the hands fidgeting as he tells me his life story in the barest details.

This novel has been scrapped, left in the Dropbox folder I have imprisoned it to, because it is just meant to be a first venture into writing, an elementary experiment. The novel is a piece of prose used to better myself as a writer and to better understand my history. Now I am more mature, and more seasoned, in my writing, I would like to believe. More grown-up about my style. Yet, just like I pursue the approval of my father in this van traveling through New Jersey, as any child would do, I, too, pursue the authority of my readers, asking for the permission to continue, asking them to validate my being as a writer. Because through writing I try to reconcile with a past I can't seem to fathom, with a void of details and images and sensations that seem inexplicable. Any writing I do is always in the pursuit of an understanding I have yet to find.

DAVID SAYS SOMETHING to the boy under his breath from the locker below. One cannot be sure what the word is because it is the end of the day and the hallway is filled with seventh graders talking and yelling out their after-school plans with friends. The boy has no such plans.

The word David says begins with an *f* based on the way

his mouth scrunches up, air throttling saliva, the tightening of the syllable around the teeth to form the word ______________:

A. "*faggot*"
B. "*fatass*"
C. "*fruit*"
D. "*fucking spic*"
E. "*fruitpicker*"

SOMETHING TAKES OVER the meekness of the boy, his let-them-get-away-with-everything attitude: he "accidentally" drops a history textbook onto David's head.

The boy immediately slams the locker, and rushes into the classroom to await the bell for dismissal. David marches through the door and rushes toward him. The boy does not know what he says but his mouth moves. David is trying to size the boy up so he puffs up his chest, and raises his head for height, trying to intimidate, to terrorize. David feels his smallness. The boy is taller than David is, bigger than he is, stronger than he is, yet their differences in proportion, David's smallness in relation to the boy's bigness, David's ability to go undetected, to be untargeted, to not be a problem, makes the boy stand out for all to see, all to scrutinize, all to blame, all to accuse. He will be the villain of the story.

What happens next the boy cannot explain: he lurches up, embiggened, all of his body hardened, bringing his fist down onto David's face. David falls back but does not fall down.

No one else seems to be around. David trembles, David pants. Neither fear, nor anger, but something else he feels. It is something the boy cannot explain because it is something only David knows, only a David or a Timothy or a John can describe to you what it is.

WE TALK ABOUT bullying as if bullying is the problem. Kids will just be kids, we hear on the news when the latest case of bullying to the extreme emerges for debate: cruel, indecent, relentless toward their peers. Kids call other kids names, punch and shove them, harass them on the internet because it's just what some kids naturally do. Campaigns against bullying are mobilized around addressing the problem of the bully, of telling the bully bullying is wrong, of explaining by not really explaining why bullying happens. What of the source of bullying, its core, the why and the how? What children are bullied about usually relates to their bodies: to the fidgety body; the too-boyish or too-feminine body; the fat body; the raced body; the impoverished body; the disabled body; the girl's body. Epithets are hurled according to the scripts of the culture the bully lives in: the Muslim child is called a terrorist; the girl who refuses to wear a skirt identified as a lesbian; the immigrant child is told to go back to their country; the child who learns at a different speed than the other children is called stupid. The cultures we live in create the bully. Bullies are not some miraculous thing that emerges from the void. They are products of a greater evil. The evil of the historical record. You can either blame the bully or the culture that produced him.

TWO CHALUPAS AND a cheesy roll later I decide it's time. It's been time. I'm twenty-one or so, and I have never told my family what happened to me as a kid. The speech pathology lessons no one had signed off on. The kindergarten teacher who silenced me. The taking away of my Spanish, and the perfecting of my English. The children who made fun of the neighborhood I came from. All the years of hurt, of depression, of suicidal thoughts, jammed into a few sentences at Taco Bell. How do I explain to my mother a past she does not know is her past, a past that is her son's past he tried to forget, a past he was made to forget? But trying to forget is always destined to fail.

She's still chewing on her crunchy corn shell, a bit of lettuce leaning out of the mouth, sour cream on the finger.

"Are you sure?" Next to us someone is getting a refill. Their large drink fills up with a red liquid, the carbonation of it fizzing and snapping and breaking through the silence.

"Yes, I'm sure."

She chews, and chews, and then finally swallows. "Why didn't you tell me then when it was happening?"

I swallow the mash of taco in my mouth. I want to keep swallowing to delay the need to produce language, to explain the boy who I was, to explain who I am today trying to explain yesterday. I think of the boy in the small-town classroom, the boy who does not know the word *language* or the fact that he is using language but language is used against him, using him. And there with the taco mash in my mouth, language, like always, like the language I did not have in my childhood, fails to articulate itself, to express itself as something representative of that boy. *"I don't know."*

I don't know what I want from my mother there in the Taco Bell. Our conversation on the matter of my beginnings does not last long. I don't know if she does not want to have the conversation, or if she does not know how. I ask her of her childhood plenty of times before this conversation and I am sympathetic. I make sure she knows I want to hear her. I want to know her story, like I want to know my father's, because her story is my story too. She tells me the comments my grandmother would make about her body, the physical abuse by her brothers, the struggle to survive when her father left them for a bit of time. She gives more emotion, more stories, than my father does though this does not mean his are not as valid or meaningful. They are just two different kinds of storytellers.

There at Taco Bell a part of me wants her to own up to some kind of negligence, taking some responsibility for the devastation that was my childhood, owning up to what needs to be owned up for. I want her to let me tell my story fully without her retreating into victimhood, without telling me I am the bad guy for making her feel bad.

Maybe what I am in pursuit of in Taco Bell is recognition, my mother recognizing my past, that I was barely given the chance to be a child.

But I don't know if my mother knows how to recognize another person.

Or maybe I am not representing myself well enough in the story I am telling her.

I don't know to think of my childhood in the first person. It feels too remote, too distant, too far from me to be imagined in that way. Third person, the *he*s and the *his*es and *himselfs*, feel closer to how I think of six-year-old Marcos, middle school Marcos, Marcos in his last year of high school.

Marcos—myself, mine, me, I—who are you?

All I get is the darkness, me and myself as this adult, this forgetful self, asking into the void how do you feel, little boy, when they say those things to you, how do you feel, little brown boy, when they touch your body in those ways, how do you feel, little thing there in the shadows, when they convince you that you are nothing, not a life worth living?

I'm looking for words to explain what words can never dream of explaining.

THE BOY IS terrified David will tell someone what happened in the classroom. He does not sleep easy knowing consequences tend to not go in favor of boys like him, boys whose neighborhood is called the Mexican ghetto, boys who are immediately imagined to be violent and aggressive and mindless. He imagines David will be waiting with his friends outside the bus stop, in the bad part of town the boy calls home, their blonde and alabaster forming a mob near his house. Their limbs ready to beat and flatten and squish and batter the boy on the road his family passes day after day, beating and battering him to a fleshy pulp like the bodies the boy sees on the Spanish news at five, image after image of Mexico and Los Angeles and Guatemala and New York City and Venezuela and the US–Mexico border, all those unidentifiable bodies and bodies identifiably brown. He imagines this vividly because he has heard of stories of boys like David who have done this to boys like him in this town, in a neighboring town, in a town in another state, another country, boys like him who will be villainized, boys like him whose pain will not be taken seriously, boys like him who will have an entire justice system ready to pound the gavel against them. He knows David and his friends will do this in the name of some great vengeance. A vengeance they are allowed to have, one they cannot describe but they know very well is their birthright and their inheritance and their duty to the land they identify as theirs.

The boy is terrified he will have to explain what he cannot explain, what he is unable to explain in English or in Spanish or in Spanglish, what cannot be rendered in any language. To tell the town David called him a _________ means to tell them who he is, who David is, who they are, and, above all else, who they do not want to be, who they do not want to be around, who they want to keep out.

The boy is afraid because he knows they will tell him violence is never the answer. They will convince him his rage is unjustified. They will persuade him all violence and all rage is unjustifiable. They will have the boy believe Davids will just be Davids, unfortunate but inevitable, boys like David being boys like David convincing the boy he is nothing, persuading him of his being nothing, nothing at all.

I KNOW THEY know. The teachers pretend like they don't hear or see anything but the words and actions of my classmates are done openly. They know they can get away with it. Perhaps all of it is just fun and games to my teachers. Innocent fun done by children. They'll grow out of it. Maybe these adults once spoke like these children, saying the things they say, doing the things they do. Some might even have children like these children. If the white adult is to reprimand the white child for the things they believe and say and do, then they are by default implicating themselves in the crime. For they are the ones who teach them to believe what they believe in the first place.

As an adult traveling on the New York City subway, my friends and I joke around about white people and their ways of parenting. "Daniel, would you please sit on your bottom? Daniel, if you sit on your bottom I will give you a reward. Daniel, if you . . ." The white mother's pleas continue as we watch from the nearby subway seats. We joke about how our mothers would give us an eye and that would be enough for us to correct ourselves, enough for us to know the fear of God. Staring over there at this woman and child who will get off somewhere below Ninety-Sixth Street and go to a playground that's well maintained and clear of homeless people slumbering, I can't help but wonder who is the parent, who is parenting who in this situation?

The white parent and child in New York City aren't so different from the ones in the small town I grow up in. There's something they all want to be, and something they all do not want to be. They want to be the affectionate and caring and respectful and obliging parent. They want their children to go to the best schools, the most segregated schools. These parents will do whatever it takes to get their children in these schools, like faking test scores or donating large sums of money, because going to certain schools comes with a kind of social capital. They believe their manuals on good parenting wholeheartedly, sparing no expense on how far they will go for advice, for guidance, for the bettering of their parenting. They do not want to be like the negligent parent who goes above Ninety-Sixth Street, or who drives into the Mexican ghetto, the parent who is a bit young, a bit financially unstable, the parent who cannot go to PTA meetings because they work double shifts, the parent who does not speak English to their child, the parent who might give an eye to their child to stop them from their antics, the parent who might even raise a hand to their child.

The white child, the child born and bred on a city block, or on Main Street, U.S.A., will walk into subways or into schools and demand a seat be given up for them, will hit their parents or peers until their request is met, and this will all be ok because they are just a child, innocent and ignorant.

The white adult allows this because no matter where in the world the white adult comes from they know the white child and their childhood is a prized possession. It is sacred, the rearing of the white child, reared carefully and reared with indulgence and reared with so many goals in mind. The white adult sees the future and wants their child to be in it, to be the future itself because, as Whitney Houston herself belts out, the children are the future, but which children, Whitney, are you belting about?

And what of the little queer and fat and feminine and neurodivergent child of color? That child is nothing more than a haunting. Haunted by who they were not allowed to be, who they had to be in order to get by, all the childhood lives they never got to live. Mine haunts the town of my childhood. New Egypt, New Jersey, robbed me. Who knows what other children it robbed of a childhood? Who knows how many other children in towns and cities like New Egypt, all across the United States, all across this globe, have been robbed or are being robbed or will be robbed of being able to be a child? Then again, in this world, amongst all this cruelty, there might be no way to ever even be a child unless, that is, you get the luxury of being born a white one, born into a world like Main Street, U.S.A., or the Upper West Side, where the rest of the world is meant to be kept out, innocently kept away and out of view.

I write this for the little brown boy. To atone, to reconcile, to ease his suffering. All my writing is for him. To let him live, to give him air, to let him feel the wind against his face. Writing to live again.

MY FATHER HAS one memory of his father. They are outside, in Mexico, and it is night. My father's little child legs are standing on a wooden post and he is being held up by his father. His father is laughing, a man who in pictures appears to be one of those men who is always laughing, never taking the world seriously. He is a contrast to my grandmother who appears in every photo to be taking the world too seriously, seeing the world as a place where you cannot let your guard down. The moon shines upon their skin, skin aglow and skin shimmering, a brown scintillation.

This one memory is all my father has of the man who he barely even got to call father. My father is but a few years old when his father dies. My father's childhood ends when his father's life ends. My father is unable to go to school and he must work the fields. What little childhood my father gets to have is encapsulated every November 1 during All Saints'

Day. His tia celebrates by making him toqueras de elote and a little mono de masa. Each year this day comes and each year my childhood father hopes against hope that this year his mono is made of pan dulce, that his tia finally can afford the materials for such a mono, a mono that would sweeten the tip of the tongue when bitten into, a mono that would go down my father's childhood belly as a sweetness divine. This, like so much of my father's childhood, like so much of his life, will never come to pass. A dream is all the mono de pan dulce will be, a dream little boys and girls like my father dream up all across the Americas, in deserts and in pueblos and in forests and in campos and in suburbs, dreams of sweetness and of sugar, that sweetness that drove empires to cross seas in ships stuffed with human cargo and ships that will fire into the brush, decimating communities. Little boys and girls across the Americas will continue dreaming of sweetness, I have no doubt, not knowing if and when their fantasy of a monito de pan dulce will come to pass, their tongues salivating at the thought of sweet, sweet indulgence.

FOR THE IMMIGRANT, the child is the American dream. Watch as they grow up, go to college, quadruple the parents' income. At least, that's the hope. My parents never told me anything along these lines. No one harassed me to go to college, no one begged me to get my act together, no one told me I had it better than they did. My parents and family were just there, getting by, getting by as they knew best. I pushed myself to pursue that most hyped-up thing we call the American dream.

I feel this burden of the American dream. The burden to do better than my family has done, the burden to make tons of money to help my family. I talk about this with my therapist all the time. That is a massive burden, she says to me, trying to persuade me to feel otherwise, to alleviate myself of such a stress. But I do feel the pressure, and it consumes me.

When I tell my family I am a writer they look at me like I have three heads. Their first instinct is to question how much that makes and I am reluctant to ever say. A writer? They want to hear I am a lawyer or an accountant or an engineer. They want to hear money in their ears because I have opportunity and I have grown up in the United States. I tell them I will get my PhD and I will get the salary of a tenured professor and I will rid us of a condition five hundred years in the making. This they like to hear and this they believe will come to pass. I, their American dream, I, with fingers crossed, will try to prove to them as best as I can that indeed the American dream exists, that in fact it is real and I am it.

NOTHING HAPPENS THE following day. David tells no one. The teacher who is the boy's history teacher, who was his mother's second-grade teacher, returns the book to him the next day in class. She does not question why it is abandoned on the floor. *"You gotta be more careful, kid,"* she tells him. Her Jewish accent is thick, and comforting. He nods his head, ready to return to his seat, but she holds him there in her gaze for a moment. She has done this before ever since his brother died earlier in the school year. She was the only teacher out of the six he sees daily who went to his brother's funeral. She senses something, something familiar, something all her own. Her husband passed away not too long ago. Is it him she sees in the boy's eyes? Her loss, her anguish, her love. Boy and teacher there in the hallway living as if living no more is all they desire.

Their exchange ends. A nod, confirmation. The boy takes his seat next to David, next to Mary, in front of John, and behind Abigail. Class is in session.

I AM TWELVE years old when my brother dies. Crushed in the passenger's seat of his friend's car by a drunk driver. Little Marcos, just a kid who has to deal with death. Little Marcos, just a boy who has to understand the forever absence of a relative who will never return home. The police enter our house and we think my brother got into another dumb fight in the neighborhood. We know something is wrong when they tell us to sit down, to have a seat. In a matter-of-fact voice, the cop tells us my brother is dead. He is dead down the street from where we live. My sister and mother immediately start sobbing. Their crying is like a shriek. As odd as it sounds, my short life flashes before my eyes, in bursts, in accelerated moving images, as if I, too, were about to die, if not already dead.

My dad, not living with us at the time because he and my mother are fighting, moves back in without question. Family swarms the house for weeks afterward, consoling my mother and sister day in and day out. Relatives around my age come play video games in my room but no one really asks how I'm doing, if I'm ok. I feel like a babysitter having to worry about the children. I'm a kid, too, but the adults think death doesn't impact us as hard. Death is for grown folks to feel. When I return to school, the guidance counselor pressures me to talk but I don't want to talk to her. She keeps asking me how I'm doing, if I need to talk, but I don't buy into her game. She has never even said hi to me in the hallway. She doesn't even know who I am. He's gone and that's that, I tell her defiantly. I keep living though living numb.

Some days I say to myself if I try hard enough, I can recreate my childhood in a different image. Make it not mine anymore. Truth, facts, reality—someone else's, no David, no Abigail, no kindergarten teacher, no speech pathologist, no words telling me who I have to be, no brother dying. After I leave New Egypt to go to college, I pretend I forget everything that happens to me all those years there. Mere ghosts in the attic. Yet try and try as I may, the memories are too sharp, the details too well-formed and distinct. There's Abigail and her laugh as I'm in the gay club dancing. There's David and his words hitting me my first time out of the country. There's Chad touching my body in the locker room as I'm getting ready for bed in my dorm room. There's Bethany telling me to grow up, Pedro, when it looks like I am about to cry on the day I graduate college. There's my brother dying again as I look out across the East River into Brooklyn, watching as the boats go by, as the traffic keeps on going, as lives keep living.

Those boys and girls and counselors and speech pathologists and teachers of that small town, my brother who lives forever in my yesterday, they are in my present life always. My memories of them materialize no matter how far into the world I go. When will it end? When will I be free? Somewhere a little Pedro is out there, a boy like me, a boy in the Americas, who is having the world bear down upon him, his world of struggle experienced in silence, alone. Grow up, Pedro, they will tell him, and he will do it because he doesn't know what else to do, doesn't know how else to get on in the world. Grow up, be a man, stop crying, Pedro, and he will think someday it must get better, someday it will all be all right. Little Pedro there all alone, hold on, little Pedro there in tears, someday will come soon enough, little Pedro there in the Americas, just wait and see.

5

WHO IS that?

The ruse is up.

The boy wonders why his father didn't drop him off further down, out of sight, like normal. He guesses since they were running late his father wanted to drop him closer to the school doors. Now the boy must answer this other boy who he calls friend, a friend whose milky complexion and blue eyes project curiosity, genuine and nonthreatening curiosity.

Tick tock, tick tock. All the boy wants to do is to almost disappear. The girth and rolls and chunks and flesh transformed into something so small, so insignificant that he can try to belong with this pale boy he calls friend, with those who look and feel and behave like this pale boy he calls friend, belonging to theirs and their kind and their—

Who is that?—the question jeopardizes, it threatens—*Who is that?*—the question asks the boy to name and identify and choose and to—*Who is that?*—the friend is able to discern the boy's father is dark-skinned and the boy is light-skinned, and this friend thinks on this difference, theorizes it in full to understand why the dark man is bringing the light-skinned boy to school, why it is the boy was in his truck, how it is possible that the man and the boy are even remotely fa—

Who is that?

What can be said? What story can be—

Who is that?

He's my father's worker.

I MAKE A very clear choice as a teenager. I choose whiteness. To try to be closer to it, to try to reap its privileges. Classmates ask that irritating question of what I am and I respond Puerto

Rican. Being Puerto Rican in my young mind doesn't have as much racial baggage as saying Mexican, particularly in a time of anti-immigrant sentiment. Though inflected by a mysterious "Indian" great-grandmother, who, along with other relatives on my grandmother's side, are a bit too dark and with hair a bit too curly to be just the long-lost Taino people, my Puerto Rican family is lighter-skinned and with more European features. They blend in a bit better in a small town. I deny my father because I am embarrassed by his dark brown skin. Embarrassed when as a kid my Puerto Rican uncles call my dad "the male Pocahontas" because of his black hair down to his butt. Ashamed of the bodies, histories, and ways of knowing that express indigenous lineage. Ashamed of my even darker brown grandparents in Mexico. Ashamed of my neighbors and family who are indigenous or of indigenous descent. At the time, I don't have a language in which to articulate why this denial exists. I just *know*. Knowing from the textbooks I read, the movies and shows I watch, the society I am raised in that brownness relates to indigeneity in some way, and the masses of Mexican and Central American people living in the United States have something to do with all that. And I, lighter-skinned, with the option to choose who I claim as my people, deny this as best as I can.

I perform this denial all throughout school. Sometimes other students don't believe me. They know what neighborhood I come from. They know it's the Mexican ghetto. They eye me with suspicion, call me a dirty Mexican anyways. I deny and deny again my darkness, nonetheless.

My therapist tells me I am just a child when I say what I say about my father, when I try to use the lightness of my skin against my father. I counter her by saying I am fully aware of what I am saying when I do it, knowing full well the logics and rationales that constitute the racial hierarchies in the United States, knowing damn well how I am putting this English I have learned, I have mastered, to use. There is no innocence with such knowledge. There is but complicity, that fantasy of proximity to that something we are globally told to desire, to value, to love, and our doing anything at whatever cost to have its validation, its acceptance.

I don't like the idea of innocence. For adults, or for children. The innocence of the child in the cultural imaginary of the United States is a thing to be protected, a thing our future depends on. There's little Billy with blonde hair and blue eyes eating his Cheerios, little Suzie with the adorable freckles combing the hair of her Barbie—these children with all that profitable innocence, all the inherent goodness, behind their white picket fences on Main Street and the doormen of their Upper West Side apartments. But Tamir Rice playing outside in a park is gunned down by a police officer because he is a Black child, as so many other Black children are gunned down and killed across the United States. Children brought over across the US-Mexico border by their parents are targets of tear gas and bullets, locked in cages or downright stolen by the US government never to be seen by their parents again. Emmett Till is punched and kicked and beaten by grown white men so badly his corpse in his casket is unrecognizable. Children watch police and immigration invade their homes to take their parents and are left abandoned across the United States as their parents are deported back to a country that might kill them, to a country that has nothing left for them.

Innocence is a value awarded to white children. Innocence is a nice way of structuring the world into who is good and who is bad, who is worthy of being protected and who is not. Children of color have never known innocence because our lives are structured in some way by violence, by precarity, by the historical record, by not knowing what will happen to us in this world.

Innocence allows for willful ignorance, willful overlooking, which becomes a weapon used by those in power.

When I choose to deny my father, to try to pass as something closer to white, I am just a child.

A child not innocent of the world amongst children whose innocence shields them from the world.

I am just a child when I do what I do to my father.

I am just a child who will do whatever he must do to get by in these Americas.

2

COUSIN OF A COUSIN NAMED PEDRO

Esteban, or is it Miguel, perhaps Santos, or quite possibly Chuy? Cousin Pedro, let's call him that, there on the porch front step with my father and me, all together in this childhood reverie.

He's my father's cousin, at or around the same age, lighter-skinned than him, though no less sun-seared than the next Pedro. He has never been to a dentist a day in his life and his teeth are perfectly aligned. He smiles and I teeter, he smirks and I totter. Lean tissue of the thighs, shoulders padded with muscle, dimples with depth. The hair beneath sheens and shines a shimmering black. His greasiness a workday sublime.

My father smiles a lot with Cousin Pedro. He laughs a lot, too, laughing like I would want to laugh if Cousin Pedro were talking to me. He brings his head down often, hiding a coy smirk. He takes off his hat every two or so minutes and embeds the nails into the scalp. Nervous tic? He keeps eye contact longer than he does with anyone else. I think these signs of subtle affection might be some kind of jealousy on my part.

"Mande?" My father asks Pedro to repeat himself. Did Cousin Pedro even say anything? He says that word so Mexican, a word that is a question, a confusion, a demanding, an irritation, a furtherance of speech. But when he says it here to Cousin Pedro it has a new meaning. There is none of the coldness in it like how he uses it on the phone or when speaking to my mother. The syllables are all affection, a playful passivity in its utterance, a tenor of the voice I do not know. A language man to man.

Cousin Pedro with mischief in the eyes replies, *"Chago, ya sabe lo que estoy diciendo . . ."*

What is this between them? The words are buoyant, light and filled with innuendo. There is a structure between them. A structure rarely seen, a structure kids are not meant to see. Their structure excludes.

Cousin Pedro and my father are much alike. Perhaps that is where this structure of theirs comes from. Undocumented, home renters not home buyers, no intentions of wifing someone up. I dance around my father, chubster me tugging on his shirt and smudging my fingers with the field-day dust, seeking his attention, his smile, his eyes, his hand on my head. I do this not knowing my father, like Cousin Pedro, never wanted children, never wanted the childhood annoyances I do to him, never wanted me.

Interruption: another Pedro passes by on the street. All eyes on this Pedro. Let him be Pedro #2 for clarity's sake. I do not know his name, and no one refers to him by his name but everyone in the neighborhood knows him. He just recently moved here after hiking himself across a continent. He's infamous for his walk, the swish in his hips, the lisping of the mouth. His name is always a description. *Ese* hombre, *that* man. He is the detail of a hand moving too erratically. He is a man suspected of curling his lashes. Sometimes he is not even *ese* hombre but simply *ese*, the definite article signaling a man and a man's life and a man who is not fully a man.

My father and Cousin Pedro say nothing of Pedro #2 but keep their eyes on him. They are intrigued, they are fascinated, they are mesmerized. A Pedro unlike the other Pedros.

"Mira eso . . ." Cousin Pedro says to my father, the words trailing off as if there is more to say, more to mean by Pedro #2 strutting down this potholed runway. What is Cousin Pedro saying to look at?

My father does not reply. There is but seriousness in his eyes. I feel a magnetism between us, as if he is now more than ever trying not to glance down at me, trying to pretend as if the something that is between us did not exist.

"Mmmmm," my father grumbles in response, continuing to watch this Pedro #2 sashay down the street. Cousin Pedro nods his head in understanding as if words are not even necessary for them to communicate, as if words might even get in their way. They do not even need words to say they do not identify this Pedro #2 as their kind of people. No one in my

neighborhood does. My uncle pokes fun at how womanlike he walks. My mother says he swishes harder than any woman she has ever met. My father says many words to describe him in order to not say a particular word.

Watching him recede from view, body but a dot on the horizon, I worry if I, too, swish my hips like Pedro #2, if I, too, am just a description with no name.

With Pedro #2 out of sight, and out of mind, my father and Cousin Pedro return to their world. Cousin Pedro's tic happens: the upper-lip lick. Every fifty seconds or so he does it. When he does it he keeps his eyes on my father. This is how one moves the tongue, I think to myself, this is how one means and makes meaning without words.

Cousin Pedro means to say something. Scratch that: Cousin Pedro always has the look on his face like he means to say something. Lips to the side, a word forming between them, air ready to sound out something meaningful. What, Pedro, is it?

"Un dia, Chago," he starts with that boyish intonation of his, the hands durable swaying in the air for emphasis, reaching close to the shoulders of my father, *"quiero que nosotros . . . tu y yo . . . solitos . . . sin mujeres, sin hijos . . . quiero solamente un cosa . . . Chagito mio, un cosa . . ."*

And I wait for the end of his declaration but the end never comes.

Suddenly, he looks over at me. No more is he the happy-go-lucky Cousin Pedro. There is a darkness in the browns of his irises. Brooding and sulky and sinister. His torso tightens and withdraws as if preparing to lurch forward and strike. Nostrils flare. My father smirks, trying to ease whatever this is, giving me those puppy-dog eyes he gives me so frequently in these childhood years. Both are now eyeing me, eyeing this blockage to their meaning. This thing like them and unlike them. This thing they see as the future, a future they are told to want, a future they want no part of. There on the porch front step, they want to resist me, deny me as the object of what they are meant to desire, but they do not know how, they know not how to be rid of us children so filled with promise, so promising of the future.

The objects of my desire are rarely men like my father, uncle, or the other men in my neighborhood. Cousin Pedro is an exception because, as a cousin of a cousin (twice removed?), Pedro is not like my father. A bit taller, skin a light caramel complexion, features more the features of the lead men in the telenovelas. He's more a Maximiliano while my dad is more a pobrecito Pedro. Pedro is rough around the edges but not rough enough to make him that class of man you set yourself apart from, make yourself a distinction to. The taboo, I convince myself (I want to convince myself), is too strong to desire men who look like my father.

They get bored. They need more. They need contact.

Mano y mano, the wager is set, elbows on the table. I am

supposed to root for my father. I do want him to win, sure, but I want Cousin Pedro to win more. I want to shout his name from the rafters. Measure the flex of his bicep. Cheerlead his unrivaled masculinity.

Three . . . two . . . one! Hand presses against hand, hard. Neck striations. Wincing of the eyes. Heavy breaths, in and out, a grunt between them. Man against man.

I am the referee of this arm-wrestling shindig. Supposed to be unbiased and fair. Supposed to call out the elbow being raised, anytime the body lifts up a bit too much. Cousin Pedro does this on several occasions and I do nothing. My father never does it and I tell him he is doing it. I need Cousin Pedro to win, need him to see I am on his side, here for him fully.

The tug-of-war grows fiercer. The muscles flex, and unflex, and then flex again. Those many, many hours the two put in at the fields show in this display of strength. Manly ferocity. Stamina more than the average human, more than enough to create a showdown to rival all the other showdowns on the block. They are superheroic to my eyes. The Thing vs the Hulk. The clasp, the curling, the palms—all force, all masculinity. There are no egos. They are playful, playing in a world of their own private meanings. Their bodies are a ferociousness only intimates can share. Edging near, edging close to—what?

My father gains ground. Cousin Pedro is weakening, the grip falters, the elbow begins to bend. He is moaning, and my father is grunting. Veins bulge. Cousin Pedro looks at my father with pained eyes, eyes meaning something direct, pure, concentrated. My father's strength overwhelms him—he gives in to his force.

Cousin Pedro flops onto the grass. His chest lunges upward then downward. I want to jump on him like I jump on my father when he returns home from work. Something, something invisible and visible, holds me back.

For the first time since Cousin of a Cousin Pedro arrived in our front yard that day, I am spoken to by my father: *"Porque te ves asi?"*

No menacing tone to his inquiry. He's genuinely curious as to why I look disappointed that my father, my hero, has lost. I shrug my shoulders. Cousin Pedro laughs at this. Is he laughing at me? Cousin Pedro's laugh does me in. The gruff guffaw, the deep crescendo at the end of it, the forward lunge of his body penetrating the air. I throw in the towel. No more, Pedro, no more.

3

THE ABCs OF MY NAME

He says my name wrong. Nothing out of the ordinary, nothing out of the blue. He is not the first, after all, and he is not the last. He is but one of many so I don't take it personally. He means no ill will by it. He does the roll call in the front of the classroom and I am ready for my shame. I think of my mother getting angry at me when the parent–teacher conference happens. He will say my name how he says my name every day in that third-grade classroom and she will revolt. Billy? Here. Bob? Here. Abigail? Here. Katherine? Here. Chad? Here. My name is next. He says it. I pause, hesitate, and contemplate how to correct him knowing that to correct him is to explain to him my difference, is to explain to an entire class the differences between them and me. Say the name out loud to this third-grade classroom and they will hear a murmur, a cry, a full nothingness. On the count of three: one . . . two . . . three. The cojones to be bold fall through. The letters spoken are their letters. Enunciations and pronunciations done in their way, on their terms. I say my name as they say my name, as they expect my name to be said.

THE *M* IN my name is a no brainer. The fornication of the lips is a true universal. All languages know the sound of lips smacking sensual, the rub of that rubbing together making the *mmmmm* sound. Anyone can get the first letter and sound right if they try, if they work hard enough to know this name. Easy peasy lemon squeezy.

My name on this lover boy's lips is treason. Any and all secrets contained within it are exposed. What conspiracy is this? He knows my name too well. Letter by letter, sound after sound, he says this name of mine with an exactness no one has ever said before. Is this what they call love? This cute boy with his intonation tells a story of my name I have never known. The rise and fall and pitch and crescendo and emphasis and stress must be addressing someone else's life. Years spent with another in such close proximity through intense joy and intense pain brings about the cruel familiarity we strive to want and, when given it, shy away from. Say it isn't so. He means to say my name in such a way, means the name to be the reason for what he has done, means the name to be a thorough explanation for why what happened had to happen. Is this what it means to be in love? He intones again to drive home his point. Who does he think he is? The first syllable stressed and cannon-like, the second syllable unstressed and clipped. His flawless twang of the fluent Spanish speaker guides the syllables of my name like homing missiles. Strike me down why don't you? He means what he is saying, this Pedro, this lover boy, he means my name in a way I have never meant my name to mean, where my name means something.

On his lips my name means love.

The *a*, *r*, and *c* of my name are easy. No need for special lip movements, the rolling of the tongue. It's the lowercase *o* in my name that trips them up. Spare them the scrutiny, they tell me, they as in those who tell you to not speak up, do not talk back, do not question, do not correct. They as in those who confirm this name is a name of accommodation. Let them say the *o* like a *u* making it ring comfortable to their tongues. These letters settle for less. What of it? This is the condition of being. My name is the name of conquest and pillage and eradication and of five hundred years of living in these Americas. The unbearable that are these letters spelling out what I think my name to be.

THE KINDERGARTEN TEACHER spits out the letters of my name like they are expletives. *M* to the *A* to the *R* to the *C* to the *O* to the *S*. She means my name as an expletive: a damning, a lack, a disciplining. Her lips like leather make this a fact to the rest of the kindergarten class that I will spend a year of my life in. I am speaking the wrong language. I am in between languages. She says my name once and never again.

NO ONE IN my family says the *s* in my name. They remove this last letter, remixing my name, their modification giving familiarity and warmth to what I believe to be my name.

A BREATH, BREATHLESS, an air-deprived somnolence. Say it loud, cutie, say it proud. Soft-sounding solitude is my name in this darkened room. He's all eyes forward, this Pedro of mine, he's all lips inward. Air, he is losing air, losing it all on his concentration. His focus is your turn-on. I want to ask him if he's ok. He's too into it, too absorbed in the moment, lost beyond the moment. He says my name, or what I believe is my name, what I have mistaken for my name, and he announces his extinguishment. Climax: he is near to it, reaching it, dreading it. He feels his futility. Our futility. He feels the futility of the body. This time-lapsed devotion nearing its unfortunate end. Through gritted teeth he says he is close, says he is ready. The brown eyes close, the face scrunches up, his back clenches. My hand grips the back of his neck where fingers feel the pump, pump, pump, pumping of the blood, the surging and seething and striating. I say his name but say it lower than even a whisper, so low the grunts drown it out. And it happens. This moment everyone waits for, everyone hypes up, what we are all taught to want. But I know this is the end of us. All returns to the normal we all want to flee. He slumps his head to the side, the body weakened from the exertion, giving no eye contact. Breath in, breath out, he is all defeat as he brings his head to your chest. One lengthened-out breath, and the brown eyes with those lashes long, close, and he sleeps.

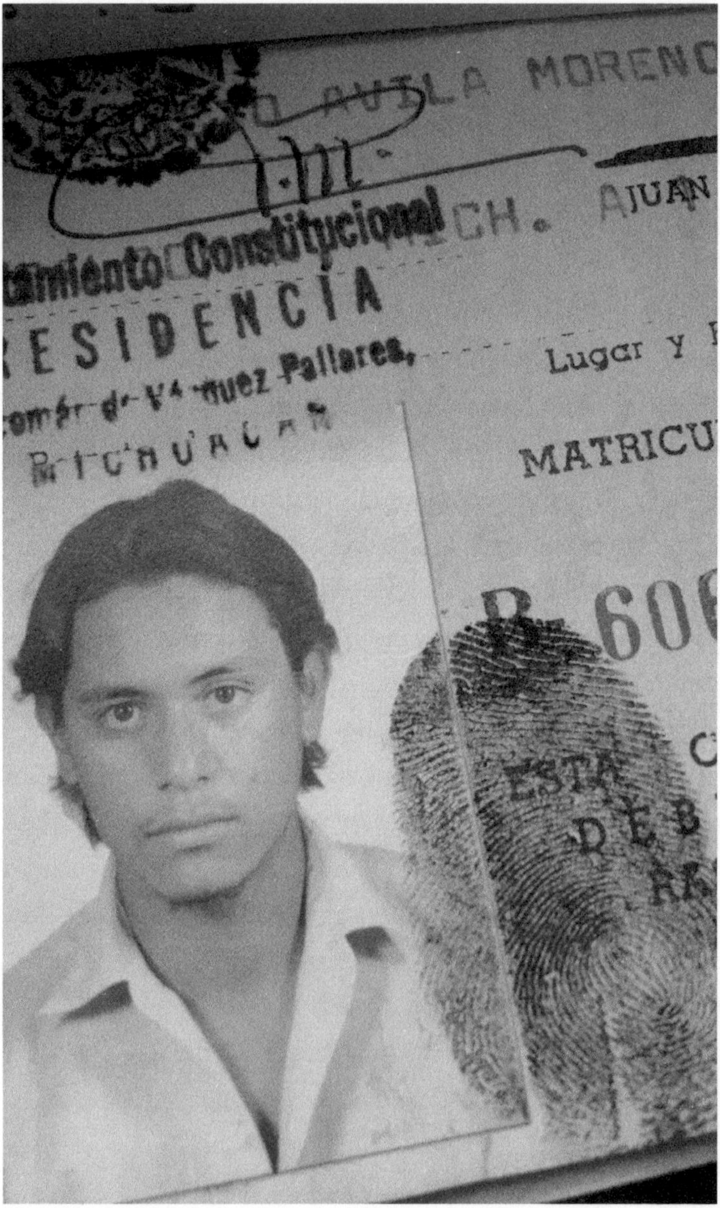

LA MORENO
CH. AJUAN
Constitucional
RESIDENCIA
Pallares,
Lugar y
MATRICU
B 606

4

TO MY FATHER

I can't look away. Youthful. Hair neat, and to the side, off the forehead. A few strands of chin hair jut out, a shadow of a moustache above your full lips. This photograph of a you I have never seen before. It is before you will undergo your thousand-mile journey across the Americas, before you will say goodbye to your mother for the last time, before you become my father. Just this photographic Adonis in brown.

But this is no glamour shot. Found amongst a shoebox containing the few documents of your life, this is an identity card issued by the nation of Mexico. SECRETARIA DE LA DEFENSA NACIONAL heads the top of the card issued in 1987, four years before my birth, followed by information with which to identify you. Birth date, marriage status, your first name accompanied by paternal and maternal names. Your occupation: campesino. Can you read or write? No. Beside your visage are two thumbprints.

What is familiar in this black-and-white photograph are the soft eyes. Doe-like, transcending time and space. I may not know the parted hair or chin-hair wisps but I know this look.

It is a face I grow up knowing. Those soft brown eyes. The lips not quite forming a frown, not quite forming a smile. The face taut and plain. Yours is the face of my father. A man I do not know.

YOU LOOK LIKE many of them in this youthful photo of yours. Many of the men and women who walk the streets of that small town of my childhood. Many are familiar faces, neighbors and cousins, and many more are simply strangers. Just people from a far-off land making something anew for themselves in a not-so-welcoming place.

Do you know the rumor, Papi? The one about the immigrant man who went missing from the town? The Pedro no one seems to know about, the Pedro everyone can't help but whisper about? When I ask the question about Pedro you say no, testily. You don't want me to keep asking, don't want me to keep badgering on about it. Why? I drop it, like we always do with uncomfortable topics, because that is what we do. Father and son.

I can't remember where I overhear it. Probably brought up while you and my mother are sitting in the living room watching telenovelas, or those rare moments you eat dinner together. He and his story are mentioned briefly, in passing. His is a story too grim, too serious, too close to home to give it duration. Maybe one of the kids from my school mentions something about it. Maybe this man is included in one of their many pranks they pull on the Mexican and Central American people living in the town. Maybe he is one of the ones they honk their car horn at as they pass him by on foot to frighten him. Maybe he is one of the ones they fling their car door out at to hit him off the road as he is riding his bike to work. Who knows?

I search for this nameless man throughout the years. Keywords all plugged in: "death of migrant in New Egypt, New Jersey" . . . "illegal immigrant death in New Egypt, New Jersey" . . . "disappearance of undocumented immigrant in New Jersey" . . . "Mexican death in New Jersey" . . . "Guatemalan death in small-town New Jersey" . . . "unidentified person goes missing from Main Street, U.S.A." . . . the word arrangements continue. Amounting to nothing substantial.

I try again. I type into Google: "immigrant death in New Jersey." The first two hits are the only ones that put the keywords together. Both articles report on deaths in immigrant detention centers. The first happens in 2005, and takes place in the town over, Freehold. Complaints surrounding the death are logged, and media inquiries receive vague and unsatisfying answers. The second occurs in 2016 and happens in Newark. The autopsy is pending, and little else is known.

I leave the wormhole that is the internet and ask my mother if she remembers a conversation with you about this Pedro. She says no. She blames her faulty memory, a bad memory she has had her whole life. She says she has never heard of such a disappearance. I believe her. She knows many of the Mexican and Central American diaspora in the area. Many of them are her friends. Some of them have been her lovers.

Is it love at first sight between you two? I always wonder this. Neither of you are straightforward with the answer probably because neither of you want to give the other such an accolade over your coupling. Both of you are so prideful. I know when my mother first sees you she can't help but not look. Your dark brown skin, your long black hair, your features of Mesoamerican indigeneity intriguing to her. Do you feel the same kind of exoticism toward her? Her light skin, her Caribbean abrasiveness, her fullness of body. Neither of you are ever forthcoming about the feelings you have for the other. Off and on again, never married, though together through so much. I have lived through all the battles of your love and still it is an anomaly to me. A kind of love I never want to be caught up in myself.

I show her the youthful picture of you. Wow, she says, your father was so sexy. She tells me how she has never seen that picture of you, that image of your time before her, before us, before any of this. She smiles longingly while looking at the picture. Is she thinking of your life before it entwines with hers? Is she recalling what your entrance into her life has done? You have to remember, Papi, the first time she sees you on the street of my childhood it is the signaling of the end. The end of her youth and her prior love, the end of a distinctively Puerto Rican barrio, the end of an era. You, her lover, you, her destroyer.

Sitting there looking at her contemplative face I wonder if she is thinking of the end, or a beginning, or neither. How would I know? I don't ask her. Some memories are not for all of us to know. Some stories are not meant for the telling.

IT IS EARLY morning on Main Street and Pedro is waiting. 5:30 a.m., to be precise. Those hours of early darkness cold and frigid. Our Pedro is next to Juan and Carlos and Pablo and Guillermo and those many other men who wait for employment, softly in dialogue with one another. Their fatigued brown faces. Mighty yawns interrupt their discussions as they adjust and readjust the hats on their heads, exposing the oily, unkempt black hair underneath. They occasionally stretch their bodies—tight necks, broad backs, firm stomachs, muscular arms, stocky legs—reaching skyward, the tired bones creaking and breaking the silence of these early morning hours.

In time a van pulls up to where they are. A window is rolled down. A hand extends out and puts up three pale fingers. They deliberate. Who shall go? There are eight of these Juans and Jesuses and Santiagos and Rigos. They don't discuss for long since they know the van might zip away annoyed at wasting time, moving on to another spot with a less contemplative workforce. Three of them take the plunge and haul open the van's back doors. They salute the other men and disappear into the van's darkness. The van lumbers down Main Street to a field, a farm, a job.

This Pedro is one of those left behind. He will be needed, surely, but for now he must wait his turn. He watches as the few cars begin to grumble down the road, off to work, headlights streaming ahead scattering the darkness of the groggy morning. A cold chill moves through him. He is thinking about the division of a continent, the collapsing of distances, the reality of space and time. His brown eyes narrow inward on a target—what is it, Pedro? A dream deferred? A dream never dreamt? A dream denied? Dime, Pedro, que ves ahí en la oscuridad de tus ojos, en la oscuridad de tus sueños? I will wait for the response however long it takes, lindo.

RUMORS HAVE FOUNDED what we today know as the Americas. But you, Papi, already know this. You, and I, live out the consequences of this rumor.

The rumor of gold, lands supposedly flooding with golden radiance and shimmer, spread across Europe. Lands mineral-rich and lands ready for cultivation and lands unoccupied were supposedly in plenty across the Atlantic. Those people forced over from Africa to work these American fields were supposedly fit for this kind of labor, their bodies biologically suited to fulfill the supply and demand dictated by some Johnson or Smith or Adams or Jefferson. Those people already American by virtue of their being here for centuries were considered unfit to live and toil on these lands, rumored to be irrational and primal and uncivilized and thus exploitable and expendable according to the whims of some Columbus or Sepúlveda or Cortés or González.

The vastness of the Atlantic made these rumors mutate, multiply, and variegate, their meanings taking on many forms, many guises, depending on who was interpreting, who was theorizing them. One tells another what he heard was across the ocean, in that whole new world, and the rumor was enough of a truth to rationalize every mission, every Manifest Destiny, every conquest. Rumors told of the bountiful, rumors sweet-talked destruction, rumors created nations. Rumors have dammed up rivers, rumors have plowed prairies, rumors have built civilizations. Rumors became laws and maxims and philosophies and truths and treaties and scripture.

The American continent is a living testament to these rumors and their many forms. The American geography chronicles all this. Imagining what is and what is not from a canyon's crumbling edge, what will be and what will not be from a drained swamp, what was and what was not from a speck of dust on the windshield. The proof of the Americas' many histories is in the pudding.

Like a rumor, a photograph doesn't tell the full story. It might mislead or give the wrong information. It is suggestive, forcing the need for further inquiry, and speculation. Those who encounter a rumor or photograph inevitably become enlisted into the pursuit of truth, into the wanting to know more. Always another aspect of the story to be found.

When I move my fingertips across the photo of you on that identification card, I feel Pedro from Main Street. Pedro the rumor, Pedro without a face, Pedro who I do not know. In order to make him more than a picture, more than a semblance of your image, Pedro must be many. Pedro has dark brown eyes. Pedro has light brown skin. Or maybe it is the reverse: light brown eyes and dark brown skin. Stick with whichever comes to the mind first. Pedro has one visible dimple on his cheek, or two if symmetry is preferred. He smiles at sexual jokes, or, depending on the temper, he smiles when made uncomfortable from these jokes. He has a significant birthmark on his shoulder, or make him have none at all. The matter of Pedro really becomes a question of taste.

What is not left up to the imagination is the redness in Pedro's eyes from the field-day dust bombarding him. What is not speculation is the soreness of the bones, the muscles, the skin, the feet, the blood, the body entire. What is nonnegotiable in this imagining of Pedro is the foggy darkness he harbors within—memories painful, the unbearable that is letting go, the unnamed crossings, the fractioning of the self, the continuing horrors encountered across a continent.

Fingers touch a photograph of a man who is not yet my father and, though identified, though named and fingerprinted, evades knowing. He is like Pedro, too, like you, like me. And I feel you, Papi, your brown, your skin, your features in papery two-dimensionality, as a hemispheric encounter. In your countenance are the brown masses across these centuries in their many forms, these Americas in their everyday tumult and revolution, their ordinary longings and intimacies. I hold your youthful image close to my face, and breathe.

IN ONE OF those rare moments when I decide to clean out my nightstand, I find a piece of lined paper with this scribbled on it: "Guat hunting—how can this happen—write on it!" I never took my own advice on writing this essay but I redeem my past ambition by immediately typing the phrase into a search engine. In 2015, a Guatemalan man named Onésimo is brutally murdered in front of his home in Florida by white teenagers. At the time of the murder, the community does not report on this crime, nor any of the other ones committed against them, because they are afraid of retaliation. The man is not a citizen, nor are many of those who were outraged over his murder. In 2018, one of the men is sentenced to life in prison but imprisonment and the prison industrial complex is no solution to the problem. Incarceration doesn't end the terror of white supremacy but merely works to propagate it. Fear of retaliation, the fear of the white nation, continues on across the Americas in the hearts and minds of those like Onésimo, his family, and community.

A link is suggested on the side of the webpage. I click it. I am now in Long Island, New York, and an Ecuadorean man, sitting outside his home like the other man in Florida, is murdered. Another link. This one brings up the history of lynchings of Mexicans in the Southwest through the centuries. Another link. This one an entire documentary about mass gravesites in Texas containing unidentified, as well as unidentifiable, bodies of migrants who did not make the crossing over the border. Another link. This one is an unidentified man known as 66

Garage who, after a mysterious accident while crossing the border, lives on life support in a California hospital with loved ones somewhere wondering where he is, if he made the crossing into the United States, if he is alive. After sixteen years unidentified, his family does find him, but the pain and trauma across lives and countries is done and over with. A few more links of violence toward and deaths of Mexican and Central American peoples in places like Florida, California, and Pennsylvania. Another hyperlink . . . another recommended video . . . another face, another body, another life gone . . .

And as that is happening, Pedro strains. He clenches his fists around a stem harder. Fingernails in palm. The puncturing of skin. Blood and chlorophyll. He theorizes. He contemplates on the afflictions of time and duress and borders and geographies and the elements on his body, his mind, his matter. His mind strays from this plant and this field and this town and this country and this continent. He feels himself as an elsewhere. He imagines Pedro cosmic. The universe in him. He thinks himself divine.

A Brett or an Abigail or a Joanne or a Bob passes on the road nearby. They may glance over and wonder why Pedro is how he is, or they may not. They may think of him for an instant as he is there, or they may not. There as Pedro is in the fields, straining and toiling as he does, thinking and theorizing as he does about his life and this town and these Americas and this universe—they may not think anything is extraordinary about it. Pedro is where he is and how they know him to be. The landscape presents nothing out of the ordinary. The scene before them is a common one on their commutes to the office, to the PTA meeting, to the mall, to the pool party, to the airport to go on vacation. All is in accordance with how they know this American geography.

And if it is the lunch hour, Papi, you are most assuredly parked in front of the convenience store, drinking a chocolate milk or eating a snack. You pay no mind to the sign that reads NO LOITERING, probably because you do not even know this sign is directed at you, criminalizes you, you unfamiliar with the letters and words of any alphabet. A David and a Bob go in for coffee. They pass by you. Some of them know your name, know your face, because you work for them, or work for their fathers. Otherwise, they know you as they want to know you. They interpret and theorize and deduce and speculate about you according to their criteria. None of them know how you live, how you love in distance, how you clear your throat in the van when you pick me up from the train, how you tense up when I ask a question about your past, how you dream dreams deferred whenever you watch boxers slug it out on the TV, wishing you could have had the chance to have floated like a butterfly, and stung like a bee.

They do not try to know you as I try to know you.

WHAT ARE THE facts of your story? My father who I barely know, my father who says so little about his life or the ideas in his head. I need look no further than the identification card with your young face. You are the son of José and Josephina. You are a campesino. You cannot read or write. The outline of your thumbprints are there in case you commit some crime and someone needs to identify you.

For people like you, facts do not tell the full story. Facts might in fact occlude the story, or give us a predefined story of who you are. Facts can be weaponized to diagnose, to terrorize, to condemn, and to justify. Facts can slowly, or quickly, kill.

Your youthful image on the identification card becomes a creation of my design. I crop out the identifying information of your life because I already know those facts, facts that for far too long a time make me feel ashamed of you. I angle it diagonally because I like the flair and drama it gives you. I aestheticize the image of you because I need you to be more than just a photograph captured by a government agency. This is the earliest photograph I have of you. There are no photos of you as a baby swaddled in your mother's embrace, none of you as a boy running down dirt paths. All I have is this. The soft brown eyes of the boy brokenhearted over a first girlfriend who rejects him because he is too poor and illiterate, because of the facts of his life. The lips forming not quite a frown and not quite a smile of the boy who does construction work in his hometown in Mexico to support his mother. The stoic face of the boy who will make a decision to leave all he knows behind for the hope that the condition of his life and those he loves can get better, does not have to continue to be this centuries-long nightmare.

I DON'T KNOW if the rumor about Pedro's disappearance is true or not. I can't confirm it and can't find anyone to corroborate. What I do know is I cannot let Pedro, Papi, bear the burden of having to let his story be the story of a tragedy. Pedro's story as just a rumor or a list of identificatory facts. Pedro's story as just toiling in the fields, crossing borders, or trying to survive. These cannot be the only stories of the life Pedro lives, and cannot be the only truth we pursue.

Let us, then, imagine another part of Pedro's story.

Pedro, there, sucking on sunflower seeds, likes to spend his time sitting outside on the cement-slab porch in his green lawn chair. Some days he whittles away at wood, carving images of animals and insects, other days he just naps. Whenever he is out there, he waves to each and every car that passes by him. His waving is not really a big deal considering there aren't many cars driving by because this road is away from the traffic of Main Street, used only for driving out to the farms. He believes each car hosts a familiar face. He believes all faces are familiar to him even though they may not share a similar complexion, a similar life, a similar outlook on his life. He sees the world in terms of commonalities. Commonalities of the body and not of language. The panicked inhale when a lover is in proximity to the flesh. The fidgeting of hands when nervous in front of a superior. The rapturous laughter after a friend lands a joke.

Let us imagine, Papi, this Pedro, yawning and stretching, massaging the crick in his neck. Pedro with eyes to the sky, Pedro with eyes on the TV. Pedro bored, Pedro flirting, and Pedro grumpy. Pedro on a Monday afternoon, Pedro making snow angels in January. Imagine Pedro living out a life of leisure and wasting away the time. Letting him live the unremarkable that is the day to day, week to week, year to year. Let us imagine this Pedro, Papi, Pedro who is also you and me, these many Pedros and Marias, these many shapes and forms our stories take, these many extraordinarily ordinary lives dotting this geography we have come to call and know as the Americas.

PART 2

PEDRO IN THE PROMISED LAND

5

PEDRO IN THE PROMISED LAND

New York is to be the saving grace. Bag in hand, printed-out directions in the other, navigating the subway system on my way to my first day at college. I am alone. My family is too afraid to drive in, their country bumpkin lives unable to handle the road rage that is New York City. This is fine by me because I am entering this city brand-new. I am not the Marcos of yesterday. The boy whose bus stop signaled him as belonging to a certain group of people, the boy whose relatives blew any sense of decency, the boy who was one hundred and fifty pounds overweight, the boy who was a bit too feminine in gesture to hang with the other boys. I don't have to be that everyday Pedro anymore.

A bird shits in my hair as I get out at the subway stop where the dorms are. Not just any bird but a New York City pigeon. Feel special, I tell myself, this is authentic city-dwelling at its best. I walk into my dorm room with white goo in my hair feeling a sense of pride, a sense of belonging. A friend tells me it's good luck to have a bird poop on you. The signs are right.

The dorm room is small, musty, poorly lit. My view outside

is of a hospital, its brown cement walls giving the impression one is living in a dystopian movie. This dorm room, though shared with another, is bigger than my room at home. I have a decent-sized closet, too. This poor kid is moving on up.

On the windowsill outside is a pigeon. Freckled in neon-green splotches, eyes ruby red, feathers tussled and ragged. I don't know if it's staring at me but I want to say it is. A hollow stare of the avian kind, a disgruntled New York attitude, saying welcome.

THEY'RE GOING TO rape you in New York City, you'll see, my grandmother says to me in Spanish with her lips puckered, head nodding in her own approval. I laugh it off because that's what I do with my grandmother, my grandmother a woman who traveled across the Caribbean waters to settle in a foreign land never to return to her island, a woman who settled in one remote location of the world because she was a bit afraid of venturing too far into it. A man sticks his finger where I don't want it in a New York City club my first week in the city and I think to myself, damn, my grandmother might be right. But I am overcome by another thought, a worse one: How does my grandmother know such things of New York City? Why is there such assurance in her prophecy?

My grandmother gets a one-way ticket to New York City sometime in the early 1950s. The whispers of the American dream are too hard to refuse. The relatives she will be staying with give her an ultimatum: She must leave her three daughters behind or she cannot come at all. A single Puerto Rican woman with children is an expensive burden to take on in the cramped tenements of Brooklyn. The single Puerto Rican woman is a burden the United States will handle accordingly throughout the century. So she makes a decision she will live with for the rest of her life, a decision that will steer lives away from my grandmother, a decision my grandmother will talk about with distance, cold remorse.

New York City was to be my grandmother's Promised Land. New York City was to be the Promised Land of all Puerto Ricans. In the span of a few years my grandmother departs from Brooklyn having met my grandfather and having had more children. New York City is not her Promised Land for very long.

My grandmother moves to a small town in New Jersey, the small town where my parents will meet, and the small town where I will be born. My younger grandmother sees something in the landscape of fields and crops and woods. It's a landscape with few Puerto Ricans, few people who speak Spanish, few people who look like her. I have a difficult time in understanding what my younger grandmother sees in that town I will grow up in. What is she after? What dream does she conceive of in this town? I am told by relatives the space, the countryside, the quiet. But is that worth the sacrifice of a community, of those whose rhythm is your rhythm, those whose history is your history? I have never lived on an island and lived island realities so I cannot pass judgement upon her. But her decision has something to do with blending in, might I go so far as to say giving in, getting off the grid. For to have stayed in New

York City, the Promised Land with those tired and poor, those huddled masses, would have meant to have lived up to an expectation, to bear the brunt of history, to stay the course of what was expected of a diaspora. To be surrounded by those in a condition similar to you, a condition hundreds of years in the making, means that condition will not go away so easily, will not be a thing of the past without a fight.

What my grandmother in her advanced age thinks of her decision is a bit harder to decipher. She has known the small-town life for fifty years. A lifetime, already. I ask why she chose this point on the map and she just smiles, her eyes hazy, far-off, far into images I cannot make out in the dim living room, images I can only speculate upon based on rumors and myth. Yet I know those images are far more complex, diffracted, are images of reasons she will take to the grave with her. What I know well is my grandmother's decision is a consequence I will live with, a decision that will bear out on my body, on my mind, on my life. Her New Jersey Promised Land my nightmare.

FRIENDS SEEM TO come quickly. I make a friend who wants to be a model, I make a friend who wants to be a go-go dancer at gay bars, I make a friend who wants to be an actor. There's glitz and glamour in each of them, an attitude of savoir faire, a Carrie Bradshaw in their step. They mean business upon the first day of the semester.

"Where you going tonight?"

"I'm so hungover."

"Brunch?"

"What are you going to wear?"

"This guy wants to be my boyfriend but idk."

"I would never be caught dead past Ninety-Sixth Street."

There's a newness in their faces. That glow that is the glow of redefining oneself, of defining oneself by what you refuse to be, what you will not be caught dead being. They were not like this a year ago in high school. Here they have molted, and wear a new sense of self, a self cultured and posh and trendsetting, a self that they think is a better self, but that is up for debate.

Maybe it's New York, maybe it's the fact I'm in college, but I, too, exude this upgraded self. I feel myself performing. I give sass on demand. I strut the angles of my face because I have never known this level of thin in my life. My queerness is paraded around like a trophy, letting every straight girl in a mile radius know I am gay, I am a gay willing to be token in exchange for friendship, for an invite to this or that event. I dish out eye rolls like a pro. I'm everything these friends and acquaintances and strangers want me to be.

There's one tricky part about my identity: my being Mexican and Puerto Rican. I don't know how to sell this in a bow and ribbon, a prepackaged gift for the comfort and benefit of others. My skin doesn't immediately give it away that I am Mexican and Puerto Rican but they always ask based off my name: "So what are you?" Like I did not too long ago in high school, that most unforgivable thing I had pulled off so well, I make a decision, a decision like anyone else might make in a situation where they don't want to stand out, stand out for difference, and I choose the lesser of two evils: "I'm Puerto Rican." They give a nod of the head, an oh cool, and that's that.

Puerto Rican as an identity, as something to cling to in white America, is less of a loaded signifier than saying you are Mexican. There aren't borders to live up to, no qualms about citizenship, no jokes about reproducing like rabbits. The days of island overpopulation prevalent in the United States' imaginary, of New York City flooded with bodies unused to the cold, of those Sharks and Marias dancing in the fire escapes to escape an overcrowded apartment, are over. Puerto Rican means something different than it used to in the time when my family came to the United States. The time of the Puerto Rican after Hurricane Maria is a time that will test the Puerto Rican identity, when their waves flock to Florida, flock to a mainland that can support the aftermath of devastation, catastrophe, underinvestment. This condition of displacement and impoverishment is by no means the fault of the Puerto Rican people. The island is a colonial holding of the United States. We have been at their mercy for so long.

The question comes time and time again. What are you? Who do you belong to? What is your difference? Each time I choose to say to them I am Puerto Rican, purely and simply. Unlike in high school, I do not have to worry if they will see my father driving up to school to get me, or if they will see him at my house. My father is sixty miles off. There are no photos of my father on my Facebook because I make sure there are none. I erase the man who has crossed a continent in my name, the man who works day in and day out to give me a better life, a man who is my blood, my reason for being. But I do not care because I want to be close to those who I have convinced myself are my people, no matter the cost.

MY FATHER NEARLY drowns in a river in order to get to the Promised Land. His brother, living in New Jersey, getting rich according to his relatives in Mexico, tells my father to cross a continent. There is work to be found, and money to be made in the fields. My father, a construction worker in his small town in the state of Michoacán, making so little, getting by on so little, decides heading north is the best step to take. Home will be home no longer. Family will be but memories in photos mailed over.

Somewhere on the US–Mexico border my father swims to get to the other side. He lets go of a backpack with his belongings in it because if not he will drown. What is lost to the waves is of the most value to him: photos. A sister in a dress, a mother with her penetrating eyes, a father never met. The preservation of life comes before the photographs. Swimming there in those waterways swam by so many, so many bodies struggling to reach another life, so many bodies becoming just bodies floating downstream to whatever ditch will harbor them, my father struggles to survive. But there is intent in his muscles. He feels some otherworldly strength. His mother's voice telling him to stop drinking when he gets into the United States, his sisters pleading to him to remember them when he's thousands of miles away. On the other side of the river there is a promise. Life anew, another kind of life, living a life a little bit easier. At what cost?

My younger father is a mystery to me. It's hard to make out the form of him. The father I know is serious, quiet, keeps his thoughts to himself. In Mexico he used to drink a lot, according to my mother, drinking in order to get over heartbreak, in order to get over the fact of his life. My father was loud, my father was a borracho, my father was a stereotype. Here is the point in my father's story where I can relate, where I can see myself in him. In my Promised Land of New York City, I, too, turn to the drink to deal with my life, to get over heartbreaks, to keep going. I drink to black out. I drink because I want for a split second, a brief moment, to feel myself out of body, to be but a body of sense and sensuality and sex, a body not having to think, to contemplate, to regret. A body being a body in full.

In a dorm-room bathroom, I chug a bottle of dirt-cheap vodka and this is all I remember. The following scene is me in a hospital gurney, a nurse demanding I wake up, my head pounding away. Alcohol poisoning, apparently, and apparently I had passed out in front of my college, short-shorts on and throw-up spittle on my chest. Epic level of embarrassment.

My friends call my mother to tell her what happened and I call her in turn to tell her to not tell my dad. As per usual, as per being my mother, she tells him. He's disappointed in me, disappointed I didn't want him to know, disappointed I let New York City do this to me. Is this not the Promised Land I asked for? My father's disappointment is the disappointment of seeing one's mistakes in another. Witnessing how fast, how far, one can fall in the pursuit of an escape, of forgetting who you are if for only a drunken moment. My father sees himself in me. History, he learns through my behavior, carries itself in the blood.

Thinking on my own experience as a twenty-something-year-old drinking and getting drunk and blacking out I can imagine my father. His form of being becomes clear to me. The boy almost a man in a bar, knocking back drink after drink, hoping the swigging and sloshing of alcohol will drown out an emotion, a memory, a reality. The boy almost a man crossing the river heading to the Promised Land, not for the money, not for the supposed grandeur that is to be the United States, but swimming against the raging current in hopes of eliminating a condition of being given to us ever since Columbus discovered the Americas, the American discovery defining a mass of people. The boy that is my father, I know him. His pain my pain, his hopes my hopes, his fears my fears—our inheritance.

My younger father makes it across the river. Panting, exhausted, he lands in the soil of the Promised Land. The soft mud engulfs him, moonlight on his face, the stars above. He counts them. One, two, three . . . continuing until the stars begin to fade, and the dawning of the day signaling the danger of capture, of men with their guns, their dogs, their ideologies. He gets up, muddied and fatigued. Sighs. His journey continues.

LOANS MAKE POSSIBLE my Promised Land. Low-income household? Check. Minority? Check. No parents to help? Check. I fit the bill and more for affirmative action, for those initiatives to include more diverse students in the university, to be a token the United States government can use for some statistic, some report, some purpose. As long as it works in my favor, I don't care: I will be whoever's token.

Loans are just borrowed time, however, as well as a borrowed experience. The student with loans knows their clock is ticking the moment they sign on the dotted line. Sallie Mae is already sending emails that the interest is accruing, the government's Parent PLUS loan is already calling for you to make payments. The student in debt tries to deny this fact of their thousands upon thousands in loans, maybe even go so far as to poke fun at it in the presence of others. Poverty is a punch line on occasion but admitting to too much poverty, to the food stamps that kept you alive, to the Medicaid that kept you healthy, is a fact best kept hidden.

When questions of financials come up in group situations I grow quiet. I give a reserved laugh to deflect attention. Plans to do this or that in the city are met by me saying I have work to do for class. I give a meek sigh to take attention away from the realities of my life I'd rather not make manifest. Attention that highlights my class or racialized existence is not something I want in these college spaces. For that matter, attention has never been something I have actively wanted. Always wanting to hide my fat body, to camouflage my feminine body, to make disappear my raced body. While at college, I become willing to receive attention for being gay, but I still at some level want to blend into the background, to be one with the amorphous crowd in white.

"*THEY'RE SOOOOOO LATE,*" Molly says, her eyes rolling in the back of her head. Her alabaster hand swings up in annoyance.

"Are you that hungry?"

She shrugs her shoulders, the freckles noticeable in the foyer lighting. "No, but it's the principle of it. They are supposed to be here thirty minutes from when I ordered and now it's forty-five."

Ten or so minutes pass and the man delivering her organic salad finally arrives. His face is windbeaten, a patchy red scattered across his light brown. The eyes are red, like those of my work- and weather-weary father. He tells her the price in his accented English, an English spoken like that of my relatives, the neighbors I grew up with, my father himself. She gives him the money, the exact amount to cover the charge, irritation in the way her wrist moves toward him.

"Thank you," she says with a clipped tone, taking the bag from his hands in one sweeping motion. She walks back to the elevator and presses the button. I, the loyal token gay that I am, trail behind her, trailing for her attention.

"You didn't tip him?"

"If a delivery boy is late they don't deserve a tip."

"Maybe he got caught up, or something happened."

"I don't know how they do it in Mexico but in America we do things on time."

I look back at him. His back is turned toward me but I can tell he's staring at the exactness of her payment, the emptiness in his hands. The white helmet protecting his head lifts up. Has his shield ever saved his life, protected him from disaster? I see him on the streets of New York City. He's there zipping through traffic, dodging passersby, weathering the elements. Long hours of labor are his days and nights. He returns to a loved one, loved ones. A sister, a cousin, a mother, a child, a friend. He pedals through the city with these people in mind. He delivers his gourmet salads and sandwiches to those suited plenty working on Wall Street, delivering meals into hands several shades lighter than his, hands that will take the plastic handle and not for a second think of the man in the white helmet, thinking not of his days, his nights, his joys, his pains, his dreams as they tip him whatever amount they see fit.

"The elevator's here," she says, not looking back at either of us.

I don't know how to keep walking, how to walk into the elevator and ignore the man in the white helmet before me, to ignore what has just transpired. This friend whom I call my friend does not feel herself doing any wrong. She is in the right. He was late and therefore undeserving. It is just business as usual, another meal delivered to her dorm, another day in the life. Whatever story defines his day, whatever life he leads, is of no concern to her.

I enter the elevator with Molly. The doors close and the man with the white helmet outside is gone.

IN AN UNDERGRAD class on modernist writings, I want to hate Virginia Woolf's *Mrs. Dalloway* much like I hated James Joyce's *A Portrait of the Artist as a Young Man.* But I can't deny the appeal of Woolf's writing, the languorous temperament of her prose, the precision of her syntax.

I let the good mood of Woolf's work carry forward into this week as we go over Nella Larsen's *Passing.* Larsen's novel is the last on the syllabus. It's the one text by any person of color, the token writer from the Harlem Renaissance the professor has chosen, as if there are not enough excellent writers of color writing in the early twentieth century to add to the syllabus. Yay for diversity.

The conversation in the classroom whirls around the topic of passing. The professor puts up a list of all the ways people are passing in the novel: passing as white, passing as heterosexual, passing as upper class, passing for happy. Clare Kendry, the woman who passes as white and marries a white man, lives in the white world thinking it is the Promised Land. Irene, the character through which the narrative is told, who can also pass as white, lives in Harlem, the Promised Land for Black people in the early twentieth century. The novel centers around the reunion of the two women and their subsequent relationship.

"Clare passes for white because she hates herself."

"Clare passes for white because being Black is a harder life."

"Clare passes for white because her father mistreated her."

"Clare passes for white because . . ."

The responses from my classmates continue. They explain what it is about Blackness Clare dislikes, about the nature of her self-confidence, about the treatment by her parents, and other theories that never mention whiteness or what whiteness is or whiteness isn't. Something is missing from their analysis, but I do not pursue the thought because a spotlight no one else can see beams on me. Fiction reflects back a truth I would rather deny. Passing? I know that well. I know intimately what motivates people to pass, why the energies required for passing seem worth it. Never have I given this knowledge words, or articulated it. Ever since high school it just was, this passing game; just is what it is.

On a second reading of *Passing*, the reader discovers Clare's Promised Land is not the white world. The white world is but a placeholder. The Promised Land is in Harlem. That neighborhood housing an entire migration, those from the southern states and Caribbean islands flocking to the north for opportunity, for a change of pace. It is Black culture and Black life and Blackness itself that become her Promised Land, her means of liberation. For Irene, this is threatening though the novel doesn't explicitly detail why this is so. Clare's Blackness and Black body in Harlem are a threat to her relations, her husband, her standing in the community, her very own conception of self. Irene, after all, is one of those accused of killing Clare in many of the theories circulating about how she died at the end of the novel.

There is no doubt Clare passes over into whiteness because of the privileges whiteness gives her in twentieth-century United States. Privilege, however, does not guarantee joy. Clare marries John Bellew, an anti-Black racist white businessman, and enters into the white world because we are all told that whiteness is joy, that to be white is to bring about happiness, fulfillment, contentment. Clare's abandonment of the white world and her integration into Harlem is an anomaly. Why? Clare forsakes whiteness by the end and something about this decision Irene does not like, perhaps not liking it because passing in the novel seems to function as a courageous act, as something daring and risky, which is very unlike Irene. Or maybe Irene does not like that Clare can so easily move between worlds, so easily get what she wants, what she desires.

The spotlight is still on me. The rays of uncompromising truth singe my skin. What is so appealing about whiteness? In this upper-level English class everyone else is white. The professor is white. The walls of the classroom are white. Even the floors are white. Maybe what is appealing about whiteness is that those who are able to locate themselves within it never have to think about it. It is the default and when you are the default there is nothing to talk about. There is no conversation about your characteristics, about what defines you, about the nature of your being. There's no excitement in that. Passing is an attractive notion because we all want to feel ourselves as the default, as the point of reference, as being understood without having to explain ourselves, as having no reason to think outside the dimensions of our bodily frame. Passing promises this feeling. This way into a life that is a life free of having to reflect on what one is, free of self-scrutiny, free of examining who and what you are.

I can sympathize with Clare and her desire to pass into whiteness and marry a racist white man. She gets close to a life where she can laugh, iron her clothes, take a shower, walk down the street and not have to think about race, about Blackness, about the realities of the world. When she meets her demise at the end of the novel, having forsaken whiteness and embraced the Blackness of Harlem, then being either thrown out the window by her husband, Bellew, for being a Black woman or by Irene, who sees Clare as too much of a Black woman and therefore a threat, Clare is a victim of wanting her cake and eating it too. She wants Blackness and she wants whiteness. She wants her husband and she wants Irene. She wants the world on her terms, but women like Clare do not get the world on their terms. If they try, they pay the price.

My professor asks at the end of the class who killed Clare. Catherine says Irene, and Meghan says John, and everyone has their opinion. I say neither, and leave it at that.

UNDER THE DISCO lights I'm Mariah Carey belting out notes. Hips in rotation, cheek to cheek, arms side to side with attitude as my mouth moves to the lyrics, the adoration of my fans a high. The alcohol rushes through the blood and the crowd of dancers are urging me to continue, to hit those high notes, to give them my diva flair. Hair flip, shoulders pointed, the upturn of the eyebrows. I am opulence itself there upon the dance floor. Untouchable in my style, impervious to mediocrity in my grace.

Boom boom boom, thump thump thump. The speakers in the club vibrate intensely, the music felt vividly, the lyrics in the bone matter. Emotions, those things not meant for the club, those things not meant for such divas like Mariah Carey, surface. The *boom boom boom* and the *thump thump thump* bringing them out, the club and the bodies and the speakers and the lights—all the past and the present. There's David from middle school, there's Abigail from high school, there's Mrs. B from kindergarten, there's Molly not tipping the man, there's that guy on Grindr who told me I was too fat for him, there's that boy on the subway who called me faggot.

I am no longer Mariah Carey there amidst her fans. I am that boy, little Marcos, tears in my eyes and a lump in my throat. I'm a boy running through the crowd of sweaty men and men with their egos, running outside into the New York City streets, running to the subway, running all the way to my dorm. Little Marcos there in his dorm, crying, all alone, all tired out, not knowing where else to run, how far to keep going, not knowing when all this running he does will end.

THERE'S DESPERATION IN her voice. A last resort in the brown of her eyes. In her Spanish I can hear the hopes and fears of my relatives yet I do not want to see similarity in her, the similarity of our lives. *"Can you teach my daughter to read and write?"*

I want to reassure her in a way she needs. She wants a miracle no one can give her in the course of several weeks. She wants her daughter to win spelling bees and most-books-read awards in school. She needs for her daughter to excel in order to confirm that the many miles they traversed across a continent to Sunset Park weren't in vain. She wants her daughter to live up to be her American dream.

"Voy a tratar . . ." I tell her in my Spanish, my Spanish that is and is not like her Spanish, a Spanish similar to my father's.

I'm the tutor. Hired by the city, an initiative the city has put in place to help students coming from bilingual homes. I am assigned those students who speak Spanish and English, students who were once upon a time me. I am supposed to be the miracle worker. Parents plead with me to help their children. Por favors are lobbed at me every time I walk through their doors. They think I will bring about the end of their condition in this United States.

The daughter of the woman wears these glasses that make her brown eyes look so large, so studious, as she moves from word to word on the page. She knows her ABCs and how to sound out some words but that is about it. She is in the third grade but she is at a first-grade reading level. I want the best for her and I have known her for but a few days.

"You have to have her read every single night," I explain to the mother, "and have her read to you. It will help improve her skills."

She looks at me with suspicion. There is something she wants to say but she does not say it. She does not trust me, this boy who is brought in by the city to help, this program implemented by the city that is a program meant to be but a Band-Aid on a very large wound. I do not tell her I was once upon a time like her daughter. The boy who could not read well, who could not speak any language properly, who was deemed a problem to be fixed by the state. I can tell her any strategy I want but she will consider my methods demeaning, a means to castigate her, a way in which to keep her daughter in the back of the bus. There is a division of language that neither of us can mend.

"Lo que tu digas," she says with eyes zoomed in on me, eyes seeing through me.

A week later I call the mother. I tell her I can no longer come at four o'clock due to a change in my course schedule and have to come at six o'clock instead. She's not having it. *"You do not care about my daughter! My daughter is never going to read or write with you! Do not come back to my house!"*

The phone hangs up and that's it. My boss calls me right after to say don't worry about it, there are more children in need, there are more mothers in their desperation. I won't see this mother again, I won't see her daughter again. Her daughter will receive another tutor, a tutor who might or might not know Spanish, a tutor who might or might not know why the mother is so insistent, so driven. This tutor will work whatever hours were left from the allotted forty hours each child receives.

This tutor will have to take the time to reassess, to identify the issues they can try to cover within the span of a few weeks, and by the time that's over they can start the real work.

I will think of this mother and daughter, a lot, I will think of this most brief moment in my life, frequently. The daughter's thick glasses, her eagerness to read with me, her quick loss of interest. The mother and her eyes doubting me, her short fuse, her desperation and hope. I will think of them as I think of all those children I will tutor through these undergraduate years. The little boy who loved wrestling and whom I will give my entire wrestling DVD collection to, the little girl who drew me a pony, the twin boys who would finish each other's sentences. Their parents and grandparents and aunts and guardians, too, I will think of. The grandmother who will tell me her dreams were back in Puerto Rico, the sister taking custody of her brother at the age of eighteen, the mother in her room too high to open the door for me. I will travel all across Brooklyn encountering lives I will know for but a moment, a moment I can be in the lives of strangers. Lives who came to Brooklyn, or have been there for generations, thinking this was to be the Promised Land, the land their children, their progeny, would do better in, would make a name for themselves in these United States. And there I am going door to door, Sunset Park to Bushwick, Bushwick to Brownsville, pencils and paper in my bag, trying to prove to them that yes here is where your dreams might begin, yes here is where the Promised Land was promised you.

MY MOTHER CHANGES Promised Lands like she changes her underwear. Before I am born it is the Bronx. A bus ticket in one hand, and a baby in the other, she flees to the city her mother fled from, the mother who had deemed New York City a wasteland. There my mother encounters the cramped tenements of the Bronx: the baby's crib an inch away from the bed, the neighbors and their tussles, the cars and their horns through the night. She sees for herself what her mother saw in the city landscape: the Puerto Rican condition. The single mothers and their plight, the broken-down cars with nowhere to go, the children in their secondhand clothing skipping cans down the street. She cannot believe her eyes. This is not the fate of the Puerto Rican people where she is from, the Puerto Ricans who do not live in such close proximity to one another, the Puerto Ricans who do not have to bear witness to the condition of their being day in and day out. The few who ventured out to the small-town U.S.A. of my mother's upbringing do not identify with the Puerto Ricans in the Bronx though they are family. These Bronx dwellers have chosen to stay within the condition of the island they have all fled.

My mother leaves the Bronx as soon as she realizes it will not bring about the promise of emancipating her from her condition. Her next attempt at finding her Promised Land, her people, will be in the island of her mother's birth: Puerto Rico. She will go there with no children, leaving her children with her mother, much like her mother did in reverse thirty years before. In Puerto Rico she will be tested. The root of the Puerto Rican condition is there for all to see. The houses without electricity, the goats giving milk, the men drinking outside and their bellies pregnant with beer. Her people? Yes, she tells herself, these are her kin and kind, pure and untainted by the mainland. Yet a gulf of difference divides them from her. These people who are and are not her people have only known this island. They did not test their luck as my grandmother did by seeing what riches, what promises, the mainland would bring. United States citizenship means nothing, and, if anything, means escaping, means letting go of the island and its people.

These kin and kind, they do not see my mother as she sees them. They will look at her with suspicion, quite possibly contempt. They see the daughter of a woman who elected to leave her people behind. They see a betrayal in the Spanish of my mother's voice. They see an island in my mother, an island slowly evacuated of its inhabitants, an island forsaken. Eventually, this will be enough to stifle my mother's interest in staying in Puerto Rico. She will leave and never come back again.

My mother's voyages across the American landscape eventually lead her back to New Jersey, the Promised Land of my grandmother, the Promised Land of my father. Around the time I am born my mother returns to the small town and to the neighborhood she grew up in. The house she will rent is down the street from the house of her upbringing. My grandmother is a two-minute walk down the road. But the houses of this neighborhood and their inhabitants have changed since my mother was a little girl. A migration from Mexico and Central America has settled in the neighborhood once filled with Puerto Ricans. The Puerto Ricans that once called this area home have left to greener pastures, to the white picket fences, to the homes that only speak English, closer to the American dream promised their parents. My mother and grandmother do not identify with those Puerto Ricans. They have decided to stay in this neighborhood, to stay speaking their Spanish to the neighbors, staying though mostly all of their kin and kind have left. They decide to live out the Puerto Rican condition in this small-town U.S.A.

Maybe my mother's Promised Land is my grandmother's Promised Land. Maybe she realized after searching a continent, a continent she thought would be hospitable to her, that the Promised Land doesn't exist, that no matter where you go, no matter how far you travel, the conditions of a life can't be kicked by just a change of scenery, a difference in zip codes.

"SUP?"

"Nothing much."

"What u into?"

"Talking . . ."

"Total top here, pnp, raw. What r u?"

"What you mean?"

"Like race? What are you? Cuban?"

It's the question that rivals all questions. The manner of my being. On this dating/sex app I have selected Latino but that is too ambiguous, too open-ended for this thrill seeker. Latino is no guarantee I talk with an accent, or have a Latin flavor. Latino does not designate anything besides some flimsy association to a person whose history derives from Latin America.

Today I am feeling bold. I want to experiment. I want to say something I have never said before.

"I'm Puerto Rican & Mexican."

The message sends. This faceless profile is the first person besides my family who knows this fact of who I am. What is he thinking? Is he thinking anything at all?

A minute or so passes and I open the app up again. His message isn't there. He blocked me. What was it? What was it about my answer that did not appeal to him? I want to ask him so desperately what it was about my being Puerto Rican and Mexican that was such a turnoff. I need to know because to know is to verify the theories I have told myself for so long about my twoness, this split confusion, my being a problem to myself and others. A part of me imagines the white daddy brought his finger to the block button to remove me from his sight because he could not see a fantasy in my body, in the strangeness of my twoness, unable to see some accented and spicy Pedro who moans and groans on cue, wailing out a *Papi* every thirty seconds or so in order to let this white daddy know he's in charge, he has dominated this naughty spic. He pressed the block button with a certainty that my being Puerto Rican and Mexican was not in his sexual appetite.

Another message, a new guy, a new set of dick and ass pics to sift through. This time around I will do things differently. I will tell this guy what I have told the others. I will return to what I have been doing for so many years, returning to this house of cards I have built for myself, this house of cards teetering on the brink of collapse.

OUR TIME IS up. It's the last day of tutoring for Maria. I have come every day after school for the last month or so. Her reading skills are better, her ability to express herself in English improving by the day. Pat yourself on the back, Marcos, because this is a job well done.

A friend texts me asking if I want to go to hot yoga at seven o'clock. I have another student to go and tutor but I love doing hot yoga with Molly, love the way being around her makes me feel so cool and hip and *Sex and the City*–like. This girl with the blonde hair and charisma and blue eyes and paid internship and house in Connecticut by the lake is so New York City to me. She is the vision of what I wanted to be when I first moved here. But deep down I know boys like me can only be peripheral to her kind of New York, the New York of the collective imagination, the New York you see on the TV and movies, the New York City where an everyday Pedro is just an extra on the set with no name.

Why do I owe these people anything? In the adjacent room are Maria's parents. I come in every day and they say their greetings and that's about it. Like so many parents, they look at me with distrust and trust, the boy who is and is not like them at their doorstep promising the cure to their condition. Looking at Maria's parents I see a stark similarity to my parents. The aloofness to strangers, the mistrust in the brown eyes, the friendly yet hostile timbre of the voice.

I call the parents of the next child and cancel. Something came up, I tell them, an air of urgency in my gringofied Spanish. They believe me because they have no choice but to believe me.

I go to yoga. Namaste my sweaty ass through sixty minutes with a cadre of NYU students, students who each pretend they are on a budget, budgeting out the few dollars that they convince everyone else is all they have. This Molly and I get a drink afterward. She leads me to a bar that is well out of my budget but I do not tell her that. My smile tells her I can afford it and that's that. Sitting at the bar with the intimate lighting, Molly tells me of her day with the guy from last night who she did lines of coke with at the club, of the fancy dinner she has planned for Saturday in the Upper West Side with an eligible bachelor who works on Wall Street. I do not tell Molly of my day. I make no mention of the fifteen-year-old girl who is reading well behind her grade level, of her parents who are unable to read in English to help with homework, of the poor MexiRican who tries to help and tries so desperately to feel he is not like his students, not similar to their struggles at all. Discussing the details of my days is too heavy for girls like Molly. Instead, I tell Molly I had to go to work, unfortunately, to a job I don't really like and a job I don't really have to go to but I go nonetheless because I would like to make a few extra bucks. I tell her everything is fabulous and dandy and oh so gay. This is what she wants to hear, after all, to hear only the glitz and glamour I have forged for girls like her. She wants to smile, she wants to laugh, she wants to revel in the stories I tell her of my well-fabricated life. Cheers to that, Molly, cheers to this New York City kind of life.

IN *PASSING* I find a scene that speaks to many of the conversations I have with Molly and those other girls like Molly. Clare, Irene, and their friend Gertrude, three women who are able to pass as white, are having a conversation. They first speak about the fear of bearing children who might turn out to have a dark complexion, then turn themselves over to small talk.

> Clare began to talk, steering carefully away from anything that might lead towards race or other thorny subjects. It was the most brilliant exhibition of conversational weightlifting that Irene had ever seen. Her words swept over them in well-modulated streams. Her laughs tinkled and pealed. Her little stories sparkled . . .

> Clare talked on, her voice, her gestures coloring all she said of wartime in France, of after-the-wartime in Germany, of the excitement at the time of the general strike in England, of dressmaker's openings in Paris, of the new gaiety of Budapest.

HOWEVER, ALL GOOD things must come to an end, as the women figure out.

> But it couldn't last, this verbal feat. Gertrude shifted in her seat and fell to fidgeting with her fingers. Irene, bored at last by all the repetition of selfsame things she had read all too often in papers, magazines, and books, set down her glass and collected her bag and handkerchief.

What follows is Clare's husband arrives on the scene. Clare is passing for white so therefore Gertrude and Irene must pass as white, too, if they are to inhabit the same spaces together, if Clare does not want her cover to be blown. The husband's entrance destroys the delicately woven conversation the women were holding because Bellew addresses Clare by the nickname of Nig, short for that awful word, which Bellew jokingly explains in this way: "When we were first married, she was as white as—as—well as white as a lily. But I declare she's gettin' darker and darker. I tell her if she don't look out, she'll wake up one of these days and find she's turned into a n—."

Everyone erupts into laughter. They laugh and they laugh and they laugh. It is a laugh so hard that Irene's "sides ached," "her throat hurt," and "tears ran down her cheeks." What else is there to do when confronted with the question, the reality, of race? A problem the women openly mask, a problem that they speak about by not speaking it? To be white or to pass as white or to try to enter into whiteness or acquiesce to whiteness, as the women demonstrate, as they demonstrate so well when Clare's husband enters the scene, is to confront the world as if the world were a thing to be denied. The delicate approach to conversation, ensuring all conversations are excised of thinking about Blackness, of whiteness, of the contours of a country. If Clare and Irene and Gertrude want to pass into whiteness then this means they must pass in the ways they speak, in the topics about which they can speak, in knowing what is sayable and what is not. They must remember to keep in mind that whiteness, no matter who is using it, who is trying to live up to it, is all about control and restraint and withholding and denying.

In the margins of the page, in black ink, are these words I write down upon the first read-through: "to make invisible race, to make it irrelevant, is to create tension."

I HAVE SOMEWHERE to be. An invitation to go somewhere uptown. Brunch, maybe, wine in Central Park, perhaps. It's a beautiful summer day and it's my junior year of college and I am living in the Lower East Side. Not the Lower East Side of everyone's imagination, of wannabe hipsters and swanky clubs, of how they sell it on every realtor website. This is Loisaida. This is the Lower East Side of the Puerto Ricans. This is Avenue D on a Friday with salsa playing, an old woman in a wheelchair fanning the car exhaust from her face, the milk carts and the dominoes being played on them. This is mazes of public housing, the bike without its wheels, the gum on the cement. This is the corner of Rivington where a Puerto Rican flag waves out of an apartment, the last of its kind, an apartment with a woman living inside who will not give in to the demands of corporate interest until she has no other choice, until she is gone from this world. This is a last hurrah of a people, of a movement, of a dream. The city of yesterday wearing down against the might of the city of tomorrow.

I walk to the subway. There's confidence in my strut, attitude in my chin thrust in the air. Some sense of being untouchable, of trying to be untouchable, exudes from my body. New York, I feel you, New York, I embody you, New York, I am you.

The DO NOT WALK sign is up. Second Avenue and Sixth. I am now in the Lower East Side of everyone's imagination. The skinny women, the blondes of their hair in the breeze, the designer sunglasses. Friends all the same color having brunch. A band setting up in the back of a bar. I revel in all this around me. I convince myself these are my kind of people.

The symbol changes: I walk. Step by confident step I walk across the city street, my stride my catwalk, and halfway to the other side a man on a bike nearly hits me. He swerves, falls to the ground with a hard thud, metallic crash of the bike. In the basket of his bike there is a bag of food. Whatever he is delivering—soup?—is now oozing onto the street.

I'm unharmed, just standing there looking at him. I don't say anything, I don't offer to help him up. I had the right of way, obviously, he did not. He's so small there splayed across the city street, so unimpressive in form. A moustache, a blue helmet, eyes red from lack of sleep. His skin is sweaty from pedaling in the heat. I am telling myself something that I don't want to tell myself by looking at him. Thoughts rapid, thoughts assaulting, thoughts unforgiving. I don't want to think that by looking at this man I see familiarity. I don't want to think that by looking at this man I see similarity to my father. I don't want to think that by looking at this man I see a bit of myself. I don't want to think of this man because I have convinced myself he is not my New York City, not my kind of people, not who I have imagined myself to be in this city. I have left men like him sixty miles away in the town of my birth, in the town where my parents met, in the town where my history was a scarlet letter upon my body.

I keep walking in order to not think the thoughts I am thinking. I don't look back but I can imagine he's picking himself up, apologizing to the cars on the road, contemplating how he will explain to his boss the merchandise was lost. I think of the soup-like substance on the ground, spoiled and spilled, like the dreams he dreamt far away from here until the day he arrived in New York City to find out dreams are just meant to stay dreams for certain kinds of people.

I get to the Astor Place subway station. People are all around: students from NYU; women in their twenties wearing designer clothes and holding designer bags; guys who look like they belong in a band. My people? Who are my people? Are they on this subway platform? Are they the ones waiting for me uptown? Are they the ones having brunch, the ones going to the expensive gym, the ones going out for the night in the East Village?

And then I think for but a second, a fragment of time, that maybe, just maybe, my people are back there on Second Avenue and Sixth trying to salvage whatever remains of the soup-like substance, perhaps back on Avenue D playing dominoes, maybe those huddled masses who live their lives on the outskirts of this city, in the borderlands where dreams bask in the hope of someday being realized.

My people? Where are they? Who are they? There's no more time to think because the subway is here and I must go, going no longer to the event I felt I had to go but elsewhere, to the last stop of the train, to the ends of the city where those masses like the masses my grandmother, my mother, my father, my family belong to live, those masses whose ebbs and flows I know as familiar, whose ebbs and flows are mine. I let myself go to the last stop. The Promised Land awaits.

MEN AGAINST THE women, and the women against the men in *West Side Story*'s famous number "America." The women sing how the United States is the Promised Land, while the men sing how it is not. Anita could care less about Puerto Rico: "Puerto Rico, my heart's devotion / Let it sink back in the ocean." For a whole musical number Anita defends the United States, shoving into the face of the men that old immigrant narrative that she is the good immigrant, the one who is thankful to the nation for saving her from her poverty, from her colonial condition. She believes wholeheartedly in the promise the United States can give.

Later in the musical, there is a change of heart. Something happens to Anita in America. The scene in the film version is Anita enters the pharmacy to confront the Jets. She is alone. They encircle her, grabbing at her, her body in their hands, their hands tossing her around and around and around as they so desire. She screams. A blood scream, a netherworld scream, and they release her. Anita (or Rita Moreno—at this point in the film what is real and what is fiction blurs, actress becoming the Puerto Rican woman she is) looks at the men with bleary eyes, eyes not of sadness or disappointment, but the eyes one gives when a betrayal has occurred, when a belief in something has died. She looks at those men, penetrates them, and her vision goes beyond them. She will think upon the song she shared with her boyfriend Bernardo, a boyfriend who will soon die by the hands of those men who grabbed her body, those lyrics her boyfriend sang narrating the condition of the Puerto Rican people in the United States that Anita counterpointed, the "lots of doors slamming in our face," or "the twelve in a room," the "one look at us and they charge twice." She will stare into the faces of men who put their hands on her because they knew they could, staring into the faces of those who she thought would accept her, embrace her, and celebrate her in the United States. There with the skyscrapers behind her in the glass of the shop windows, those skyscrapers she saw from the deck of a boat launched from San Juan, those skyscrapers blooming and promising in their height, Anita stands in the rubble of her Promised Land, staring at the faces of men and a landscape that no longer has any promises to give, if genuine promises it ever had to offer.

A FEW FRIENDS and I are waiting in line at the Union Square movie theatre, waiting to see *Batman* or some other superhero movie. It's my final semester of undergrad. Next year I will be heading to grad school. A fully funded PhD program in English Language and Literature awaits. A new journey in academia, new trials to endure. Professor Gonsalez soon to be.

These friends are friends who have been around since my first semester. They are gay men, men of different races and backgrounds. They have seen me in my lowest moments, consoling me through drunken stupors and heartbreaks and STD scares. These men know so much about me yet they do not know an important part of me, do not know my father works the fields day in and day out, do not know I stem from a darker race of men. It's about time to tell them about this part of me. Unlike Molly and those many other Mollys, they will be entering this next part of my life with me so I want a clean slate. I want to start graduate school without secrets, without having to lie about the nature of who and what I am. I don't want an identity of erasure to define me anymore.

"There's something I have to tell you guys . . ." I say, the words reminiscent of the first time I came out to my family. When I started college I never had to come out—I was just out. I made it a fact I was gay, made it something I wore on my body like a badge of honor, knowing being gay in twenty-first-century New York City was something to be celebrated, commodified, tokenized. Now I am coming out, again, coming out as the one thing I have been most ashamed of being: Mexican.

"I'm . . ." The word has a hard time coming out, the tongue doesn't move, the vocal chords don't know how to say it. This will be the first time in my life I will say what I am about to say. Their eyes look at me with total bewilderment. They know there is a secret but have no remote idea what I could have been withholding from them. Expectation in the lips.

"I'm . . . how do I put . . . I'm Mexican."

"Oh," one of them says, eyebrows raised in a mild surprise. *"I thought as much."*

"Yeah, me too."

None of them make a big deal of it. None of them really say much at all. They just let this fact of my being Mexican settle and naturalize. Within a few minutes we are up and rushing to get seats in one of the middle rows of the theatre, like we always do.

MY THERAPIST SAYS I need to forgive myself for passing as just Puerto Rican, for saying to that friend who I thought was my friend in high school that my father was my father's worker, for denying my father was my father for so many years. You have done your penance, she says with a gentle firmness, and I meet her resolution with polite negation, a swift turning of my head. No. Forgiveness must be earned, even the forgiveness one gives oneself.

So I write a path to forgiveness, reader, writing to you, writing to myself, writing to right my wrongdoings. To write wrongdoings, to write the details of how I have wronged, citing the causes and the effects, is to realize the potential in forgiveness, in making forgiveness a means to actually change my life, to make my life mean something for the better. Or so I want to believe.

I do not want to be Clare Kendry by the window, death an enigma, details of her life uncertain. I want an ending with some kind of clarity, to have my demise written of in its glorious specificity, knowing full well who I am and what I have done at the time in which I meet my demise. I want to be able to tell someone, anyone, I have reached the Promised Land, the land promised to me to bring about my salvation, my emancipation from my past, and once there, once in its bustling avenues and busy streets, turned away from it.

IS NEW YORK City my Promised Land? At some point in my life it definitely was because I needed it to be. New York City as my Promised Land served its purpose though not the purpose I had foresaw. Like all Promised Lands, New York enabled a fantasy of who I wanted to be, of where I wanted to be at, of how I might be in the world. But I have come to learn in these Americas, as a child born from differing histories of the Americas, there are no Promised Lands. History has denied us that, as history tends to do. There are just coordinates on the map that provide temporary refuge, giving us a moment in time in which to collect our bearings and go again, going so we can tell the next generation of where we have been, how we have been tested.

I remain in New York City as I write this, but someday I will not—I cannot. Other landscapes, other horizons, call me. Go, keep going, go to a sanctuary that may harbor you, to New York City the city of refuge, beyond and forward past it, go I hear in my body. Just go, as Maria and Tony say to each other in West Side Story, someplace different than the American landscape they find themselves in, somewhere like a real Promised Land where meaning does not have to mean as it means in the Americas, somehow, someday, somewhere.

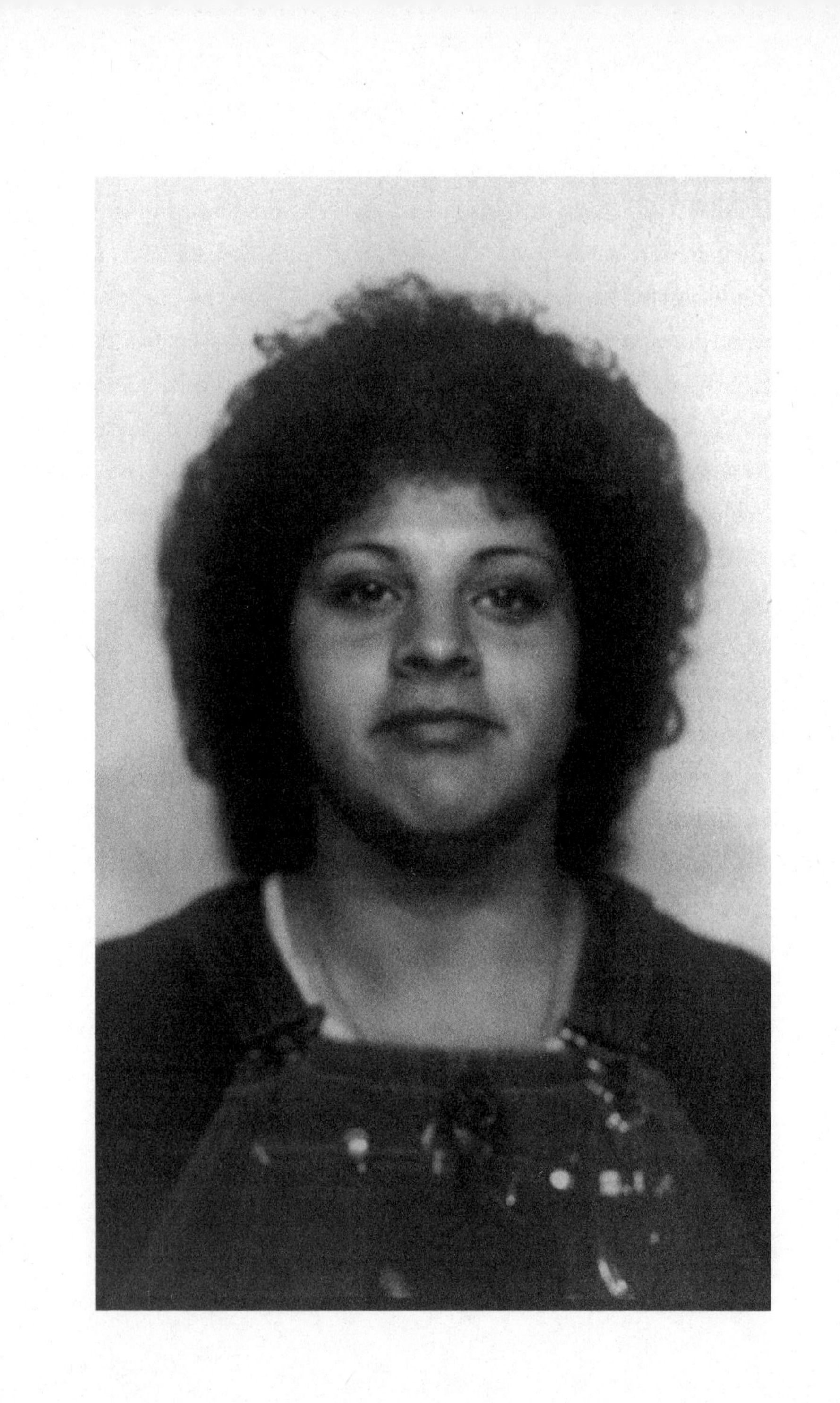

6

TO MY MOTHER

I have never known you to be a quirky person. Hotheaded, yes, assertive and never wrong, certainly, but never quirky like the photo of you suggests. Where is this taken? At the movie theatre, the carnival? Is it the late seventies or early eighties? The overalls, the curly hair, the frown-smile figuration of lips. I can't stop looking at this black-and-white photobooth picture of you because I can't make heads or tails of your countenance. I don't know what your face is trying to tell the viewer. This is not the mother I know.

Then, and now, you have always loved photobooths. Anytime we go to the movie theatre, or the mall, you pop your head in the booth to check the prices. Odds are you find them too expensive, which they are. There is a photobooth photo of us from around 2006, when I'm first starting high school, and we are both smiling. My cheek is squashed up against your cheek. The flash is too strong so the image makes us look like we are drowning in light. We look content. I'm sure we are, in that exact moment, but the photograph masks the historical context in which it is taken: the recent death of your son, my brother; you losing your job due to the depression, the unimaginable mourning; I, the fat and feminine son, the one with too much swish in his step and verve in his voice, am the only son left, a source of pain for you; you taking out your frustrations and pains on me.

The photobooth stages an encounter of participation. The person being photographed knows it is coming and they want it. They have paid for it, after all. So they smile, so they pose, so they do their thing, whatever that thing may be, hoping it will give them the best photographic outcome. Serious, if you want, goofy, if you like, a little bit mopey, if you so choose. Whatever look you want to give, you give it, because it is just for an instant, a moment. By doing so you create another self. One that is not your everyday self, perhaps, not riddled by depressive frowns or the happy-go-lucky smile. The photographed subject doesn't have to give the same look they give on a daily basis. The photobooth lets you play a character, an emotion, a style, where you can become a stranger in a familiar body for a brief moment.

But you know this better than I do, you chameleon. Your younger self, there in the photobooth, with quirky countenance, the only example of such a look in your photographic archive I can find. All the other photos I find of this period of your life, or of you at all, are serious-faced poses, staged smiles. That's the mother I know. The mother who acts first and thinks later. The mother whose mood and attitude can change like the flick of a light switch. The mother quick to use her hands to solve her problems.

But in this black-and-white quirkiness you become unfamiliar to me. You are the oddball photographer. You are the Puerto Rican girl as artist. Not my mother I have come to know.

HAVE YOU HEARD of the photographer Diane Arbus, Mom? Having wanted to be a professional photographer yourself, you probably have. She was famous, and one of her most famous photographs is *Puerto Rican Woman with a Beauty Mark, NYC* (1965). The black-and-white photograph is of a Puerto Rican woman looking straight ahead, a black scarf wound around her head, and, as the title of the picture denotes, a notable beauty mark is on her cheek. Her face houses an expression passing as horror, surprise, disgust, anger, annoyance. Perhaps all of them at once. Her gaze is not at the camera but rather over the photographer's shoulder, the expression directed at an object or event beyond the photographic framing. Arbus seems to capture this moment, whatever this moment even is.

This moment of capturing, though perhaps inflected by a touch of fetishization on Arbus's end, is not untruthful. I have known these visages. I have seen these Puerto Rican women caught in a moment. The photograph of a tia in Puerto Rico looking out from her porch into the distance, face contorted into an expression of irritation or disgust at whatever it is she looks upon, sugarcane stalks jutting out beside her. The confused or pained countenance of my dying grandmother as she looks on at me, bedridden, with the glazed eyes of dementia, not knowing who I am, not knowing my voice, not knowing I am the grandson she took care of once upon a time. I have witnessed your face when the police tell us my older brother, the man's man, the Pedro of every Latin American mother's dream, has died, and your netherworld scream, your face a distortion I can never not forget.

There are two photos I find among your albums that are reminiscent of Arbus's *Puerto Rican Woman with a Beauty Mark, NYC.* They are two photographs of your mother, my grandmother, a woman who I also call my mother.

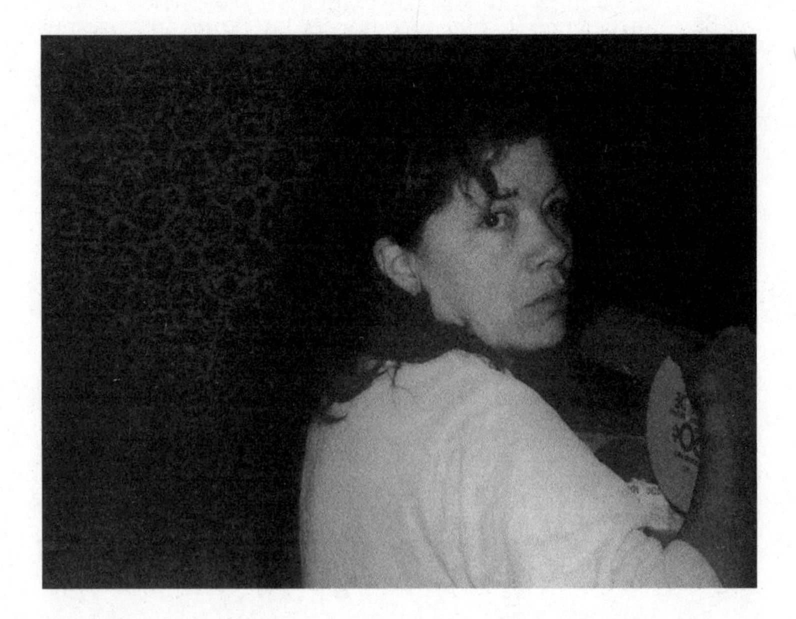

THE PHOTOS ARE obviously taken before I am born because I have never known her that young. The sepia tone designates the seventies. Not to mention the wallpaper. In both of them, she appears to be caught off-guard by the photographer, as she looks over her shoulder in surprise standing in the kitchen. In the first, she is in front of the sink looking back at the photographer, washing out a bowl in her one hand, and in the other there is the large metallic spoon she uses to cook with. On the stove next to her is her caldero, where for decades she makes her rice and beans and stews and bacalao, her cooking a staple of how you, and I, will come to spend time with her. In the other photograph she appears to be opening something above the stove. It is night, evidently, because the flash of the camera becomes a deluge of light against her surprised face while the rest of the photo is encompassed in foggy darkness.

Though you can't remember, and I can find no one to confirm, I know these are taken by you. The staging of the over-the-shoulder look of your muse is distinctly your photographic touch. I can see you waiting patiently for the right moment to snap the picture, to get her just so. Pose, Mama, I can hear you saying in Spanish, as she looks over her shoulder at you, at her daughter the photographer. I want to believe these are photographic attempts to get closer to your mother, to your mother who was cold and indifferent toward you, to your mother who didn't know how to say I love you to you. Mama, I can hear you calling, as she looks back in both, the flash of your camera a labor of love, an attempt at loving her.

Unlike in Arbus's photograph, there is a tenderness to these photographs of my grandmother, a Puerto Rican woman. A certain kind of knowing of the photographed subject, the intimate knowledge of how they will react to the camera flash, to your familial surprise. This intimacy and tenderness manifests in many of the photos you take throughout my childhood. Many appear to be captured in a moment of surprise, like this one of me.

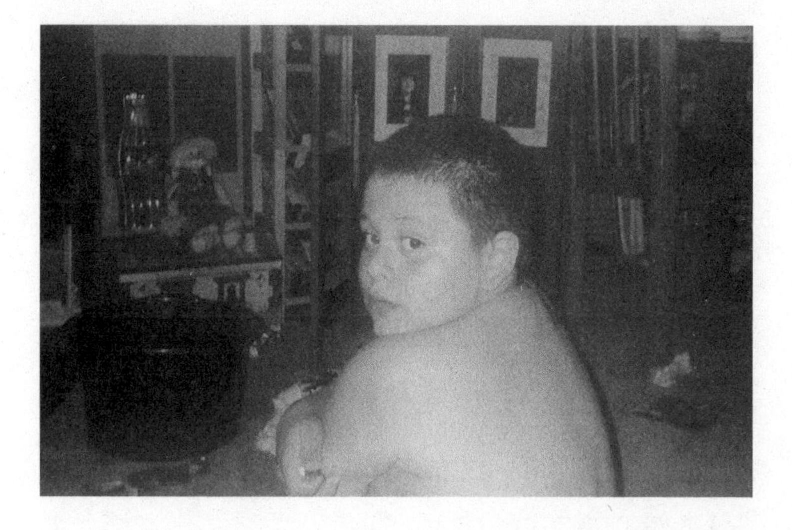

MY CHILDHOOD SELF is looking over the bare shoulder with what appears to be a surprised face, like my grandmother in the kitchen, wondering what you are doing, why this photo here and now. But you know why. You are a photographer. You can see the perfect picture in a moment. The careful attention on my exposed body, the turning of the shoulder the turning into a posed vulnerability, my face suspended in disbelief or wonder or something else. I am grateful to you for this photograph, Mom. This photo gives me a different portrait of myself to work with. One that does not just have to be the ridiculed and violated body my classmates make of me in school. In this photograph I can be the fat and shy and feminine and brown body made beautiful, aestheticized for all that I am. The tenderness and intimacy of your photographic aesthetic is an unusual emotional register for the mother I know. I get to know you differently this way. I get to have a different relation to you than the one we must have day to day. Here is the quirky photographer of the photobooth. Here is the overall-wearing artist paying close attention to scene and subject, the wanting to produce a certain kind of photographic effect, the distinctive capturing of the moment where suspense becomes surprise, where mother sees daughter and mother sees son, where son sees his mother as the photographer, as the artist creating him in a moment gone by.

THERE ARE NO photographs of you two together. Mother and daughter. The two women who raise me. There are group photos with other family members but those aren't the same. To be together with another in a photograph, posed and proximate, is to try to capture the intimacy harbored between the two. An intimacy that allows the viewer to spot the foundations of some story untold, some tension unexamined, or some narrative going against the grain of what is visible.

I have no such photo to work with and this saddens me. Saddening because you two raise me. Because in my memory you two are always together. Sitting in the kitchen gossiping as the mists of the meal being cooked envelop you both. Folding clothes together in the laundromat. Grocery shopping for hours to my impatient childhood annoyance. But ever since

I can remember, you have let me know that you and your mother have a rocky relationship. How she would make comments about your body. How she would always side with your brothers. How she never really showed you affection. And my grandmother mothers me in a way she does not do for you. She sponges my childhood body in the bathtub, the transistor radio playing songs in Spanish from the Caribbean, telling me to close my eyes before she pours the soapy water over my head. She cooks meals especially for me. She has told me "Te quiero." She is a different mother to me than she is to you. We do not experience the same person. My portrait of her is different but I must account for yours, too, because there are many truths to a person. We are all composite and contradictory beings.

You have said it yourself: She has always favored her male children over her female ones. The evidence supports your claim. She treats her sons like overgrown babies. Her four daughters she treats with a detached coolness. We, like my grandmother, have all been taught to value boy children more than girls. Pedros are bloodline, Pedros are the decision-makers, Pedros are to be the future itself.

My brother is everything a mother could want and more in a boy child. He is overwhelmingly masculine. He gets girlfriends easily. He wants a family someday. All of this is cut short one quiet October day in 2004, and there is no longer the son of the collective imagination within the house. I am too feminine, too fat, too gay, too introverted to be anyone's dream of futurity. So much so that the summer before I am to go away to college, in the heated moments of an argument about my departure, you say, "I wish you died instead of him."

We mean what we say the most when we are in the heat of rage. I know you meant those words that summer day. Those words that will never leave me. I know I am not the son you wanted. I can never be the son you imagined me to be in the womb all those years ago. It has taken me a long time to come to terms with that fact but what has helped this process of understanding is knowing this is not exclusively of your doing. We all have inherited a common assumption of what it means to be a son, a boy, a Pedro in the Americas. Pedros are tough. Pedros don't cry. Pedros are to keep the bloodline going. If this is followed, then the Pedro and his family can be closer to being respectable, perhaps even survive, maybe even get out of the colonized condition.

What if I tell you, Mom, that you and your mother have more in common than you think? Your mother favored her boys because she, like you, like many, believed in the inherent value of the masculine, of the man-child. You can see, right, how the mother's cherishing of the boy carries down to the daughter who becomes mother? Though how they value the boy, and the masculine, is different, taking shape to fit the context and situation. The way my childhood body moves and how I speak is picked apart by you. Boys don't cry, you will say to me, boys don't play with dolls, you will tell me. Don't walk with such a swish in your hip, don't hang your hand like that, don't do this or don't do that that might give it away you are not the little macho Pedro, the little Pedro every mother fantasizes about having.

After my first year away at college, I return over the summer to tell you I'm queer. You cry and ask me why I didn't tell you sooner. I find this response disingenuous given your track record of policing my body. From where comes this sudden change of heart? I think my year away from the house gives you time to reflect on my absence, to come to terms with my feminine and gay body, to think upon the subject of your little failed Pedro, of your Pedro who wanted to get as far away from you as possible. I know you are afraid to lose me. You see how eager I am to leave the small-town life, how easily I acclimate to being away in the urbanity of New York City, and maybe you think my grandmother is right. That I am an andariego, a wanderer. That I can pick up and go where I need to, leaving behind who I must to live truthfully, to live free. A year away in college and you never make remarks again about how I walk or how I move my hands or how I sound or who I date. Whatever prompted your change of heart, I am grateful for it.

I am not the Pedro you wished for, Mom, and I will never be. I cannot be my brother, and I have no interest in being a man's man as my brother was. I am the Pedro who swishes his hips. I am the Pedro who gestures with his hands a bit too much, a bit too extravagantly. I am the Pedro who does not want children and does not want the white picket fence. I am the Pedro creating my own story as best as I can in these Americas with this body and this life I have been given.

As the world has come between my father and me, so the world comes between us. As it does for everyone. If this photobooth image is but a moment for you, Mom, a happenstance capturing of quirkiness, an exception to your norm, then I write especially to this image so as to give us another timeline, another way of being together. Writing to the young quirky girl in the photobooth who will someday become my mother. Writing to the quirky photographer who I have never known and can only know as a black-and-white image. The girl who likes to have fun, the girl who pays dutiful attention to details, the girl who celebrates the differences in others. The girl in the photobooth who reminds me we are many selves, and some of those selves get lost through the passage of time. Writing to the lost girl, knowing what it is to be lost, to have a version of your childhood self taken from you and not know how to go back and reclaim it. I write this to the photographer in the photobooth. I write this to the Puerto Rican girl as artist, to the girl who I will someday call my mother.

7

PEDRO FULL OF GRACE

He's such a Pedro. Across from me, on this 4:30 a.m. Queens-bound N train, on my way to get my stomach cut open, skin excised, and flesh stapled shut, is this Pedro I name Pedro. My cousin Pedro lives in Mexico. Cousin Pedro is a photograph to me. One Cousin Pedro among many that I have. Another brown face. Pedro, as a name, as an idea, as syllables on the lips waiting to be sound, gives comfort but I cannot explain why.

Did I mention I am alone? A friend asks, "This is a cosmetic surgery, are you sure about this?" I tell myself that over one hundred pounds lost should award me the golden ticket into 100 percent body positivity. But this is not that movie. My movie is the movie of too many dollar-menu cheeseburgers, too much poverty, too sad too bad. Boys on Grindr: "How does your skin do that?" They are curious how the skin hangs over a Play-Doh–like circle, physics against flesh, but this is if I get lucky enough to not get blocked after sending them a shirtless pic. My boyfriend cheats with a guy from every borough, race, and religion but none are boys with over 10 percent body fat. Proactive, I dial up the plastic surgeon, list the routing numbers of my savings account, and watch as a few thousand dollars transforms into a few thousand pennies. I convince myself I am doing this for me.

Behind Pedro's head is an advertisement for the HIV prophylactic PrEP. I have seen this before. They stand out in their open displays of a man holding another man's hand, in Spanish and in English, all kinds of men represented except for those in white. But where are the men kissing men, the men-and-men sexuality? These posters lack desire, they lack the thing they are selling: sex. The skin against tongue against ass and the foreplay wordplay through text message and videos and photos are all missing. This doesn't represent me at all. My doctor, funded by Medicaid, asks me questions about topping and bottoming and if I use drugs and alcohol during sex and if my partners are cis or trans, and all this data is used for these kinds of ads. There I am holding hands with a partner, happy-go-lucky that now I can marry, that now it is legal for me to express my love. Little do the advertisers know I want the sex, too, the raunch and the kink and the bareback penetrations.

They say ads never work but these do. I am convinced. I try out PrEP, or as it is also known,Truvada, for a few months. In my hands the Truvada blue is a universe. Entities large and small are contained within it: the rising percentages of Latino men infected yearly and Gilead Sciences, Inc., and Magic Johnson and New York City and ACT UP and the Black gay man criminalized for being seropositive and NGOs and my tio who died two months before I was born from an unidentified yet fully identifiable "illness." All are atomized, made molecular, compounded together, and contained within this capsule the size of my fingernail, entering via the molecules and substrates and compounds dissolving into my bloodstream. A few months pass and my interest in the little blue universe dissipates. The doctor asks too many questions, the doctor controls so much. I end up being managed by the doctor who uses my bodily data for some pie chart or statistic or pamphlet. One pill, once a day, no exceptions—I am tired of it.

Does Pedro there on the opposite side of the subway car worry about HIV as much as I do? Think upon the legacy of AIDS? Does he desire other men? Wanting their subtle movements, their lips across the body, the particular way in which they orgasm?

None of this matters. I am here before this Pedro on the subway, this man with eyes like my father's, eyes red and sleep-deprived, eyes the eyes of the overworked and underpaid, eyes of men who must live out in the body the five hundred years of American history Columbus set in motion when he sailed the ocean blue in 1492. My father doesn't know I am on this train. He thinks I am sleeping peacefully in my New York City apartment. He thinks I am living the life of the upwardly mobile son of an illiterate and undocumented farmworker. He thinks I am the American dream. He doesn't know I am floundering in my PhD program. He doesn't know I am not heterosexual. He doesn't know that I hear voices in the quiet of my bedroom. But I just want my father. That man who falls asleep minutes before his motherland wins the World Cup, that man with the stutter divine, that man who contemplates the metaphysics of the universe while trimming the lawns of some corporate complex, some Mr. and Mrs. Cookie-Cutter America, some Princeton/Rutgers/Montclair State University. Mi papa, Papi, my hero in dark brown.

Pedro named Pedro is across from me. Eyes half-shuttered, head doing that wobbly motion New Yorkers make when tired. What geographies hospitable to him does he dream up? He's so photogenetic, so precise in his features, so alike to a cousin of a cousin I crushed on in childhood secrecy. I want to take a photo of him but then I think of the European tourists I saw yesterday, who shamelessly spotlighted a sleeping houseless person with the flashes of photography, thinking to myself how alike they are to their ancestors, their parents, themselves, who photograph the Other in hopes of knowing the secrets of being, the secret to their own being. But I am not like them, and no longer like Pedro. Neither and somewhere between. Pedro on the Q train, the flutter of the lashes are flash enough, Pedro Full of Grace, your Queens-bound eyes my comfort.

8

POBRECITO PEDRO

A hashtag on Twitter: #FirstTimeISawMe. The hashtag is for underrepresented Twitter users to tweet out the first time they felt represented in popular culture. I think on the moment this happened to me. The first time I felt represented. The first time I saw . . . me?

#FirstTimeISawMe . . . the *Selena* movie? No, I might have cried at that final scene with the photo montage, but it wasn't my life, no resemblance to my life. #FirstTimeISawMe . . . *The Brothers Garcia* show on Nickelodeon? No, might have gotten a few good laughs, but the family dynamic is far from mine, too ideal. #FirstTimeISawMe . . . the one character in that Goosebumps book? No, even though his name is Carlos and he's described as light-skinned, his one-liners are awful and his dialogue is too choppy and I pride myself on my witticisms.

#FirstTimeISawMe . . . think, man, think . . . #FirstTimeISawMe . . . aha! There it is, there is where, there is who: Pedro from the film *Napoleon Dynamite.* Pedro the side character in the 2004 comedy about a dorky white boy from Idaho which, as noted on the film's website, is centered on this plot: "When his friend Pedro decides to run for class president, it is Napoleon to the rescue to help him triumph over adversity."

Pedro, the reader may or may not ask, really? Pedro the brown side character who has to be saved? Pedro the stereotype? Pedro is so unremarkable, so unmemorable. Pedro is just . . . well, he is so . . . Pedro . . . such a pobrecito.

Who wants to be him?

LOCKER ORANGE-RED AND a doorframe with an eighties-blue trimming to his side, Napoleon's eyes are semiclosed as he listens to a man's voice barking out of the frame, not at him but at someone else: "You do understand English?" The camera then pans from Napoleon to the principal of the school, who is staring down at a teenager the viewer will soon find out is named Pedro. Off-screen and immaterial, language, and its meanings, introduces this Pedro. Before Pedro is a body he is words. The principal, off-camera before, but now fully framed within the filmic gaze, says, "This isn't that complex." More language, more meaning, more cultural baggage. Pedro stares up at him, facial features and brown eyes full of still expression, his response the response of indifference. Whether this indifference is an imposed indifference or a strategic one of his doing is not known. He just looks real pobrecito-like, like when I am a kid getting injured or some kind of slight happens against me, and my mother and grandmother say, "Ayyy, pobrecito." They emphasize that word *pobrecito*, accentuate it in their tough Caribbean womanliness. That word meaning something like "Poor little you." A word to give comfort, a word to playfully chastise. The use of the word *pobrecito* is always circumstantial, a word with different uses for different contexts.

Pobrecito Pedro there before the camera in the film *Napoleon Dynamite*, pobrecito Marcos there all alone hurt and damaged.

Before I go to New York City for college, my grandmother ominously warns me, "Pobrecito. No sabes lo que te espera allá." My mother says something similar. They don't want me to leave. They fear for me so they both give their warnings. Pobrecito you, pobrecito me. There the world awaits you, boy, all its uncertainty, all its cruelty. Are you even ready for it? For what awaits you out there in the world?

All I know is New York City cannot be as awful as where I am. Nowhere can make me feel as lonely as I feel here, I tell myself. I have one or two friends here in New Egypt, New Jersey. I don't feel like I belong. The politics of the world are in small towns like the one my family reside in even though my mother and grandmother think they are not. They believe they will not be harmed living in such small places. That the poverty and hardship and the inherited colonial conditions they know in Puerto Rico and Brooklyn do not apply there. That somehow they can be exempted from their condition of being, their being Puerto Rican women with a particular kind of history that colonized islands bring with them.

I understand their desire to believe in this. This fantasy that a place can be devoid of politics, of the brutal and unfair history that defines the United States, Puerto Rico, and the Americas. I tell this to my mother today. These little places are but a fantasy, I say, a way of trying to keep the world out. I know, she says, forthright, but I prefer this. I feel safe. I feel comfortable. Who am I to judge her? My mother who lives in her little house in the woods. My mother who wishes she had more people to speak Spanish to besides my father. My mother whose world, with the exception of two brief excursions of living in Puerto Rico and the Bronx when younger, is a world contained within a fifteen-mile radius.

They are both right: I do not know what awaits me in New York City.

I soon find out it is a reckoning.

The reckoning is that Pobrecito Marcos does not even know who he even is anymore.

IT IS WELL known that *Napoleon Dynamite* is a cult classic. I have only a vague idea of what being a "cult classic" means but when I say the words to prove a point, or state a fact, or to engage in dialogue, I pretend as if I could define it. Some rapid-fire Google search I do ten seconds before I write this sentence identifies cult classic as "something, typically a movie or book, that is popular or fashionable among a particular group or section of society." If a movie is a cult classic, then, this means it has some kind of cultish following. Are these fans behaving in this cultlike devotion engaging in an identification, identifying with this movie in some way? Or is their fandom worship and devotion? We worship to feel ourselves as puny, as so small, so insignificant, that we are no longer ourselves. We cannot see ourselves in God, in the Divine, in that which we worship. We are, perhaps, not meant to.

This theory is contested by those conquistadors and pilgrims and nobodies from Europe who arrived in what they termed the New World and saw themselves as representative of God. They were *his* messengers, *his* voice incarnate on this continent foreign to them, *his* model of humanity all planetary inhabitants were to aspire toward. God bestowed upon men with enough reason, enough wealth, light-enough skin, the gift of being representative of a higher order of consciousness. God said to all, according to the doctrines, interpretations, decrees, reports, and laws of the conquistadors: Be like these kinds of men, act like these kinds of men, think like these kinds of men. They became God upon anchoring in the New World.

Hundreds of years pass and our altars are still dedicated to a God crafted in these men's images. He, for he is always a He, is a God representative of us. We pray hoping to feel closer to His image for He is holy and Himself divine. But the people who those conquistadors did not consider people enough to make their own decisions, those people who are now the people like Pedro and me, people unlike Pedro and me, found a way to feel more represented in this New World. They worshipped a Virgin Mary a little closer to their color. She didn't make them feel as inadequate as the priest of the pueblo would. She did not speak only the language of pillaging and conquest and conversion and forced labor and dispossession and slashing and burning. They saw the evacuation of themselves, the no longer being themselves, but they could be so particularly themselves in worship, be a themselves not determined upon what degree they were or were not representing some ideal, have a relationship to the divine denied to us ever since 1492, in this icon we call La Virgen de Guadalupe.

La Virgencita is everywhere for those poor, unfortunate souls who need her. She is in the telenovelas my grandmother and mother watch, prayed to particularly by women, all the dreams and aspirations that aren't happening in real life sent to the little plastic icon they keep on a nightstand. My dad has a key chain of her on his car keys but I am not sure if he prays to her. I have never seen him even pray. I keep one of those dollar-store candles with the image of La Virgen in my apartment and I'm not sure why. I don't pray. I don't believe in a Christian god. I don't believe in the miraculous conception of Christ. Maybe it has something to do with the fact La Virgen is for the less fortunate. That those like me see her as a beacon of hope. Something to kneel before and say some words to, telling stories about the day and week and year had, telling dreams unfulfilled, hoping against hope she is listening, she might consider them.

My mother thinks my father keeps La Virgen on his key chain because it is a way of connecting to his deceased father. He has to believe in some higher power if he is to believe someday he will see the man he can't even remember knowing, the man who dies when he is too little to even have memory. Que pobrecito. The father who is fatherless, who has never known a father. This is why he has never been the kind of father who expresses emotions, why he could never open up to you, she announces to me, as if this fact is an epiphany. I'm not sure if I want to believe this is the sole reason why my dad is the way he is to me. I don't like ascribing to such heteronormative notions, notions that a boy needs a father, that without a father he doesn't know how to be a man, that a child is lacking something by not having a father. I think my father is the way he is with me because it is how he has had to be in the world. Detached, and indifferent. Emotionally reserved. On edge. Withholding his thoughts and history from me. If not, if he dares be a little more honest, a little more brazen in what he thinks and feels, there will be repercussions. His mother, he tells me in passing, treated him similarly. A parenting in distance. This kind of disposition seems to run in the family.

When I am a child, he's immensely affectionate. He does push-ups with me on top of him as I pretend he is a roller coaster. He puts me on his shoulders and takes me around the yard. I lay on his chest and fall asleep there. I use my fingers to outline the keloid scar on the right side of his chest, creating elaborate stories of how it happened. A bar brawl, an alleyway robbery, him playing superhero while defending a little old woman from a robbery. He's my quiet hero.

When I'm nine years old, he moves out of the house. Another argument between him and my mother. He'd moved out once before a few years back but it was only for a few weeks. This time it's longer. He visits me when I'm over at my grandmother's house a street away from where my mom lives. He asks me how I'm doing, watches me play video games in the living room, and gives me some spending money before he leaves. I remember how sad I get each time he goes. How my heart breaks to have to see him leave not knowing if I would see him again.

At this age, I cannot expressly identify what it is I fear when he leaves. All I know is I hear in school from my classmates how they pick on "beaners" and "illegals." They throw garbage at them from car windows. They encircle on their bikes those walking to the fields, and sometimes do more than just that. I know how immigration and police show up unexpectedly at night, dragging people into their vehicles who look like my dad, their dogs chasing people into the woods who we know and could very well be one of us.

When my father leaves my side, these are the dangers that run through my head.

Dangers that I know include me but I only understand this fact when I am in my teens, when I start putting the pieces of this most American puzzle together, piecing together the horrifying truths that dot these lands.

Around this time of my father not living with us is when I stop laying on his chest. I stop rubbing the keloid scar and creating fictions around its emergence. Around this time is when the full onslaught by my classmates begins. When I begin to fully make sense, though still not in language, in words I could explain to others, of what it means to be a child of color in relation to whiteness, to despise who and what I am.

The intimacy with my father is never the same after. After he moves out for a little while, after the outside world enters to shape how I feel about my dad, after the "all-American" town I grow up in makes me believe my father is nothing more than a fieldworker, a brown nobody, I begin to think of my dad as cold, unaffectionate, and indifferent. A statue unalive and uncaring, an idol from a foreign land, a primitive lifestyle dead and gone. I tell myself, you do not identify with people like him. People who live backward lives, who cannot read or write, who are not of our modern world. I want to identify with the kids in my school. I wish I had their parents. I wish I lived in their fancy, new housing developments. I wish I had their history as we learn about it in the textbooks: noble pilgrims from Britain searching for religious freedom, brave explorers traveling westward in pursuit of riches and freedom, brilliant men and women who fought for liberty and justice for all.

This is the view I hold for more than a decade. One that will take a total undoing of what I know, and how I came to know it. Many hours alone as an adult laboring to know why I feel so terribly about myself. Lots of hours with writers and artists, thinking on their work, and, in turn, thinking on how those ideas map a path for understanding who I am. A view that will require a total reimagining of how I know the world, how I know my father and family, and how I know myself.

Pedro, on the screen, can you hear this?

Pedro, there amongst all that white, can you feel me?

Let us remove ourselves from this prewritten script and be a different kind of Pedro.

***NAPOLEON DYNAMITE* IS** a film in minimum. Facial features are still and uniform, each character remaining in one register of emotion. Vocal intonations lack range, each character speaks with their own minimal expressivity. The plot is without much plot, those elements the viewer so depends on like rising action, climax, and falling action are downplayed, if there at all. Even the camera angles follow the filmic formula of everything in minimum: each scene fixates on its characters and scenery with a lethargic stillness, transitions lackluster, a humdrum effect culling all the components together to pull off a film basking in its glorious underwhelmingness. The impression on the viewer is no impression.

This is my hypothesis as to why the film is considered a cult classic. The underwhelming excess of the film is its charm. No character really impresses us, few aspects of it stand out as exceptional besides its unimpressive appeal. To identify with such an unimpressive and underwhelming aesthetic is to admit to identifying with the loser, the nobody, the one who is not remembered. Our sensibilities are trained to identify with the loudmouth, the go-getter, the courageously adventuring hero. This sensibility makes it hard for us to want to identify with a character like Pedro—there is so little to him. He is unimpressive, underwhelming, unimposing, and any other word you can think of with the prefix *un-*.

He is just a Pedro, after all.

I am all Pedro-like when it comes to trying to understand my father. He is a force to be reckoned with. Inscrutable, something primordial that rejects me. Pobrecito me has to have my mother be the middleman. She speaks his language. He is most comfortable with her. She knows his most intimate details that he has never told me. She is the closest person to him, and this has something to do with my mother being the polar opposite of him. She lets you know how she feels. She expresses herself. She likes to talk about her past. Their differences balance one another out.

My years in New York City during college expose me to being affectionate with men other than my father. Some who are like him, not very talkative, not so forthcoming. Others who are not like him, very talkative, telling their stories on a first date. Each one becomes a kind of mission, of figuring out how to approach them, how best to meet them at their comfort level. They challenge me and my beliefs. Men of all sizes, all colors, all religions, all levels of femininity and masculinity. Not all men are like my father, and this becomes a grounds for understanding who he is better.

These years in college going on dates and hooking up, I realize my life can be on my terms. I might not be able to change who my family is, or the material conditions that structure my life, but I choose who I spend my time with and how I spend that time with them. Dating and hooking up make me more aware of the systems of thinking I bring with me from New Jersey, and the ones I am confronted with by New York. The racism and fat-shaming and femme-hating and transphobia rampant in queer cultures I encounter in New York rub up against the ideas of my childhood. How do I care for these different kinds of men I encounter? How do I honor their lives and their stories on their terms? These two questions surface again and again during these years of contemplation, these years of figuring out how it is I will come to think and wonder and analyze the world I live in.

I admit I'm a little jealous of my mother. Of the access she has to his feelings. The access he has never given me and I don't know if he ever will be able to. In my own relationships with people, I see myself doing what my father does. I withhold. I don't let anyone know if I am hurting or if I am happy. His stoicism is mine, too. I don't know if I want to change that. If I want to reveal myself all the time, to have to announce the state of my emotional being. I can understand my father not telling me as much as I would like. Because in him I see myself. But does he see me in him like I see myself in Pedro? Does he see me his son, his Pedro, standing there needing to be loved? Needing to be recognized?

THE FILM IS near its end and Pedro is so close to becoming class president. Who could even believe the boy from Juarez would become the next class president in rural Idaho? The climax, insofar as this film can be said to have this customary storytelling device, is upon us. However, like in all good storytelling, a wrench is thrown in to shake things up. Each candidate for class president must perform in the talent show but Pedro does not have a performance ready. Stage fright consumes him. He does not know how to be a star. Poor Pedro.

Fret not, Pedro, Napoleon is here to save the day. Donning a white shirt that says VOTE FOR PEDRO, Napoleon dances to Jamiroquai's funk hit "Canned Heat." Napoleon slides, stomps, and twirls in the most lackluster manner. His hands move about, point, and punch, all with the most banal of gusto. The entire time the face doesn't move, the light reflecting off his glasses out toward the audience. After Napoleon's impressively unimpressive dorkiness, the audience, delayed in their response by disbelief, applaud. Napoleon is a hero, Napoleon is so cool in his uncoolness, Napoleon saves the day. Pedro, can you even believe it—success! Napoleon has made your wildest dream of being president on this side of the border come true.

But a plot twist is thrown at Pedro. Did he really think this story on the big screen was all his for the taking, his for the telling? Right before the student body is to vote for class president, Pedro, as if prefacing Napoleon's YouTube-iconic dance for the crowd, gives his final speech:

> I don't have much to say. But I think it would be good to have some holy santos brought to the high school to guard the hallways and to bring us good luck. El Santo Niño de Atocha is a good one. My aunt Concha has seen him. And we have a great FFA schedule lined up and I would like to see more of that. If you vote for me, all of your wildest dreams will come true.

Their wildest dreams are, apparently, the moronic dorkiness of Napoleon's dance moves. Pedro, in this moment of the film, is at peak pobrecitoness. On the big stage, so unimpressive, so unable to hold the crowd with his tone and emotions and movement in minimum. Does he not know politicians are enthusiastic? Well-spoken smooth talkers? Using hands and face and all kinds of body theatrics? Poor Pedro, Napoleon must think, I must come to the rescue, I must save him from himself. And he does with his awfully funny white-boy dancing.

This moment in the film doesn't feel like what we typically identify as a white savior narrative, a trope where a white person saves a person of color who otherwise cannot save themselves. The stakes are much lower, banal, overwhelmingly dumb. Who cares who wins a high school presidency? There's something more to say about how certain kinds of moods, dispositions, attitudes, and bodily comportments are deemed unworthy or unacceptable. Pedro, as he is, monotone voice, flat facial expressions, slouching and stiff, is not presidential material. Who cares what he thinks, if he can even think? He's so unimpressive on the main stage and he needs Napoleon's dancing antics to get the crowd on his side. He's not meant to be taken seriously.

Pedro must contend with a culture that values the showy, the heroic, the spinning of elaborate yarns with words. Pedro is simple. He speaks simply. He thinks but does not say. A philosopher, Pedro? No, how could he be, when the philosopher wants to be known as such, wants to be heard and seen? We have our philosophers on CNN and Fox and the BBC debating policies and rhetoric and other very important matters. We have our philosophers at Columbia and Oxford and Harvard with their nice tenured salaries shaping the minds of the select few who get to grace their classrooms. Quiet Pedro, Pedro of few words, Pedro so unimpressive in his way. Pedro a philosopher? Not in this day and age.

Like Pedro there before his classmates, before the filmic audience, I am at peak pobrecitoness when I have to call my parents for money to pay the remainder of my tuition the first semester in college. I feel like a loser, like a letdown, needing someone to save me. This isn't the New York City experience I fantasized about before coming. Where I am big and bad, in charge of my destiny, not needing any help because I am the star of my show. If I do need some help, at the very least, where is my Napoleon? Where might my dorky white savior be? My life is no movie. My white savior is nowhere to be found and all I have are my parents, tucked away in New Jersey, on the end of a telephone line, and my pathetic crying. I owe around three thousand dollars and this is a surprise because I had thought the tuition was fully covered. The loans I had to take out were supposedly meant to cover it all, being that my family has no means to support my education. I, a first-generation student with no help navigating this process, am wrong. I call my mother crying, telling her they will kick me out. I call her reluctantly because I anticipate she will tell me I told you so, and telling me I should have never moved to New York or went to such an expensive college. I am ready to persuade myself she does not understand what I have to go through because she has never been in my position, has never had to traverse the unfair systems of higher education. I expect her to make me feel worse than I already do.

On the other end of the cell phone line, unexpectedly, is my mother with sympathy in her voice. Her tone is one of care. Her breath is lined with worry as I cry there hysterically sixty miles away from her. Here is her youngest son, the boy she warned not to leave, coming to her in his hour of need. A boy she tells the prior summer before his departure to New York City, in a moment of heated exchange over why he wants to leave his hometown, that she wishes he had died instead of his older brother. He knows deep down she means this. That he, the effeminate one, the queer one, the one who has no desire for children and a wife, should be dead instead of the masculine brother who brought home girls and wanted children someday. He knows these words are true and he must accept them because, if not, he will only perish under the weight of their sincerity.

Despite our complicated relationship, maybe I call my mother at this point of crisis because I want to be comforted by her. My mother is not the affectionate type. She is not the mother you go to when you are feeling hurt or scared. Yet she is the first person I call, wanting her voice, her understanding, despite believing I will not get it, that she is incapable of this.

She proves me wrong.

This phone call I hear how her voice breaks, extending to me through the telephone an urgency equal to my own, and it is welcome. Calming. She assures me we will figure this out. Not to worry, she says several times, and I believe her because she has never said something like this to me. Not to worry when she has never tried to hide from me the struggles of paying the rent, the arguments between her and my father, wondering if my father will get deported.

She knows I am not calling to ask her for the money given she has a hard time holding down a job. I am calling her so she may ask my father on my behalf. I don't want to ask him, but I have no choice really. My father, the man who works in the fields before the sun rises and finishes well after the sun sets. My father, the man who has never had the opportunity to receive any kind of education. My father who has known nothing but the cruelty of living in these Americas.

My guilt swells while waiting to hear back from my parents. Here I am needing the woman who I think does not understand me, and the man I disavow. The woman and man who signify so much that I do not want to signify. Where are John or Molly or Abigail or David when I need them? Why won't my allegiances to whiteness save me? Poor me. Pathetic me. Here crying in the lobby of my school, in front of strangers, alone again like the boy I was not too long ago, the boy who I said is no more. I want to be like my new friend whose parents pay for his tuition outright with no need to drown himself in student debt. I want to be like the others who live in my dorm who don't have to work several jobs like I do. But here I am foolishly believing in a system that will not rescue me and was never intended for me. What to do with such a realization? What to do when the structures you believe in fail you as they were always intended to do?

Here, in this lobby in front of my school's financial aid office awaiting my parents' phone call, a sense of doubt—over who I want to be, over how I want to think about the world, how I want to perceive people like my father and mother—appears.

My mother calls me back, and tells me my dad wants to speak to me. He asks me in his typically stern way how this happened when I had guaranteed them the tuition was covered. I can't explain to him why this happened. I can't explain to him how this system works because I do not know myself. I can't explain to him in words how this system is rigged against people like us. Those who do not have parents who are citizens or have parents who are too poor to be eligible for a loan. Loans with outrageously high interest rates that students like me will agree to because we have no other choice. Loans that will go unpaid, giving the government permission to criminalize you, to deem you unworthy of shelter and food, labeling you a failure. He asks me to confirm with him this won't happen again because he cannot pay something like this. I promise him yes, and he says he will send over the money in a few days.

Problem is, the following year of college, the same issue arises. Some tuition isn't covered by the loans I take out. The same conversation ensues between my father and me. The stumbling to explain something I cannot at the time explain in words to him. Explaining to him why this has crept up on me again, why it has to be so hard for me to receive an education. Though he says my freshman year he would be unable to pay these thousands of dollars if it were to happen again, my father does. He pulls through for me.

To this day, I don't know how my father gets these two large sums of money. It feels taboo to even ask. All I know is he does the extraordinary for me. During these two moments in my first two years of undergrad my perceptions of people like my father, mother, family, and the people in my neighborhood, constructed by the world I grew up in, begin to shift. Who are my people? Who am I in relation to these Johns and Abigails I encounter in places like New Egypt, New Jersey, and even New York City? What systems of thought and structures of power hold me captive in their enticing gaze? The slow undoing of white America's stranglehold on my thoughts, my consciousness, my very existence happens there in front of the financial aid office. In tears, unsure of my future, alone with the uncertainty of not making it in this country, on this continent, this place we call Earth. Happening when I realize these systems and structures of white supremacy will not be the ones to save me because they are the ones that have put me in this position to begin with. As they have put those who came before me, and will put those who will come after me, unless something is done about it.

In this film that is my life, this most unremarkable scene that is so common, there will be no white savior. For the white savior trope has always been a myth. A myth disguising the devastation and humility and hurt and suffering that comes with the impulse to save us dark and huddled masses, to save us from ourselves. No white savior is coming, for no such thing has ever existed. Nothing more than a centuries-long fiction.

MY FATHER WHO, with pen in his hand shaking, its thin body an unfamiliar tool, signs on the dotted line of my birth certificate. Pobrecito. Those hands of a man used to the handle of a shovel, the grip of the hedge cutters, the soil of the Earth. My mother's grip steadies him. She directs the wobbly spelling of his name. His name he knows only as a pronunciation, as sounds in the air, the impact against flesh. She guides him in this ritual proving lineage, this ceremony of patrilineal descent. But it is not enough. The hands of my father are too wild. His name in letters is unknown to him. Language for him is not the language of the written word. These five hundred years have given him (us?) a different language. The disciplined posture, the stonelike face, the cruel indifference of our brown eyes leering. In these Americas our bodies are what speak language, not the pen and the written word, not signatures passing down the name of our conquerors or signatures agreeing to pay back thousands upon thousands of dollars so we could have a chance to go to college.

When the birth certificate arrives in the mail, my last name is spelled incorrectly. The first *z* in my name is mistaken for an *s*. This is the first time my father has ever written the letter *z*. At least the *z* at the end of my name is interpreted correctly because by this letter my father must have had enough time to feel the pen in his hands, the rhythm of angles and lines and slopes and loops on the page growing familiar, enough practice to make the *z* of his name legible as a *z*. He is an incredibly fast learner. The spelling of my name for the first time is the first time my father spells his own name. It is the first time he feels his name in his hands, feeling the weight of each letter, the process of naming us the naming of all that that has been denied him, all of that that shames him, all of that that has conquered him, all of these five hundred years in the letters of our name.

PEDRO IN *NAPOLEON DYNAMITE* mentions his aunt Concha has seen El Santo Niño de Atocha. According to Wikipedia, this is an image of the Christ Child, a small Christ who roams the landscape of Mexico, and the United States Southwest, helping those in need. He helps so many, across so many miles, he wears his shoes out. Selfless, indeed.

Pedro, if he is elected president, promises he will bring this Christ figure into the hallways. This santo will help these people with their needs. But what are these students in need of? Will these students let Santo Niño de Atocha represent their needs? Pedro might say whatever Pedro needs to say to win. Pedro does what Pedro needs to do to get by.

If we take Pedro at his word and believe Aunt Concha saw the Christ Child, then she must have seen the feet of Christ. The feet of the Christ bloodied, scabbed, and exposed from walking all these Americas to help those in need. His holiness brought to such humanness. Sounds unlikely. Saints do not represent humans and their trivial lives. Was Aunt Concha mistaken? Maybe who she thought was Christ was just a Pedro, or maybe even a Maria, one of the millions of Pedros and Marias walking and running and swimming and climbing and burrowing through these Americas. It's likely she saw in the darkness what she believed to be the representation of Christ, the Messiah who had promised to deliver us from Evil since 1492, but what she actually saw was probably the ordinariness of a mortal in movement, some Pedro or Maria who had abandoned their worn-out shoes somewhere along the journey from one end of the continent to the other. Who knows? Maybe Aunt Concha did see Christ. The divine in the everyday Pedro, the saintly in the average Maria. The feet of those most Holy who must walk the miles upon miles of the Americas in search of someplace to try and call home.

Home, for some of us, can only ever be a matter of trying to find it. The perpetual pursuit. I am born in the United States. Born in a little town most would believe is homey. Moved to a big city so many fall in love with and, through time, call home. My queer body, my fat body, my raced body, my conflicted body. Home for me? None of them, really. Where, then? Where is home for someone like me? Whose body has only ever known turmoil in any place he has chosen to go?

I am not even at home in my own name. A name I have only ever known as a mispronunciation. Instead of the fuzzy slipperiness of the *z* on the tongues the pronouncer of my last name sounds out the wetness of an *s*. When they call out my name during my college graduation, they say the first *s* like a *z*.

Who is this boy they call? Who is this Marcos they expect to walk across the stage?

Pobrecito me.

My parents, sister, cousins, and boyfriend are sitting in the audience watching. My boyfriend and sister both text me how my father is crying profusely. They have never seen him cry before. I have only seen him cry when I am eight years old and his mother passes away in Mexico. He contemplates returning for her viewing, though he is undocumented and knows the journey will be dangerous. He makes the painful choice to remain in the United States. Seeing him crying so hard over his mother is the first time I feel heartbreak. To see a man so stoic, so stonelike in disposition, break in such a way, impacted by the person he cares for the most before I come into the picture, is hard for my childhood self. His silhouette breaking the news to me I will never forget. These tears at my graduation, though, are tears of joy, as he will later tell me. I do not get to see them and this hurts for some reason. As if the witnessing of his joy is an event I need to see. Perhaps because it is so rare for him to express anything to me. My successes are his, he reminds me a few months later, as if knowing I had such a desire to witness those tears, as if he knows something in me yearns for more. Me, his only child, the first to graduate college in all of his family, pursuing my dreams of becoming a writer when he never had the chance to pursue his dream of being a boxer—his success.

There in my cap and gown, all I feel is guilt. The guilt of knowing that for so long I wanted to disassociate myself with people like my father, with the idea of my father, of all that he symbolizes and signifies and represents. Perhaps this guilt is what I need to feel in order to redeem myself, in order to move on from all these years of confusion and denial. I would pity myself but that feels too generous.

Pity is such an odd emotion. You can pity others, feeling sorry for them, a kind of compassion for their plights and suffering. The one pitying seems to be in a privileged position, as observing the sufferer from an outside position. Or you can pity yourself, which seems gratuitous in a way, self-deprecating. A way to feel sorry for all the unfortunate things that happen to you. When my mother and grandmother call me a pobrecito as a kid, and introduce me to the act of pitying, it is an affirming gesture. Not the belittling one that I so frequently associate with the act of pitying. For instance, the way nice white folks pity people of color who don't have what they have, or the way rich people pity the poor. Pitying when done by certain kinds of people seems antagonistic. My mother and grandmother's use of pity is a form of care. Me, the pitiful child, and them, the pitying adults, telling me they see my suffering, they see my pain no matter how trivial or intense it may be. Calling me pobrecito and by doing so recognizing that I am a thinking and feeling being, that I feel pain and know suffering.

I pity my dad in this kind of way. I pity my mom, too, and my grandmother. All of my family, really, those I like and dislike, those who have hurt me or could care less for me, those whom I have never even met. Pitying them in that way I came to know as a kid that recognizes their pain and suffering. That recognizes what they are feeling or thinking or believing is worthy of recognition. Feeling sorry for them because I wish the world were different.

I pity the little boy that is Marcos. Walking across the stage as a man in my cap and gown, I think of him there in another timeline alone with his thoughts in his kindergarten classroom, in those middle school hallways, in his bedroom, in the woods near his house. Pitying all the beliefs about his family and himself that he holds to be true because others convince him to. Pitying him because in another timeline he is living out what I, my older self, have already lived. What I am reconciling, atoning for, figuring out how best to live with. He is right now in the eye of the storm. How to rescue him? How to let him know he deserves to live? Pitying myself, pitying my parents, and all of those like us, helps me better understand what has transpired in my life. I can look at what I have done and not let it destroy me.

Say the letters of my name are corrected, that I went through the process to legally change my name, what then? Is this closer to the truth of my lineage, my familial roots, the composition of my body? Does this answer some question that my younger self and adult self and my future self need answering? I would be merely "correcting" one mistake for another. My father's last name is a mistaken last name. Some irritable civil servant gave his father's father and his mother's mother and her mother's mother and all their mothers and fathers and all those other people living in these mistakenly named Americas more European or Christian names. Our names were given to us to make it easier for some conquistador to pronounce us into existence during forced labor roll calls, or to overenunciate the names of those humans who would be forcibly removed from their homes, or to call out the name of one of those many bodies that worked too slowly, that didn't give up their home fast enough, that never became fully Christian, that refused to be a human like the oh-so-modern, oh-so-civilized humans who were drafting up the laws and ordinances and decrees and language to forge a New World.

I don't identify with a name—I identify with the history that named me.

To call my father's spelling of my name, guided by my mother's hand, a mistake, is wrong. A mistake is an oversight, something that was unintended and unfortunate, something that strays from the truth. Though surely unintended, the spelling of my name bears the weight of history, history's movement between what was, what is, what will be. The conquistadors on the shores of a New World, scabbards and crosses and hands pointed toward my ancestors, ready to take. My *s* supposed to be a *z*, my *z* absent in place of an *s*, is a testament in letters. History's tenses alive in the body.

Ours is a name not ours but imposed upon us. Not in our language for our language, the language of the colonized, the language of the pillaged and the raped and the dispossessed and the impoverished, the language of the historical record erased, the language of those searching for refuge across this inhospitable world, is no language.

The impossibility of pronouncing our names is our possibility.

Call it our American dream.

Not the American dream as it stands in the popular imagination. The dream that in this country you can be whoever you want to be as long as you work hard and do everything right. I have known too many people in my life, and too many stories of those I have never met, of their unending days of work. Their unending commitment to paying taxes, to paying bills, to doing everything they are told to do in order to get a better life. And in the end, the ultimate end that is death, they are met with nothing more than inherited debt, sickness, and pain, and all their unfulfilled dreams. I don't identify with the American dream. I don't identify with the false meritocracy this settler colonial country likes to imagine itself being. I identify with Pedro from *Napoleon Dynamite.* Pedro off-screen, outshined by the buffoonishly impressive Napoleon. Pedro with the posture and countenance of a most minimal indifference, Pedro the thought unfinished. Pedro the on-screen manifestation of the historical record. Pedro is the #FirstTimeISawMe.

9

A BRIEF AND UNEVENTFUL HISTORY OF BURLAP

In order to save themselves some extra cash, the British Empire, at war with their colonies in the New World, hire German mercenaries instead of the much more expensive homegrown British soldiers. The number of these mercenaries turned deserters is high. Disastrous for the British efforts at suppressing their ungrateful subjects, among many other forces working against the British in the wild lands of the Americas. Historians note these deserters had no stake in the Americas, no reason to fight besides the wages already given them, whereas the revolutionaries were fighting to be a nation, to be alike and unlike their counterparts across the Atlantic, to be the symbol of freedom itself. Parts of these mercenaries' attire were constructed from the jute plant, the fibers coming together to create a fabric that was named hessian, after the distinct group of Germans who wore them. Hessian fabric in the United States is known as burlap.

August 4, 2017: mounds of it in the front yard. One after

the other stacked up in three piles, slightly lopsided, nearly ready to topple over. Frayed edges of the fabric hang loose. Some are much longer than the others, jellyfish-like tendrils dangling down, split fibers curling at the end seams. Different shades of tan and brown. The coarseness of the material gives a hardness to the yard, the softness of the soil and the smoothness of the leaves in the trees making the burlap stick out, an artificial menace. It'd be an eyesore for those inclined to visual aesthetics but our house has never been meant to serve such a purpose. The house is a roof over the head, brick and wood and panels and Sheetrock to get by in, a means to try and make it on this continent vast and sprawling.

Burlap is the most constant item in my father's work. The burlap is used to protect the exposed roots of a tree or shrub when it is being transplanted into the earth. To be moved from one place to another for a plant is a dangerous, even lethal, affair. The burlap keeps the moisture in the roots, protects them from any damage the world might try and inflict. Burlap cares for the most vital part of the plant as it prepares for shipment to its final resting place: a middle-class home, a corporate complex, a private business, a university lawn. Burlap is needed until it is needed no more.

WILLIAM CARLOS WILLIAMS'S 1925 book *In the American Grain* is a collection of microhistories about the Americas. Each essay-history is an origin story, a retelling of origins, an experimenting with any surefire notion of origins. Riffing off the idea of the conquistador logbooks, in his microhistory titled "The Destruction of Tenochtitlan," Williams itemizes and lists in pages-long detail the gifts sent to Cortés and his compatriots by Moctezuma, who hopes to stop them from destroying, pillaging, stealing, creating a New World: "a gold necklace of seven pieces, set with many gems like small rubies, a hundred and eighty-three emeralds and ten fine pearls, and hung with twenty-seven little bells of gold . . . several shoes of the skin of deer . . . a shield of wood and leather . . . a large mirror adorned with gold . . ." and on and on do the gifts come. But as History has proven, nothing is enough for these foreigners. Gift after gift, plea after plea, treaty after treaty, the cataloging of pre-Spanish beauty, the splendor of the Americas before they are named the Americas: "But Cortez was unwilling to turn back; rather these things whetted his appetite for the adventure." The Americas are more than enough for the Cortéses and the Columbuses. Insatiably enough.

USING MY UNIVERSITY'S subscription service, I search the word *burlap* in the *Oxford English Dictionary.* History of words: etymology. Roots and beginnings and origins traced back to the first documentation of a word's usage. According to the *OED*, the etymology of the word *burlap* is uncertain. The dictionary speculates the word derives from the Dutch word for "rubbing-clout, linen." The dictionary also goes on with its speculations: "The first component may have been confused with *boer* peasant."

Another word, another etymology: *peasant.* Unlike *burlap,* the *OED* entry for *peasant* is more extensive, has a longer genealogy. The nicest entry: "A person who lives in the country and works on the land, esp. as a smallholder or a laborer; a member of an agricultural class dependent on subsistence farming." The definitions get a bit . . . rougher. "In negative sense: a countryman or rustic, regarded as ignorant, crass, or rude. Usually with derogatory modifying word." They get worse: "As a term of abuse: a person of low social status; an ignorant, stupid, unsophisticated, or (formerly esp.) unprincipled person; a boor, a lout; (also more generally) a person who is regarded with scorn or contempt, esp. by members of a particular social group. Cf. farmer, villain."

My father's identification card, containing his youthful visage in black and white, and issued to him in Mexico, lists his occupation as "campesino." My father's job, his occupation in life, is a peasant.

ASSIGNMENT IN MY junior year of undergrad: "Create a museum installation representing your life." Found objects include: a pill to control diabetes; a black-and-white photograph of an unidentified woman; miniature boxing gloves; a black lipstick container; a photograph in sepia of hot-air balloons in flight; Goya seasoning wrappers; a piece of burlap.

CAMPESINOS, PEASANTS. I know them. They are the men and women who live next door in my childhood years, they are the men and women of my family, they are the men and women in my house, they are my neighbors in this Washington Heights apartment. Does this make me a campesino? Campesino is an identity category in places like Mexico, across Latin America, and other parts of the world. In the United States the word sounds rude, archaic, carrying the weight of the many *OED* entries. No one goes around identifying as a peasant unless they are trying to make a joke out of their poverty, or crack a joke at how lowly they are being treated by someone in a higher social position. The United States versions of campesinos are probably "the poor," "the downtrodden," "the needy," "welfare dependents." Born in the United States as I am, in the borderlands of Main Street, U.S.A., in the borders of nations my family and friends and neighbors have brought to me, what am I?

IN HIS NOT-SO-MICROHISTORY of the Haitian Revolution, *The Black Jacobins*, an important study of the largest revolution by enslaved persons against a colonizing nation, C. L. R. James writes: "There is no drama like the drama of history."

"FOUR FISHES, TWO ducks and some other birds of molten gold . . . miters and crowns of feathers and gold ornamented with pearls and gems . . . several large plumes of beautiful feathers, fretted with gold and small pearls . . ."

1989: THIS IS the year my father stops sleeping on the petate, a bedroll made from the palm of the tree *Leucothrinax morrisii.* The bedroll looks like a woven basket unfurled, laid out, turned into a sleeping apparatus. *Petate* is a Hispanicized word from the original Nahuatl word *petlatl.* The bed doesn't look comfortable but my father says otherwise. It looks a lot like burlap, in fact.

In this year 1989, the same year my father finds himself sleeping in a petate in Mexico, my father risks everything, leaves behind everyone, nearly dies, crossing over to the United States. He cannot remember the date he left his home in Mexico and the day he arrived in his living accommodations in the United States. Dates are not my father's specialty. In the United States there are no petates, perhaps no need for them. Tucked away in a pocket of the Americas, a part known as the armpit of the United States, my father transitions from the durable fibers of the petate to the much more cushioned material of the spring mattress. He identifies mattresses as pinche porqueria, pieces of shit.

Objects made in the modern world are not meant to last. They are to wear down, break down, wear you down until you break down and buy a new one. The petate can last for decades and decades, my father says to me, almost bragging. He notes how the metallic springs in mattresses lose their rigidity fast. Petates do not have springs, nor mass-produced construction. They are woven by a mother, a tía, a grandmother, a sister. They are the products of hands of those who are familiars, those who are loved. The palm leaves in the hands of these women, the hands twisting and braiding and mending and weaving, is memory at work. Memories of a time before time, of grandmothers and their grandmothers and the grandmothers before them. The rough hands meeting rough material is a skin history: a history of campesinos and illiteracy and dispossession and conversions and assimilations and impoverishment written into the hands weaving a bed, a blouse, a life. My grandmother weaves my father's petate.

On a mattress, in the nowhere lands of New Jersey, he does not sleep comfortably for a long, long time.

WIKIPEDIA ENTRY FOR burlap: "In Jamaica and certain parts of the Caribbean (where it is only known as Crocus) many enslaved Africans who used to work on the plantations were not often given pleasant materials with which to make clothes. Some had access to cotton which was spun, woven, cut and sewn into serviceable clothing (often called homespun) whilst others had to make do with clothing fashioned from roughly hewn sacking. Enslaved Africans used their resourcefulness to recycle discarded sacking and fashion them into garments that although fairly uncomfortable by all accounts provided protection from the heat and dust." The words are copied and pasted verbatim from the website of the Costume Institute of the African Diaspora. The website notes how burlap is now used for fashion and art. Innovation is using what history has wrought to your advantage. Innovating a history that will not be forgotten.

A PINK POST-IT flag. Sticking out, waving proud in the bibliography section of James's revolutionary history. I always read bibliographies. The development of thought, how one worked their way to an idea or study, what someone disagrees with and what someone agrees with, is fascinating. Scouring the cited history of how something came into existence gives me an inexplicable thrill.

Underlined in green pen is this entry in reference to two books on the antislavery movement: "Both these books are typical for, among other vices, their smug sentimentality, characteristic of the approach of Oxford scholarship to abolition. As the official view, they can be recommended for their thorough misunderstanding of the question." In green ink, undated, my marginalia beside this bibliographic entry reads: "Reading the official text knowing it will be wrong the value of official History is its wrongness and therefore we are more [word illegible], critical readers."

". . . two wheels, one of gold like the sun and the other of silver with the image of the moon upon it, made of plates of those metals . . . a variety of cotton mantles . . ."

SANDBAGS ARE SOMETIMES made from burlap. On the news you see Floridians prepping for a storm every other summer, propping the bags up on their patios, complaining about another storm they have to prep for. The circulation of images from Hurricane Katrina shows storefronts piled high with sandbags, thinking they are ready, though in the end the sandbags prove useless against the waters that will engulf them, wash them away to distant locations. When Hurricane Sandy hits, I am in Washington Heights staying with a friend. The mayor of New York City tells us to stay away from the windows, in case they shatter from the wind speeds. No such thing happens. When we walk outside for the first time in days a bodega storefront sign is on the sidewalk. The shards of its neon lights are scattered in all directions amidst the many leaves and branches. My mother calls me after the storm passes to ask if I am ok, to express her concern, and to inform me an old man has died in Manhattan. The man's name is Frank M. Suber, he dies in the basement of a building, and *The New York Times* reports, "It appeared that he had been walking on a sidewalk when a surge of water carried him into the building." He dies on Broad Street, a block away from the dorm I was going to ride the storm out in. I keep thinking I am so lucky, I am so lucky, but I don't know why.

2005: PILES OF empty burlap are littered across the back of my father's van. The many tools he uses throughout the day—

shovels and loppers and hedge clippers and scissors and machetes—are carried around in a burlap sack. Trees soon to be transplanted are standing straight up in the back with burlap wrapped tightly around the roots. For some reason or another, burlap is also the cushioning of the front seats, and the floor mats. My father has found many uses for this inexpensive material. No corner of his dusty van can escape it.

The scent is overwhelming, pungent, distinct. Every morning ride to school, every evening on my way home, every ride to the train station, this is the scent of these voyages. As soon as the doors are open, it hits you, the odor a force, a sensation upon the body. I worry the other students during these high school years will catch the scent, walk by and experience the odor, make assumptions. The odor of burlap tells them my father is not a firefighter, not a cop, not a fancy NYC corporate head honcho, not a business owner. The burlap scent pouring out from the van lets them know my father works for their fathers. The aroma of the burlap tells them stories of who I am, and who I do not want them to believe I am.

The scent of burlap lingers on the clothes for the rest of the day.

ONE SOLITARY EYE, pure white, horrifyingly white, is exposed through the burlap sheathing his head. I aim for this eye. I think myself a digital sharpshooter. His closeness makes it hard for me to get the shot I want, the shot I need for a faster kill. I shoot. He is still lumbering toward me, chainsaw revving up in his hands, a bloodthirsty gurgling emanating from the burlap-sacked head. I shoot again, and again, and again—too late. He has reached me, he has cut me in two. Game over.

I am playing the video game *Resident Evil 5*, set in an unidentified country in Africa. On the Resident Evil Wiki, the recurring enemy is identified as a "Chainsaw Majini," a steroided villager-zombie wielding a deadly chainsaw. He is an enemy appearing many times throughout the game, reminiscent of the terrifying villain from the *Texas Chainsaw Massacre* movies, Leatherface. Besides this, there is little else known about the enemy, about where the enemy lives, about the enemy's life before being infected with a bioengineered virus. Africa, and whatever unnamed country the player is in, is without history. This is just a video game about zombies, pure, unadulterated shoot-'em-up fun. Any seeming allusions to real life are incidental.

Yet, nevertheless, history surfaces, history engulfs. The histories of corrupt African politicians, of monstrous African warlords, of backward African peoples are histories learned from a clickbait article or a cursory news segment or a government tweet or an NGO website or an outdated textbook. History, and history-making, always derives from a particular perspective. We live history at all moments, we choose sides at all times. Just like there is no one history of an event, there is never no history. Me shooting an African man with a burlap hood over his face, or throwing grenades at men all named Omar in a desert town with fake Arabic script on the signposts, or sniping narcos from a rooftop in some unspecified Latin American country, or mowing down mobsters with a machine gun in a teahouse decorated with dragons and bonsai trees, is history. Shooting bodies in virtual worlds only makes sense when we are doing it to certain kinds of bodies in certain kinds of places, while violence against other kinds of bodies in other contexts might terrify us.

". . . a number of underwaistcoats, handkerchiefs, counterpanes, tapestries and carpets of cotton, the workmanship superior to the materials of which they were composed . . ."

THE SCISSORS HAVE a hard time cutting through it. The material is resistant to change. What I cut ends up fraying the edges, warping the squared shape I intended. No matter. This assignment for class, this found-object history of me, will do.

The piece of cut burlap is in my hands. Coarse, no moisture in its fibers, rugged. From what little I can remember of my father's rough touch, this fabric feels a lot like it. Burlap on the skin invites history, that strange and volatile and metamorphic thing I call my history. I think of myself as a boy, holding his hand in the farmers market, at the summer fair with all the rides. I think of myself as not a boy, as a twenty-something-year-old, holding his hand, our hands around the same size, our hands rough and cragged from our labors. Two men, especially those related, especially those brown, do not hold hands. Perverse, perversion, not allowed. Intimacy as an adult is no longer that of touch. Whatever intimacy between a father and son exists, it must be in the shadows, unnamed and unnameable, a stare a mumble a goodbye through the phone a hug during a special occasion, if we are lucky enough. I want to believe the words intimacy and perversion are not mutually exclusive categories—together I want them to form the word love.

I realize I am gripping the burlap, hard. Gripping it as if it were a hand, palm against palm, my fingers extending to weave between the fingers of another, muscles and tendons and ligaments and flesh trying to grip, to contact, to feel. I loosen my grip, tack the burlap to the box displaying my other found objects, and go to class.

BEFORE JANE AUSTEN becomes Jane Austen, she writes a short history of England for her sister. The Historian, as a title, as a role, as an occupation, is to know history. Facts on the ready, textbook-style prose to be administered in the name of Truth. The Historian should be able to recount, to give dates, provide a sequence of events, what happens where and when. But the Historian that is Jane Austen, young Jane Austen, Jane Austen before she is Jane Austen, plays at being the dumb Historian, plays up in a playful manner *herself* writing history. Concerning Henry V: "During his reign, Lord Cobham was burnt alive, but I forget for what." On the apparent notoriety of Henry VIII: "It will therefore be saving *them* [her readers] the task of reading again what they have read before, and *myself* the trouble of writing what I do not perfectly recollect, by giving only a slight sketch of the principal Events which marked his reign." Her final entry is on Charles I: "The Events of this Monarch's reign are too numerous for my pen, and indeed the recital of any Events (except what I make myself) is uninteresting to me." She does warn us in the beginning this history is done by "a partial, prejudiced, and ignorant Historian."

In this day and age of Wikipedia and high-speed internet and Google, history is an easily retrievable thing. It is ready for us to access, ready for us to manipulate. In her history, Austen does what we do today: omitting or bypassing facts to humor our audience, to win them over; mocking or poking fun at the political parties we do not agree with to disparage them; exalting at all costs our political allegiances no matter the faults or misdeeds they commit. History, and how one writes it, creates a world in an image of our liking.

Austen's history is prefaced with this note: "There will be very few Dates in this History."

"AND BOOKS MADE of tablets with a smooth surface for writing, which being joined might be folded together or stretched out to considerable length, 'the characters inscribed thereon resembling nothing so much as Egyptian hieroglyphics' . . ."

ANY YEAR BETWEEN 1989 and the Present Day: the slamming of metallic doors. Sun in the sky. A bird in flight, shadows of wings extended on the earth, on route to whatever point is its destination, whatever worm is to be its feast. Muscles straining, bark against skin, burlap in the palms of my father's hands. He lugs this tree weighing forty pounds or so across synthetic grass. One of his friends, or a stranger who looks like a friend, installs the grass, cuts the grass, maintains the grass. He waves to these friends and strangers when he sees them on the road. He waves to the mother of three trooping down the street, stroller in hand like a tank, three pairs of small hands firmly bound to the stroller's side. He waves to the man who owns the gas station, turbaned each day in different colors, beard white as snow. He waves to the man who hangs out in front of the local Wawa, a man unlike many of the other men in this small town, hair in luscious coils, hair a lustrous black. He waves to the shadows in cars passing. In all brown faces my father sees friendship.

He stops in place. The tree is put on the synthetic grass. He goes to his van only to return momentarily with a shovel. He digs. Striations up and down the arms, bicep bulks, downward plunging of the shovel head. He's so fast. Unnecessarily fast, it seems. What is the rush, my brown Atlas? The features of his face are solid, rock-solid concentration. Everything is being put into this digging action, everything for him is in this moment. An explanation, a saying: time is money.

Soon enough a hole is in the ground. A foot or so of negative space. He lays the shovel on the ground with an unusual thoughtfulness, for some reason he is attuned to the impact of shovel on earth. He walks over to the tree, and bends over to the roots. Fingers maneuver at the twine binding the burlap to the roots. The intricacy of the knots explains to me why my father keeps his nails so long: they must be used to quickly and efficiently work their way through the durable twine. He yanks, he loops, he wiggles. The twine after a minute or so of laboring is off. The burlap lays on the ground in a crumpled flatness. The roots of the tree are exposed. The dampness is visible.

He lifts the tree and places it, gently and carefully, into the hole. He scoops up the soil with the shovel and chucks it back. In no time at all the tree is in its proper place, its new home. The leaves bright pink, the thin, extending branches, the greyish-black bark: they give a newfound quaintness, a sense of orderliness, to whatever space they settle in.

He picks up the burlap. Pause in action, a beat in time. The material is familiar in his hands. Years upon years of history in the gripping of its rough texture, the coarseness of the fibers in the palms a history of a life. Burlap is a provisional fabric. It is not meant for permanency. Its function is transference, to be a transitory component in the process of cultivating life, its use value dependent on a situation, a circumstance of vegetal vulnerability. It takes no part in the ultimate design of a landscape. It is what enables the aesthetic, what allows for its existence, the hidden-away actor in creating the beauty of some sprawling home or university campus or corporate complex. When burlap can no longer serve its purpose, to protect and to enable and to transfer and to store, it is exposable, disposed of. Burlap exists to exist for others.

Burlap's history is the history of enabling history. What would Princeton University be without its lawns, its sprawling greens and browns on the university website, the foliage and shrubbery so exquisitely maintained to create the most appealing tour for incoming students? Imagine Google headquarters without its foliage, the trees so exquisitely shaped for employees old and new to take pride in, the bushes so tamed for potential business partners to enter thinking how respectable, how put-together, these partners appear to be. Try to think of Main Street, U.S.A, without its potted plants in intricate design, the waxy leaves welcoming as one passes by in the car believing nothing could be wrong about such attractive places, the well-maintained grasses appealing to the eye for the human eye is trained to believe such displays in the landscape are symbols of cleanliness, respectability, goodness, community. History is written into the landscape. History in a place tells us how to view the place, or how not to view a place given the history of its creation. Burlap fosters history and history-making without anyone even knowing. No one remembers how burlap takes part in the cultivation of life, much like no one remembers History—not one history of one particular thing, but all History, Histories of the many, History itself—is tended to by those excluded from it, erased from the very History they cultivate. History excludes the history of those who labor at creating it.

"AND THEN THE end: Cortez had demanded gold . . ." is how Williams concludes his listed extravagances. He narrates the killing of Moctezuma, the fall of Tenochtitlán, and the restructuring of the city according to Spanish tastes. I can't help but linger over the solemn syntax of his list's conclusion. The fatigue in the writer's voice, knowing it was always the gold Cortés wanted, and it still is for those many modernized and corporatized Cortéses who come after him. Their feverish pursuit of the gold that is the extraction and the exploitation and devastation of the lands and bodies of the original peoples of the Americas, still here, still trying to make pathways for indigenous life, land, and community. We must not follow in Cortés' greedy footsteps. A search for home, for place, must be with the knowledge these lands in the Americas belong to the many nations, the many groups, of indigenous peoples. We must situate ourselves in place with that understanding. And, by doing so, we labor with the ever-renewing urgency of eroding these boundaries of settler nations, these violent and violating logics of settler states, dictating what is and what is not, who can exist and who cannot. Any sense of home and belonging must be, always, with that in mind, for there can be no more pursuits of gold, no more Cortéses, no more conquests and colonization. No more. No more.

10

TO PEDRO MY NEIGHBOR

There are no photos of you and me. None of us playing basketball, or running through the woods, hanging out on the block. My family and I have no pictures of you at all in our albums but I know where to find you: the school yearbook. There you are. Contained within a small square frame at the bottom row amongst your classmates. Your head is tilted down, demure, the brown doe eyes. Is your gaze direct, or askew? I cannot tell but I know the lips form into what is supposed to pass as a smile but looks instead like a frown.

But that is not your photo either. It is a photo of you taken by the photographer hired by the school. Taken in the school library, or the cafeteria, our white classmates staring on as the flash ignites in our eyes. Stay still, Pedro, they'll say to you, to me, let me capture this moment of you. We will sit still and quiet lest they think we are disruptive. We will listen to their commands to smile, diverting our eyes as best as possible, inside roiling with anguish and pain and humiliation as the camera flash ignites against us.

There are no photos of you that I have access to that are

beyond this capturing. Instead, like a slideshow, in my head are moving images of that boy who lives down the street from the childhood me. Image after image of the boy you no longer are but to me you will always be because I do not know your older self. Maybe, in order to write this, I need you to stay the little boy. To just be that boy named Pedro.

Pedro whose house at the end of the street isn't falling apart but sure gives that impression. The blue-paneled walls chipping and the bent-out-of-shape screen door. The cemented walkway leading to the door lined with fractures, weeds in the cracks, cement chunks the size of Skittles tossed about. The occasional tuft of grass in the dirt yard. The chickens running around, uncaged, pecking madly at the ground. Each window wide open, a darkness on the inside, a darkness sometimes broken by the brown eyes of an unnamed child peering out, brown eyes eyeing freedom denied.

You have a big family. Your younger brother who trails after you wherever you go. The three sisters who, like you, are always so quiet, so withdrawn, never saying anything. Your mother whose name I have never known carries a child in her arms wherever she wanders, the tiny body swaddled in a mass of cloth, little brown hands clinging to its mother's shirt neckline. Cousins and uncles and aunts and family friends and acquaintances and neighbors and strangers go in and out of this house.

My childhood self passes this house each day. I play with you for the many years I spend in this small farming town in

New Jersey. I play with you, to be totally honest, out of desperation, when there is no one else. You do not invite me over to your house, nor do I ever want you to invite me because I do not want to have to invite you over to mine. I do not call you a friend, not even an acquaintance. I do not say hi to you in school, and, in fact, I pretend I do not even know you when we are there. I only want you to be that boy who lives in my neighborhood, a boy with a permanent black smudge mark on the cheek and lollipop residue outlining your lips, a boy who is a boy with a last name similar to mine. You are not a boy I think of as my kind of people. My kind of people are the Johns and the Abigails and the Bethanys and the Chads but that is a little bit hard to make happen considering they live on the opposite side of town, fifteen or so minutes away, in those new developments, with those spacious and well-manicured yards tended to by men like my father and your father, men who might very well be our fathers.

Your father is so unlike my father. Papa Pedro hangs out on the street drinking beers. Papa Pedro lobs around his curse words, loud and boisterous, without care. Papa Pedro works sometimes, when he feels like it, when he feels up to it. Stereotypically stereotypical of him. He says hi to me when I pass by the house and I offer up a weak smile, barely cordial, amicably hostile. He knows my father, and he knows my family, but I pretend as if he is a stranger to me, a nobody before me. My father is nothing like your father and I feel blessed. My father promised his mother before coming to the United States he would never drink again and he has never broken that promise made nearly thirty years ago. He is the guy you ask for a loan knowing you will never have to pay it back because he is too nice to remind you to pay him. He is the guy never idle, never able to relax, because he is too consumed with work, with laboring.

But the ruse is up when I glimpse your father's eyes. His eyes, the shimmering soft browns like my father's eyes, like so many of these men and women's eyes who live in this neighborhood, lined with thunder-like streaks of red. The red is an effect of many causes: the field-day dust; the sweat stinging the eyes; sleep deprivation; the sun's relentlessness; the straining of the vision to see if an ICE agent or police officer is entering the farm, the neighborhood, the street, the yard of the home, the home itself, the bedroom while asleep. Our skin, our names, our physical features, our accents, our everyday mode of being gives us away as being in relation to you and your father in some way but we are of a different stock. Or, at least, I want to tell myself we are different from you.

You talk about how you will someday be a drunk like your Papa Pedro. How you will hang out on the street and never work. You drink canned soda and pretend you are drinking a Modelo. You rock back and forth, slurring speech, gyrating your hands around in mayhem. You wriggle your thin waist around chaotically and call it dancing. I find the rehearsal of your future self funny, grotesque, and, somehow, thrilling.

Watching as you feign drunkenness without care of what others think. Choosing to laze about and drinking and having a good time though the world around you expects you to be an overachiever and self-hating and exceptional. When I, childhood self and future self, am always so composed, like my father, so moderated and so in check.

Pedro, my antithesis, Pedro, all I wish to be.

MEMORY IS LIKE a slideshow. Not smooth and seamless like a movie. No well-edited transitions and cinematic scores and narrative coherence. The images come one after the other, in no particular order, jarringly, each momentous and catastrophic in its presentation of what was.

Pedro passing me by in the hall with his head held low.

Pedro laughing quietly in the woods.

Pedro running down the pothole-riddled road.

Pedro, how do you remember me? Am I quiet, like you, reserved? Do you think me too feminine, too fat, or do you think I'm a bit weird? If, that is, you remember me at all. Forgettable because childhood me wants to be forgotten. Do you know, Pedro, that I throw away my seventh- and eighth-grade portraits because I find myself so repulsive to look at? I want to erase myself so others may forget about me, so that I don't have to stand out so very much. You probably forget about me, Pedro, because I want to be forgotten. Wanting you to forget how I don't speak of my family. Wanting you to forget how we don't even look at each other in school. Wanting you to forget what I will do to you that day.

It's any day of the week, after school, like usual. You are tied to the pole of the basketball court with a rope. We are playing some kind of game to kill the boredom. You have been there for some time. You squirm, you thrash, you resist and I find it funny. I'm not sure if you are over the game. I can't take what you say seriously. I walk away for twenty or so minutes and leave you there, squirming, trapped. I return and the look on your face becomes one of worry. The game has gone on for too long, clearly, but not for me. I don't want it to end.

There, tied up as you are, has me surging with a feeling indescribable. This feeling of dominion, of having one's way, of having the world operate according to your whim. Your body, and what happens to it, under my possession, and how pleasurable it all feels. Is this why John M. or Catherine with a *C* or Chad do as they do to us? This feeling without a name. Representing no single emotion, representing no reasonable reason, just the deliciousness of a body there before you that you can claim as yours, as consumable, as disposable, as violable, predisposed to whatever whim or fancy because his body and those like him mean a particular something, a body disposed to meaning, full of meanings, meanings shifting and meanings transforming but meaningful as a bodily representative and representation representing a fantasy of belonging and purity and patriotism and power and whi—

Screaming. It is you. Yours, this scream. So unlike you, so out of character. The mouth is a gaping wideness. The tonsils pulsate, and enlarge. The scream careens into the nearby woods, the leaves tossing and turning in an uproar, the birds in a many-winged disarray.

The feeling I get from what I do to you must be what they feel when they do it to us. Not an isolated feeling, not a modern one either. No one name or concept for it. Old, and ingrained, though ever vague and amorphous. Back, back, and back we can go to identify it. To the first booted footfalls into Africa, into Asia, into the Americas, into and into go the feet of men backed by theirs guns and scabbards and dogs. To the miles of roads walked by the indigenous peoples of the Americas who are forcibly removed, killed, and then sequestered into designated parcels of land. To the ships full of Black bodies crossing the Atlantic who will make the modern world. To the subsequent days and decades and centuries of revolutions, genocides, dispossession, starvation, lynchings, incarceration, and impoverishment.

And in them all, in their specific sites and contexts, there is pleasure. The smiling white faces of the lynch mob printed on a postcard. The neat and sometimes quite beautiful prose of Christopher Columbus announcing the removal of the indigenous peoples of the Caribbean. The scenic weddings on former slave plantations. The strategic photo ops with poor and hungry children taken by the philanthropist or the aid worker or the congressman who will never step foot again in the poverty-stricken neighborhood, town, or country. The wearing of blackface, or indigenous peoples' clothing. The list can go on and on.

Round and round the rope goes around Pedro's body and I feel it. Him there wriggling and twisting, I feel how easy it is to fall into the trap. To let this age-old feeling normalize within me. To let it normalize to the point where I can walk away and not think twice about it, letting it solidify into the practical and rational and logical, becoming a cruelty of willful ignorance and oversight I can no longer name as such. And it will pass on to all I know and come in contact with and will go on unquestioned, becoming common sense, becoming just the way things are.

But your scream, Pedro, breaks me from the allure of this hold. Your scream materializes in sound what I cannot find language for, cannot represent in words, cannot bring to bear. This scream, which is the breaking. The breaking across time and space, your scream the scream of all those Pedros and Marias who have lived and died through these centuries, the Pedros and the Marias who are our parents and siblings and relatives and neighbors and strangers on the street, all those Pedros and Marias dotting these Americas screaming at this exact moment in time, yesterday and tomorrow, there and here, then and now.

This scream, which is the scream inside of me right now.

I rush up to you and untie the rope.

Are you ok . . . Pedro?

THIS PHOTO IS of you and me. Our arms are slung around each other. I loop my arm around your neck because I am taller, and your arm around my waist. We are both smiling. Behind us, the potholed road, the chickens running about, and the younger kids riding their bikes as the sun begins to set on the street of our childhood. Someone from the neighborhood takes this picture because we ask them to. We want this picture of us. Our posing, our timing, our moment. Ours.

But we know, Pedro, this never happens. This photo doesn't exist. There are no photos of us together as children and there will never be. Our history has already been written.

Like a slideshow, all I can do is imagine snapshots of us having a different childhood.

You and me eating cake at one of our birthday parties.

You and me passing each other in the school hallway and saying hi.

You and me playing video games in my house.

You and me having dinner with your family.

You and me together.

I need us to have another timeline besides the one we must have. One of our devising. One of our creation. I need to dislodge us from being stuck in time and space because that is to allow others to write our story. These scattered-about images in my mind of a past that never was is an attempt to imagine our past not defined by shame, humiliation, and the desire to be liked or close to the white children and adults who govern how we feel about ourselves and each other.

Can you see it, Pedro? Our arms across one another. The cemented ruptures in the road. The soft light of day's end. See, Pedro, how our eyes have in common that soft sheen of brown, the gentle scintillation. Look, Pedro, how we are together on the street neither of us live on or visit anymore, the street of our childhood. Are you reminiscing, Pedro, as I am, on this image of us, this portrait of our friendship?

11

PEDRO'S THEORY

The camera records his theory. The dexterous chubby hands in the air, the upturned palms, the pointed forefingers. Follow him as he goes point by point in unintelligible discoursing. He moves his mouth and tongue like his grandmother, his tias, his mother, all of whom he studies so closely, delivering bits of words and scattered phrases in English and Spanish. He theorizes with flamboyant surety, laying claim to some mystic knowledge, a subject he knows so well that he doesn't stop to see if the camera or his mother turned cameraman understands it all. There, in the moving image, he is animated by the desire to theorize.

But what *exactly* is the theory being explained? He mumbles incomprehensible words and sentences, all gap-toothed and smiling, seven-year-old glossolalia. He breaks off midway through a thought, pausing at length in what appears to be bored idleness. It's hard to follow the line of thinking he presents to the mother-cameraman as he meanders through the house, leisurely picking up knickknacks and toys along the way, demurely resting hands on the wood-paneled walls. His discoursing is so casual, and aimless, disinterested in the camera's desire to know him, to document him.

I can't decipher what my childhood self is saying, and neither can my parents, as we watch this home-video footage of this day in the nineties. The footage is remarkably captioned in all capitals as THE EVERYDAY. Just my mother recording the goings-on of life in our tiny rented house. She makes a lot of these kind of recordings in the 1990s and early 2000s. The bulk of these are birthday parties, baptisms, and other special events. But some of the footage is more random documentation of my siblings and me. When my brother dies in 2004, however, that all seems to stop. There's little, if any, footage after that year. Much of the footage that I'm in is of my younger self discoursing on unknown topics, in the same wandering manner, and it always seems like my mom catches me unaware. As if she is merely trying to document what I am doing unprompted and unwarranted by the camera's gaze. I cannot place myself in the child's head, in his thoughts, though I want to. I cannot decode the elaborate theories of garbled words and nonsense concepts he expounds though, technically, they are mine. I want to *know* him in the most definitive way but he eludes me, the little chubby feminine brown boy, in the moving image of yesterday, theorizing his embodied knowing, his broad imagination, moving yet further and further from my understanding.

THE FOOTAGE IS different from the photographs I have been analyzing of my childhood self. There is sound, the timbre of voices, static. There are dialogue, scenes, and movements. But like the photographs, I describe these moving images of my childhood self because I want him to speak to me. Wanting him to breach the barriers of time and space so as to give the words context, the moment, the life as it was lived. I want to know more than the pain and trauma of my childhood. I want more for that little boy who was and is me. All I can do in that pursuit is this ekphrasis, this description of images, a speculative imagining of a childhood past gone by.

The art of description has been around for a long time. Homeric description established it as a literary style, and then it was popularized in the tradition of blazon poetry pioneered by Petrarch and Elizabethan poets. In the eighteenth century, description became closely aligned with the rise of empiricist science, and was put to use as a means of taxonomizing and classifying the world according to European epistemologies.

The Hungarian Marxist philosopher Georg Lukács, in his 1939 essay "Narrate or Describe?," is critical of description as a literary form. Undertaking a Marxist critique of the work of Zola, he links the dehumanization of capitalism to description, where the automation and assembly lining of human life is like description. To him, description's function is one of generating static, immobile, and inert scenes. Throughout the essay, Lukács criticizes description for producing still lifes, being "superfluous," doing little more than "emphasiz[ing] the picturesque and superficial aspects," and, in the boldest indictment, creating a "dreary existence without a rich inner life, without the vitality of continuous development." For Lukács, description is a form of decadence, feminized and passive, a wasteful indulgence in details, whereas narration captures the inner life of people, providing a connection between the past and the present to articulate the development.

But I disagree. I examine these photographs and footage of myself in pursuit of the detail, precisely because of the inner worlds it might unlock. "Description," as Mark Doty notes in his book on description's poetic force, "is a mode of thinking." Details and describing tap into ways of paying attention to the everyday living that is overlooked, deemed unimportant, written off as insignificant.

In *A Map to the Door of No Return*, Dionne Brand, writing in lyrical and critical prose the dilemma of the Afrodiasporic person living out the afterlives of slavery, explains how "cartography is description, not journey. The door, of course, is not on the continent but in the mind; not a physical place—though it is—but a space in the imagination." For Brand, returning to the African continent is not a guarantee of belonging and self-realization, not the Promised Land delivered. Rather, belonging and self-making are practices. One must describe, critically imagine, the cartography of life and life-giving one needs for oneself, for others, for another world.

If I don't practice this descriptive imagining, then there is no way to reach out to that little boy, to know a different narrative than the ones imposed upon him, defining and limiting how he understands himself. Indulging in the detail lets me relive, or live anew, the ordinary, what my mother has so eloquently captioned as THE EVERYDAY. In a world that demands the pain and trauma of marginalized peoples, in a world that requires us to be exceptional and overachieving in order to validate our worthiness to exist, the detail and description's commitment to the ordinary, the excessive, the unimpressive, the ornamental, allows us another way to be. I want to relish the details of images I barely got to live because that lets me get closer to that little boy, closer to another life, closer to the many selves I need to forge my path from here forward.

Tina M. Campt, a scholar of photography and critical race studies, explains the act she calls "listening to images" as "the practice of looking beyond what we see and attuning our sense to the other affective frequencies through which photographs register." Campt explores what photographs taken of Black subjects through dominant frameworks and institutions can do to foster a "quotidian practice of refusal" that is "defined less by opposition or 'resistance,' and more by a refusal of the very premises that have reduced the lived experience of blackness to pathology and irreconcilability in the logic of white supremacy." The Black feminist method outlined by Campt is one prioritizing the haptic, and the sensory, experience of photographs and images, an analytic connection to the image that examines the event of the photo, the conditions surrounding its moment of instantiation. This method takes into account the seen and unseen, the past and present, of what constitutes the image. The photo becomes an interpretive event in and of itself.

Campt's work provides a means for me to listen to the images of my youth, scoping out the details, in order to describe them. To amplify the ordinary and the everyday, to speculate upon the scenes and contexts of the images of my youth, to imagine in prose a life lived and yet never lived. I let the detail lead me down paths I never knew possible.

IT'S AN EXTREME close-up. Shaky though, because the camera begins the recording zoomed-in, zeroing in on the brown of my childhood eye. The camera is zoomed in so closely you can see the speckles of honey-color in the eye. Slowly the camera pans out to reveal the full face. He's laying against the side of the couch, the left cheek all squashed in, gazing blankly at the camera. What is he thinking? Is he wondering why this camera is interrupting his solemnity? No commentary is given by the mother-cameraman.

After twenty seconds or so of this facial close-up, the footage abruptly cuts to my brother and me wrestling. I'm squealing because I cannot bring his large frame to the ground, and he laughs at the futility of my effort. This recording rolls for about four minutes. I appreciate this footage because it is one of the rare recordings I have of my brother and me. It is one of the rare recordings that documents his voice, his humor, his full body. This few-and-far-between documentation of him bolsters the sparse memories I have of us together. Though I don't know if the footage supplements the memories, or if it creates them.

I can't help but wonder if the close-up prior to the wrestling footage is a mistake. Simply a test to check the audio or visuals of the camcorder. Twenty seconds is so little time for such a portrait. I rewind again to view it. I slow it down. I triple-check the footage after the wrestling match to see if there are more tapes like the one of me on the couch but find nothing. I find nothing other than the longing for a few more seconds, a minute more, of the child in repose, poised for contemplation. If I rewind and slow it down a part of me believes I will give him more time to think, more time to laze about in his own thoughts. I want more footage but maybe what I truly want to know is the impossible—the moment before filming. Before the intrusive red of the camcorder light, before the camera's all-knowing gaze, when undisturbed by the presence of another, just there with thoughts in quiet rumination, what figures of imagination dance in the eye, what worlds do the brown of the iris conjure?

THERE IS A sentence-scene in Justin Torres's *We the Animals* that is a tangle of details. An accumulation of specifics into a single syntactical construction, exuberantly detailing an average moment in the life of a queer Puerto Rican child:

> "This is your heritage," he said, as if from this dance we could know about his own childhood, about the flavor and grit of tenement buildings in Spanish Harlem, and projects in Red Hook, and dance halls, and city parks, and about his own Paps, how he beat him, how he taught him to dance, as if we could hear Spanish in his movements, as if Puerto Rican was a man in a bathrobe, grabbing another beer from the fridge and raising it to drink, his head back, still dancing, still stepping and snapping perfectly in time.

The film version of this sentence-scene in the family's kitchen pales in comparison. I go to the movie theatre ready to not see this scene, but to experience it. I hope to feel its rhythm manifested in the cinematic, its worded twisting and binding emanating from the screen. But it's not there, and it's not the film's fault. Language does something else. In the syntactical construction loaded with details, the abrupt clausal breaks one after another, is the coalition of words, emotion, and body. It is an instance of recognition by the child of the father's trauma and yet it is also a moment of intense joy and bonding. They are together there in an intergenerational and diasporic embrace fueled by the detail. The queer child of color makes art out of a sentence: a still-life portrait with the father as the centerpiece, moving from the present of the kitchen to the parental past in

Brooklyn, the strokes of loving precision upon the details of his father's dancing, his father's pain, his father's biography, holding the child in attention, holding him as his thoughts spiral in poetic embrace.

I FIRST ENCOUNTER the work of performance studies scholar and queer of color theorist José Muñoz in a queer theory course taken my sophomore year of undergrad. We read an excerpt from Muñoz's first monograph, *Disidentifications: Queers of Color and the Performance of Politics*. We turn to Muñoz in the class, obviously, for his ideas, for the theoretical contributions he is supposed to impart to us. Yet what strikes me the most, what lingers in memory, is an autobiographical passage from his youth. A moment in which the queer child of color becomes theory.

The excerpt is from the final paragraph of the chapter focusing on the gay Cuban American cast member from MTV's *The Real World: San Francisco*, Pedro Zamora. Here we have another Pedro to factor into our theory, and one of the first Pedros living with HIV/AIDS to be portrayed on US television. Zamora is the focus of chapter six in the monograph, where Muñoz examines the ways in which Zamora presented a defiant and out queer life on the television screen.

> As I sat in the living room with my parents, I marveled at the televisual spectacle of this young man and his

> father, both speaking a distinctly Cuban Spanish, on television, talking openly about AIDS, safe sex, and homosexuality. I was struck because this was something new; it was a new formation, a being for others. I imagined countless other living rooms within the range of this broadcast and I thought about queer children who might be watching this program at home with their parents. This is the point where I locate something other than the concrete interventions in the public sphere. Here is where I see the televisual spectacle leading to the possibility of new counterpublics, new spheres of possibility, and the potential for the reinvention of the world from A to Z.

This paragraph is merely an ordinary moment of a queer kid in front of the TV screen with his father. Anecdotal evidence, anecdotal theorizing. Nevertheless, I am struck by this paragraph the first time I read it, as well as by the rereadings afterward, because it confirms to me, the queer child of color, that our everyday reality, our embodied living, can be the stuff of theory. Our minds and bodies can theorize this world though we are rarely allowed such recognition. This concluding paragraph breaks from the monographic time, breaks from the regimented prose of the scholar. The flaming staccato of the opening sentence, which asks us to luxuriate over it and to notice what he is doing. The jerky rhythm of the clauses documenting the body and its relations, the affinities and intimacies the scholar feels for the object of analysis. Where the queer Pedro on the TV screen and the queer Pedro in the living room meet, in writing and thought, across times and mediums. This Pedro-to-Pedro theory becomes an instant to unmake and remake the world as we know it.

THE CAMERA FILMS from above, an aerial shot of curly brown hair, as the boy does, well, nothing. He's just seated on the floor with crisscrossed legs, murmuring out ideas the camera can't make out. The mother-cameraman-narrator asks, "What are you doing?" He gives no answer and plays coy by seeming to not notice the camera. There's no doubt when the red of the camera's light flickers on he becomes more performative. You can see the slight intensification of his mannerisms, his expressions, his vocalization. He wants the camera to see him. He wants us to take notice.

There's something about the disinterest of my younger self I admire. His flirtatious disregard of the camera. The resolute intention to discourse on a topic, to use a lexicon and grammar no one can interpret. He must feel so free there in the everyday footage my mother records. It's a version of my childhood self I don't really know. I only know him as the quiet boy, withdrawn, and perpetually afraid. This boy in the footage is carefree, unbothered, letting his thoughts and ideas wander without the worry of what others may think. He's a stranger to me.

Much of what constitutes memoir writing is the concentrated attempt to recover and reconstruct the past into a cohesive narrative. Whether overtly expressed or subtly implied, a sense of wholeness and realized identity is typically the end goal for narrativizing one's experience. Far too often, such attempts rely upon neat and tidy understandings of identity, histories, and places. The many images of my younger self, however, put pressure on these conventions of autobiographical writing. The more footage like this I see, the less I seem to know of him. Every attempt at pinning him down, my efforts to piece him together into some completed and whole being, only move me further away. Dividing the boy into fragments and fantasies, into many pasts, many selves, all in relation to different contexts and people. We exist in complicated worlds, intricately enmeshed in numerous unperceived ways, and the writing of our lives must reflect that messiness.

Maybe that's the theory my younger self is going on about all the time in the footage. Maybe he's informed by what Audre Lorde coins in *Zami: A New Spelling of My Name*: biomythography, a method of writing combining history, biography, and myth. In it, the voices and stories of the many women who have made her who she is appear. "The term," elaborates scholar Karen Weekes, "reflects the biography of the figure who speaks for collective experience, along with a mythologizing impulse that enlarges this quotidian figure and inscribes it—in its both mundane and legendary aspects—into a contemporary cultural mythology." The biography of a life is many lives informed by those who shape us. Dionne Brand echoes this thinking in different terms: "A map, then, is only a life of conversations about a forgotten list of irretrievable selves." Brand poetically relays how the pursuit of self-making and knowing is a constantly changing process. Sometimes we forget selves, sometimes we edit, but we keep going on in unending search because there is no one self, no formative identity. Many, always more than one.

Lorde and Brand guide me in thinking of how memoir writing is about composing selves. Stylizing oneself according to what is available, what might have been, and what is yet to be. Adorning a past with the real and factual, but also with the desires unfulfilled, the rage and pleasure disavowed. Imagining a geography of self, memory, and collectivity that otherwise might not come to fruition. Particularly for marginalized people, especially for queer and trans people of color, we must compose a life to our suiting. Where the past, present, and future are always together, shaping one another and shaped by the many voices of our communities and ancestors, imagined in ways to allow for our pleasure, our ordinariness, our revolutionary thinking. The rupturing of time and space, photographic and filmic memories that aren't really ours anymore, though they become something else, something proliferative, expansive. Perhaps this is what Pedro's theory is all about. These efforts in prose to compose a life, the living out of many selves and conversations in the hope to compose another Americas, another world that does not have to be this exact one, that might be another one right on the surface of a photograph or a home video or a sentence, right there awaiting its graceful articulation, its sumptuous detailing.

IN A DITCH dug out in the front yard by his father, the protagonist of *We the Animals*—unnamed in the book but referred to as Jonah here in the film adaptation—lies in the mud. There is no language in this scene. Just sensory details. The supple sounds of mud against body, the rustling of the trees, a breath in and out. Alas, the urge for language, the need to explain in words, overcomes me: What is he thinking? This little brown boy buried in the mud, in a ditch, in a grave, what is on his mind? What thoughts does he think there amongst the worms and tree roots, if, that is, he is thinking anything at all? Little brown boy building systems and fantasies and processes and universes in order to prepare him to leave this mud, this ditch, this grave of solitude.

I read language and words onto the slight muscle movements of Jonah's face, the staring straight ahead of his eyes, a question in his blankness there in the mud-like grave: "How do I become free?"

Little brown boy, free? Little brown boy who desires other boys, little brown boy with this inexpressible rage, little brown boy beat down by words and hands, little brown boy with this unthinkable hurt, free?

Against all the odds, all the rules of physics, the boy rises out from the ditch. Into the air, and sky-bound. He goes beyond the screen, the town he lives in, his family, the film, my imposition of words. He's but a shadow across the treetop canopy. An effect of light and darkness, air and matter, presence and absence. Jonah does not say anything about this surreal moment as it happens. In fact, for most of the film Jonah does not express himself in language. The film's composition alludes, touches upon, suggests on his behalf. There is a case to be made that the film portrayed this languageless Jonah in order to highlight how the queer child of color has little room to speak up for themselves, and to emphasize how their thoughts and ideas must always be monitored.

And yet I also find this refusal of language a welcome relief. The relief from having to explain our trials and tribulations, or to represent our identities and cultures for an audience presumed to not be like us. In the absence of language, we can be embodied beings, bodies of sensory expression and sensory intimacies. We can be bodies that imagine other possibilities through the banal and the mundane like laying in the mud, the surreal and absurd like soaring in the sky. Films do this work best, and especially films by and about Black queer experience like *Moonlight*, *Looking for Langston*, and *Tongues Un-*

tied, as well as shows like *Pose.* These examples demonstrate how filmic depictions can tap us into the ordinary, the embodied, and the fantastic. Our theories don't always have to be proposed in language.

THE CAMERA RECORDS a convening of the family members, their chitchat and laughter, their togetherness on the couch at the grandmother's house, all is well until the slight turning away by the cameraman, an instant of the slightest shift in perspective, there, out of the frame and out of the scene, it's the boy, eleven or so years old, big-bodied and hunched in the nearby hallway archway looking in on them, wallpaper, a minor detail of the room momentarily captured on footage though the camera doesn't know what to do with him, doesn't know how, or if, he even fits into the frame, and, as quickly as he appears, he disappears.

IN THE QUOTIDIAN, the everyday mundane like having a Coke with a lover in poems by Frank O'Hara, or in the sketch of a Coke bottle turned vase by Andy Warhol, José Muñoz finds traction for his theories on queer utopia. "Queerness is essentially about the rejection of a here and now," Muñoz asserts, "and an insistence on potentiality or concrete possibility for another world," where hope emerges for queer relations, queer living, and queer world-making. In his most-read book, *Cruising Utopia*, Muñoz offers a thoroughly expansive critical attention to what the quotidian can do, and how we can use the quotidian moments of the past for a present and future queer politics.

Muñoz's theoretical ventures are prefaced by an epigraph from Oscar Wilde: "A map of the world that does not include utopia is not even worth glancing at." The cartographic terminology is sustenance for the theorist, a way of formulating his own theory: "queer world-making, then, hinges on the possibility to map a world where one is allowed to cast pictures of utopia and to include such pictures in any map of the social." Brand, too, uses cartographic imagining, cartographic theorizing: "To travel without a map, to travel without a way. They did, long ago. That misdirection became the way. After the Door of No Return, a map was only a set of impossibilities, a set of changing locations." We must devise our own maps. We must draw out the world required for queer and antiracist potentialities. The cartography of another place where our relations toward one another are ones of mutual care and generosity, not bound to systems of exploitation, distrust, and violence. Queer of color childhood in films, photography, and home videos does this cartographic work imagined by those like Wilde, Muñoz, and Brand. Where the quotidian like the shot of the face, the detail, the angle, the expression, and other minor forms become sites for what can be or what might have been or what is yet to be. Another time, not this one, maybe one that never was, but it can be if willed, if needed, if imagined as the coordinate on the edges of the map, verging onto another map entirely, a map worth glancing at, a map of worthwhile impossibilities.

THE ROLL OF film winds out into the VCR before we can see what the contents of the tape hold. My mother delicately takes it out to see if it can be salvaged but most of it is shredded, a tangled cluster of black ribbon. Thankfully, we get to see all the other home videos with the exception of this one.

I wonder what might have been on the tape. Might it have contained the secret to activating some other understanding of my childhood self? Some other portrait of my family, neighborhood, myself? I am so desperate to find another past, a past verifiable with concrete and material evidence like film footage, that a sadness clouds over me at the thought of the ruined film. I need the film to authenticate myself. I need the film to be the proof of a past existence.

The desire for all the answers, for the foolproof and definitive, is a powerful yearning. It is ingrained deep into how we are supposed to learn, grow, and authenticate ourselves. For many of us, however, we don't have records or evidence. No recorded family histories, no documents to attest to a former life, no ephemera. Many of us don't get the luxury. Sometimes all we have is the little chubby brown boy rambling out ideas in a language the camera cannot decipher, the little chubby brown boy wandering from the camera's view in a way my adult self cannot interpret. Following the traces of the cinematic presence, off and on the screen, has to be evidence enough.

THERE'S A CHILD in the New York City neighborhood I live in who looks like my childhood self. The moving image on the screen comes to life. When the child in my neighborhood runs too fast, they lose their breath but they keep smiling, still in the rush of chasing a mouse down the block. They laugh with an effeminate loudness, they gesture extravagantly with their hands. The child speaks in Spanish and in English.

Anytime I see children who look like him in public I feel something. Not a nameable emotion or thought. It's more like a sensation, an embodied response of seeing a familiar stranger. Seeing myself in the flesh, and the subsequent desire to reach out to them so I could have a sense of what it would be like to hold my childhood self. To embrace myself, to whisper affirmations, to let myself know it will be ok despite knowing my childhood will not be ok.

BUT, PASSING THEM by on the sidewalk, I remind myself these children who look like younger me are not me. They are their own story. They are their own many selves. Their own journeys in laughter, crying, and living. They will have to find the language in which to express these stories and selves. They will need their own theories to transform the world.

THERE IS A particular montage quality to many of the home-video recordings done by my mother. The effect is not intentional, being that my mother doesn't know how to use any video-editing software. It is just her default filming method. She never keeps track of what each tape has recorded, so often many are overwritten or, in some cases, bizarrely spliced together. For instance, a tape will open with a cousin's quinceañera in 1998, and then halfway through we are lounging in the living room of my grandmother's house in 1994. Different events and years are haphazardly conjoined. There is no voice-over narration for beginnings or endings, no narrative stability to frame recorded events. Jump cuts abound. One moment I'm quietly playing a video game in the living room, and then the next I'm wrestling with my brother in a bedroom. All of this combines to form jarring displacements of time and space, few narrativized scenes, and sequencing run amok.

My mother keeps all these tapes in a plastic bin. There is no order to them whatsoever. Thrown about, undated, they are bits and pieces of our collective past. When I inquire into the many montaged videos and the archival disarray of the tapes my mother has no problem with it. "I just wanted to record as much as I could," she answers. She feels no need to catalog or order them. There is no urgency to digitize them and preserve them for later years. I guess you can say I'm more like my mother than I think.

My mother's unusual filming methods, as well as her

haphazard means of archiving, give me a way to think about composing these selves. Montaged, uniquely brought together, incidentally at times, at others purposeful. There is no single approach or method to examine memory or life, as the tapes of my childhood and their storage demonstrate. Throughout my twenties, I have desperately wanted a way to speak to my younger self. I have wanted to know him so totally, so determinately, believing this full knowing would somehow allow me to tell the little boy he will be ok, he will make it through. Instead, in every attempt to reach out to my younger self I find him only reaching out to me. Not saying something profound, or epiphanic, but merely quiet murmurings, deep contemplations. Where his reaching out becomes the form of this book. But he is more than just a book. He is an ongoing project, a universe of thinking. The compilation of writings that didn't make the final cut, the writings published elsewhere, the scribbled writings in notebooks and unfinished writings in files scattered on my computer. His reaching out to this present of writing, the many selves and many forms, across the space-time continuum, these plentiful I's that are always an us, an ours, this future writing yet to be.

This is his theory.

PART 3

PEDRO OF THE AMERICAS

12

DISSERTATION NOT IN PROGRESS

Idle, and in bed. My body won't move. I should be writing my dissertation, I should be working toward the completion of my doctorate, I should be productive instead of at this impasse, this near-sleep. I am supposed to be the American dream, right? I distract myself by scrolling down my newsfeed on Twitter. Tweet after tweet, article after article—bombardment. Apocalypse now, or has the apocalypse already happened for some us? Finger swipe, finger click, finger tremble. "Children of Undocumented Parents Left Behind After . . ." "A Man Killed by Police for Selling Cigarettes on the Sidewalk . . ." "Death of an Undocumented Immigrant in New Jersey Detention Center Finds No One . . ." "Hurricane Maria Devastates the Island of Puerto Rico, Killing Thousands . . ." "What They Left Behind: Online Database Tracks What Migrants Left at the Bo—" Enough! a voice says.

Which voice is it today? You or you or you or you? The finger in my brain points in no direction at all for this brain is a cave is a labyrinth is an underworld is nowhere and everywhere is a metaphor interchangeable. Voices scream at activist friends and strangers that enough is enough. One voice, whisper-like, threatening and singular, says: These articles must be lived day to day, why let the phrasings consume you, why let the terminology nag at you, why let the narratives do things to you against your will, why why why? Another voice says: You will this pain into being, you suffer because you know your kin and kind suffer worse, suffering brings you closer to those like your father who works the fields day in and day out, filial piety, psychical desecration, you thrive in this pun—

No time for voice identifying. Energies required on the *D* word, the *D* that all my living family and all my dead and gone ancestors could never even dream of: Dissertation. The dissertation is the proof of your ability to be a doctorate-worthy person, worthy of the accolades of civilized society. The *Oxford English Dictionary* does not define *dissertation* in this way: productivity, the means out of poverty out of colonial legacies out of my own racialization, inadequacy, my therapist diagnosing me with "imposter syndrome and survivors' guilt."

No idea what I am trying to write, what I am trying to argue, what it is I am researching, who I am citing, who it is I am trying to be. Idea-less. A professor suggests, "Less ideas, more writing." Filled with ideas (am I?). Good ones, half-baked ones, regurgitated ones, and undeveloped ones. All ideas, all kinds. I am a thinker not a doer. Pedro the wanderer. I try at writing like I try at being a filial son—try and try and try but am always not quite good enough. Trying is all I do well. Darling, I am PERFECTION at trying. Attempts at stalling, almost-but-not-quites, lingering on a thought for too long, scribbling down a concept, whi—a thought interrupting, no, a voice, not my voice but memory now makes it mine, a voice of my memory: *"Marcos, I don't really think you are ready for grad school, then."*

Broken-record memory. Same imagery: her the professor of literature at her desk in front of me, and me, the poor student of color, behind her desk, at her mercy. It's my junior year of undergrad and I am contemplating getting my doctorate in English Language and Literature. Foolish. The audio is what changes in this memory. The phrase repeats but it repeats at a different pitch, inflection, tempo, rhythm, emphasis, intensity. Memory-making a remixing. The question of "Did the memory happen in *X* way, or was it actually like *Y* way?" is irresolvable. Too many variants to represent the Truth. But what master does Truth serve? Not mine for mine is the truth of this variance, these many styles of how the scene went down, of how the event has impressed itself onto my body. Her truth? Her story is probably different than mine, if, that is, she remembers it at all. Her Truth is the truth she was being nice, trying to help me, reduce the disappointment I would feel when the nos started pouring in, her Truth is the Truth of the whi—

I break down the worded memory:

"Marcos": An attempt at sincerity, the linking of the familiar with kindness, a pseudofamiliarity and a pseudokindness. She knows my name therefore she knows what is best for me.

"I don't think you are": An opinion with the gravitas of truth, her PhD hanging from the wall her Truth, an assessment based on prior knowledge, assumptions, and her experience about the nature of my being, about who I am as she sees I am based on how she knows the world.

"really": To emphasize the degree to which she believes something is real. This "really" is what gives the statement its intensity, the frictive rub of enduring for almost half a decade after its nonexistence. The "really" exists well beyond its prime.

"ready for grad school": What constitutes readiness? Are my words on the page not argumentative or factual or pretty enough? Is there a barometer to gauge the activity of my brain? Can you count the many voices in my head? To not be ready for graduate school means . . . it means . . . to further develop the thought requires a separate close reading, an entirely new hypothesis.

", then.": A reply in regards to something negative I said. I can't remember what was said that prompted the statement and this concluding ", then." Maybe I mention reservations about my ability to keep up at the graduate level because I didn't take enough courses on "canonical literature," maybe I present doubts about my abilities to actually do five or so years more in school because I will be the first one on both sides of my family to finish undergraduate and then the first to go to graduate school, maybe I worry about funding and having more tuition fiascos like I did in undergrad, which required my underpaid and overexploited farmworking father to bail me out . . . maybe I . . . maybe just . . . maybe this . . . no more maybes.

"Marcos, I don't think you are really ready for grad school, then.": A disciplining, a limiting, a deferral, a not-quite-good-enough but, like they tell my family, like they tell my lovers and friends, like they told my ancestors, like they tell those like me, someday it will get better, someday you will be good enough. Always someday.

To write the dissertation is to recall this memory. I have come to embody its multitudes.

The clickbait articles on Twitter are more appealing.

MY MIND THINKS erratically. Sometimes irrationally. My brain moves so fast, thinking so many thoughts at the same time, as if overcrowded, as if at a very loud concert, as if I might be going insane.

What is happening to me?

I am no longer the boy in the small town, or the young man in New York City. I am in my mid-twenties and about to get my doctorate. I am twenty-three years old teaching college classes. I am proud of being Mexican and Puerto Rican. I am proud of being gay and femme and fat. I feel in control of my own destiny. I am well on the way to upward mobility. Feeling like my life is mine, authentically so, at long last.

So why is my brain like this?

I should feel whole. Healed. I should feel like I have everything together.

But all I am is a body with too many ideas. Too many ideas at all times of the day, too many ideas never letting me concentrate and focus, too many wayward and unrelated ideas.

It's my second year in my doctoral program, and Pedro from *Napoleon Dynamite* is still on my mind. I can't shake him. This Pedro from a film I watched as a kid, an idea in my adult head. YouTube videos are watched, Pedro fan theories are read. Ideas happen. I write a semischolarly article on him for class. "Catchy title," my advisor says, approvingly. "This idea might be a good lead for the dissertation." Dissertation: the golden ticket to upward mobility, my family and ancestors' wildest dreams.

Draft after draft comes out of me. New outlines form each day. Paragraphs and sentences and full-length essays concerning the filmic importance of Pedro litter my Dropbox. I open one saved file thinking this is the file I need, the words that I needed to continue working on, and they are not. Doesn't matter to me. I continue from the thought I last had, laboring in whatever direction Marcos from last week, last month, last year might have been thinking. Each file opened becomes a whole new theory. Pedro on the brain.

One of these ideas, I convince myself, will be the one I need for the dissertation. The dissertation is the key to my upward mobility. Key, as my parents note, in helping them in their own struggles with poverty and making it in this country. But what I identify in Pedro at one moment, when I seem to be on the precipice of some groundbreaking new piece of cultural criticism, changes. Thoughts taper off, die down, drift slowly yet surely into another half-thought, an undercooked thought, the thrill of a thought in the process of formation. In one draft, Pedro is identified as making this literary contribution, in another draft, Pedro represents a certain kind of thing in this cultural context. More drafts, more outlines, more of Pedro. Pedro: stoppings and goings, half-started treatises and half-finished theories. For the sake of some scholarly article, a definitive dissertation, and a full-time teaching job, I need Pedro to mean more definitively, represent what I need him to represent, be representative of one thing. The scholar I am, if scholar I am, is too fussy, all over the place, too finicky, a hot mess dot com.

My father never finishes his thoughts. Each idea begins authoritatively, hardened pauses and gruff intonations, he overemphasizes to let you know he is proving his point. The vocal masculinity gives him the credentials he needs to back up an idea he feels he is not qualified to give because he is, as he so graciously inserts into his theories, illiterate and has never had the opportunity of a single day of schooling. These pumped-up speech-thoughts deflate midway through completion, becoming a flimsy arrangement of grunts, stutters, half-words and nonsyllables. An afterthought might happen, if I am lucky.

Though speech halts, the eyes still wander, the facial features slacken contemplatively, the body slouches into another thought. Something is clicking in him. These bodily movements happen when he is in the deepest of thoughts, when he needs the solitude to think, to be alone, like he does every other day in the backyard with body forward, body thinking on the trees, the stray cat, the moon, the weeds, the sun, the frogs in the grass. The thought in speech wanes into the thought of the body because another thought has struck him, an addendum to a prior thought, a thought needing the time to be outlined in the depths of his brain. He tells me if he could write he would write down the memories of his past so I could read them. I dream of reading notebooks upon notebooks of my father's writing. His penmanship I imagine to be ornate, a bit blocky, noticeably undersized like my handwriting has been accused of being. Trying to pronounce the words needed to tell the story of these Americas, the story of my father and mother and family, our lives the story of a continent divided, sounds like an impossible labor for a mouth and a tongue and a set of lips to do. Perhaps on paper the incompletion of my father's thoughts might find completion. Perhaps this Pedro's theory is what we need.

ANY GIVEN MOMENT in the day. Reaching for a book, on the subway going downtown, eyes on the ceiling while in bed, scrolling on the newsfeed—voices. They do not discriminate. They are a diversity. Listening to loud music or running along the water disperses them for a bit of time. These solicitors have no sense of the law. They are not bound to my jurisdiction. Repeat offenders without knowing it. Concentrate on the dissertation, a voice of reason says, please because time is money, time is what will rid you of this post-1492 condition, time is what will lift you and those others who rely on you out of this, time is how whi—

Concentrate is related to the word *concentric* and both derive from the root word *circle*. *Circle*: a loop, an endless infinity, a returning, a repetition, no openings for escape. The most common harassment from the voices: Marcos, you are moving in circles.

THINKING: THAT'S ALL I do, all I'm good at. Wasted hours, wasted days. I do not think on the dissertation as I should be doing—or am I thinking on it? Are these articles I come across on Twitter leading me to a thesis? Will these internet wormholes lead me to, finally, at last, conducting research?

The newsfeed entraps. One article after the next. Videos, images, hashtags, the whole internet shebang. Reading as those like you and unlike you, watching as those like your parents and unlike your parents, those like your friends and unlike your friends, are struggling/suffering/living/thriving. I am trapped between extremes of nonbeing. Twitter is not respite but proliferation, the bending of my mental and material energies, a rubber band on the verge of snapping into two. Two; or the process of becoming two of myself, two of this life, two bodies harboring these many voices simultaneous jumbled competing and at the same time fragmented. Two distributes the burden. Two ameliorates. Two on the tongue is refuge.

DESPITE TELLING MYSELF constantly I have my life together and how proud of myself I am, my mind behaves otherwise. It doesn't believe the mantras. But I persist in saying them as if if I say these things enough, if I shout it loud enough, it will stick in my brain.

I'm not sure how trauma works but I think how I think is a result of trauma. An unaccounted-for aftereffect my brain is now living. All those years denying my father and family. All those years creating an elaborate lie of who and what I am. All those years believing in the fantasy that white America will save me from my family and my history and myself.

If how my brain thinks is a result of trauma, it makes sense. I mistrust white people. I find it hard making friends with white people. I listen carefully to what white people say and do and how they do it because I am not sure of their intentions. I debate what they are capable of doing knowing they are capable of doing so very much.

This trauma, though uniquely mine, is nothing new. My father and mother know it, my relatives know it, my neighbors know it, my friends know it. It has been told to me either directly, or indirectly. Writers of color, and those white writers throughout time writing about people of color, document this.

James Baldwin's essay "A Stranger in the Village" is exemplary of this. Baldwin's experience in the small Swiss village is telling for how trauma knows no borders, transcending the trauma of white supremacy in the United States, following one as far as a remote village of white people who seem to be removed from the world. Baldwin thinks about how they think of him, how they have come to think of him as a result of the history of European enslavement and colonization, a trauma that transcends all space and time. And I think this speculative act, of what the white man is thinking and how he comes to think it, is a form of paranoia. One that gives those people like Baldwin and me a particular acuity, a weariness and wariness, that only the historical record could have given us. A defense mechanism of sorts. Our brains knowing this kind of heightened state of being—this being on edge, this overthinking brain, this perpetual state of unease, this trying to know what people are thinking—is what has to happen living in this world. A hypervigilance that is the only way to survive.

This trauma of the colonized is an inheritance.

This trauma firing in our neurons at all times and in all places.

ONE OR TWO articles make me really think. The scholarly good-good kind of thinking: jargon in abundance, syntactical structures bloated with clauses and commas to fit a massive idea into a sentence, the mandatory peppering of "therefores," "howevers," and "rathers." A good sign: the voices in an uproar, in all directions and at all times and in all pitches. Onto something. Thinking with these voices makes me forget any sense of being an "I." Of my body and out of it, I am not singular nor contained within an "I" or "me" or "myself." This chaos of voices is spurred by Others, thinking on Others, those Others unlike and alike. Are these articles with particular words and phrasings and images dissertation-worthy?—how? The personal is political but the personal is not scholarly. Dissertation begins with the sound *di-* not unlike the words *division* or *dissection* or *disintegration* or *discipline.*

"DESCRIBE THE VOICE," my therapist demands of me.

"Well," I start, feeling like I must answer because she has her degree on the wall behind her, her legs crossed so tightly, eyes blue surveilling, the alabaster skin the skin I associate with knowledge, like those Greek statues imprinted into your memory though you don't recall how they got there, symbols of Wisdom, Truth, Beauty, Authority: "it's like yours . . . ya know . . . no offense, but like *Stepford Wives* meets academia . . . a bit detached, knowledgeable-sounding, cool and collected and authoritative . . . well, if we are being honest here, if I'm not beating around the bush about this, then it's like that of a whi—"

"Marcos, I don't really think you are ready for grad school, then."

This voice that was a person in a moment in my life lectured on literature. This person was paid a salary my family and I could never even dream of, a salary outmatching the combined income of at least seven of my adult family members, a salary given to discuss a dead white man for three hours a week. Sigh. I grew to love the work of this dead, white man. In class, I had ideas. Many. Most went unsaid because I felt the other students (students whose names ranged from Meghan with an *h* to Katherine with a *K*) had already said some version of what I had to say. However, when I did muster up the literary cojones to say an idea, an idea that forced the class to think about the white characters and their being similar to those characters, or about the plots and their relation to colonization or enslavement or empire, an idea forcing them to think about themselves in full, the reception was a polite silence from my peers and an even more polite grumble from this voice that lives in me, a protracted "Mmmmm."

THE TWO ARTICLES. One discusses a documentary that investigates why migrants from Central America and Mexico are dying while crossing the border, and another is about an unidentified undocumented man who becomes fully paralyzed while crossing into the United States. Ideas. Too many, too close to home. My advisor asks: "Are you sure you want to put yourself out there like this?" I don't tell her this but this is what I want to say: "I just don't know how not to."

I GO TO a psychiatrist for a little while because I cannot control my thoughts. They move so fast. I feel disoriented in my apartment, walking down the street, or while teaching. I hear voices while lying in bed, I see floating eyes in the next room. I am unable to think a thought but instead think random words, phrase fragments, unintelligible sounds. Is this what has become my ordinary, this insanity?

The psychiatrist diagnoses me and gives me a prescription. He does all this gently, unjudging. This will calm you, he says. Will it fix it? Will it heal me? I ask pathetically. No, he says, what you feel, how you think, makes total sense. What you have been through, what you are living with, it all makes total sense. No healing, just managing, he remarks sympathetically. This is one of the first times in my entire life where I feel like someone gets me. Where I feel someone gets what is happening in my brain. Where I am not the problem to be fixed. Where I feel I don't have to try to explain myself in words over and over again like I always have to do.

I am tired of having to explain myself.

I am tired of searching for words to explain all *this*.

I'M TRYING TO be more forthcoming about the state of my mind. I tell my boyfriend and some friends about the voices, the hallucinations, the near nervous breakdowns, and it feels good. I tell them, as best as I can, how my brain works, though giving words to such an irrepresentable thing feels impossible.

But I try, nonetheless, to find words to relay what is happening to me and they are affirming and understanding. I tell them I don't want to have to discuss this all the time, don't want them to ask me how I'm doing, to bring it up. They get it, and let me discuss it when I so choose.

It feels good to be open about how I'm doing. Before this point, how I am doing and how my brain is thinking is something not to be talked about. Boys don't cry, boys don't express their feelings, boys don't show weakness. I don't have any words or language in which to talk about how I am doing until my mid-twenties. I tell myself for years what I am feeling is a result of my own flaws. If I just work harder, if I just stop letting my emotions and thoughts get the best of me, I can be normal. Think more positive. Not let the conditions of my family and my life get in the way from my success. Overcome, just get over it.

Not until I realize this most American attitude is actually detrimental to me, to us all, can I finally be a little bit more free. More free to let my brain and body be how it needs to be, move how it needs to move, write how it needs to write.

SEVERAL MONTHS, TWO articles, countless ideas. Pages and pages of outlines, rough sketches, incompletions. One draft thinks about sympathy and human rights, while another thinks through the environment, global warming, and racialized bodies. Various ideas in other outlines but they are much more abbreviated, truncated. Each outline cites my life. A citation in particular: My Father and Me. Our lives, our being him and me, our plural ours. The body and the borders of the body and the body of the Americas and the Americas of borders. A one-page intro recounts how my father clears his throat, trying to clear the field dust accumulated from across the Americas, while driving me home from the train station. A brief concluding paragraph details my anxieties about my father's deteriorating health, the impossibility of getting him insured, and my desperation to "make it" in order to pay for his medical expenses. Tears on the keyboard, the half-started opuses, the stoppings and the goings, half-finished masterpieces, the thoughts unformed and forming, all these many outlines citing the motions of father and son through the Americas, our post-1492 condition, our survival our pain our generational divide our loving in hard times. This might exceed the bounds of this scholarly endeavor.

THE PERCEPTIONS OF my classmates haunt me to this day. I hear their thoughts in my head. I see the world how they see the world. I know what keeps them awake at night because they once made me believe what they believed. Their idea that the neighborhood I grew up in, all those neighborhoods like my neighborhood across the United States, across the Americas itself, are zones of wildness, savage and untamed. These are the ideas they hold that are the foundations of modern American attitudes toward immigrants and people of color. That we, the dark horde from below the US border, and within it, pose a menace to society. That we are too unlike them. That we will undo their way of life and their systems of belief. Fearful we will become the majority. Fearful that countries like the United States will no longer be theirs.

As they should think.

But this is not uniquely an American attitude. We see this fear of the dark races in places like the United Kingdom or France or Australia, fear of those already in and those trying to get in. All of Europe watches from their satellites and drones and oh-so-modern technologies as Black refugees crossing the waters from Africa drown, in search of refuge, in search of life. The mass shootings and public lynchings and private assassinations and bomb strikes, some legal and some illegal, in every corner of the globe against those deemed dangerous and expendable. These places like Europe and the United States and Latin America and Australia and South Africa, built from the glories of colonization and enslavement, cannot stand that their dark subjects are so unruly. Cannot even fathom those dark and huddled masses are so unwilling to sit still in their place, in those places the white race exploited and manipulated and then abandoned. We cannot name white supremacy and colonization as the culprits in these different locations, and how the structures and systems of white supremacist colonization are to blame for these interconnected violences, this global suffering and death. We flounder in language, floundering in the ability to identify precisely and clearly what is killing us, what is making us live these unlivable lives.

My experiences in the world, the experiences of my family, all the writings of those like and unlike me I have encountered, have given me a language in which to understand this better. A way to better know how to feel out the systems and structures that contain me, that seek nothing more than to annihilate those like and unlike me. And I think that is the work at hand. To figure out what the structures and the systems holding this unbearably cruel world together are and, in the process, to imagine others, to imagine freedom for all of us.

A WORD: "PSYCHOSIS." The icing on the word cake: "Schizophrenia." The therapist sees the panic forming in the pursing of my lips. "No no no, these are just symptoms, doesn't necessarily mean wh—"

My father purses his lips, too, whenever he says the word *mande*. He also purses his lips when he stutters. I used to stutter upon a time but they took that from me like they took my Spanish my confidence my people my wild tongue. They may have taken the speech and the speech tics but they could not take this pursing of the lips that is my father's, our inheritance from the moment those conquistadors and pilgrims and missionaries and those many other alabaster men landed on the shores of a New World, the pursing of the lips our defiance when they demanded in a language we did not know, the barrels of guns pointed in our faces, ship masts in the near distance anchoring in shores they will name the Americas, "Become like us but never fully us or else . . ."

DETERMINED. OUTLINE AFTER outline of dissertation-worthy material is open on my computer. Word soup. I sift through the printed articles I amassed from Twitter. Nada. No lightbulbs flashing above my head. Is it scholarly, this idling by? This waiting for something to submit to me a treasure trove of knowledge, words to be interpreted and argued? But the voice of the therapist intercedes the thinking—

"Sounds like you and your father are a lot alike(?)(.)"

Statement of fact or a question? Hard to tell. Being human for the therapist is a science, and my being human is an experiment. Too many variables, not enough controls. A tad bit resistant to her method. Experiencing life an experiment in being alive. The therapist says (asks?) this because I mention to her how my father felt survivor's guilt over leaving his mother and sisters behind in Mexico. She makes sure to emphasize I might be projecting this guilt onto him but she does not know my father, she does not know his inherited silence, his stonelike posture of body and face and voice and mind that has helped his survival in these Americas. She does not know how he told me, with the most subdued undertones of grief and bitterness and anger and regret lining his face and coloring his voice, how he and his family were mad his older brother did not send money back from the United States. My father once remarked—said in Spanish and translated here into English—"He was living rich in the North and we were living in our continued poverty." Knowing this pain of abandonment, my father does the opposite. He sends money, he calls, he remembers in diaspora.

"You project a lot onto your father(?)(.)"

Is the accusation I analyze, study, and interpret my father, scrutinize and examine the dynamic between him and me, hypothesize and theorize how we are and how we were and how we will be in these Americas? Then I am guilty as charged, madam.

"You love your father a lot(?)(.)"

This dissertation: thesis, body paragraphs, theoretical backgrounds, transition words, bibliography, concluding chapter: a study on our revolutionary love.

IN MY HEAD are voices. Voices of my parents who live tucked away in the woods of New Jersey. Voices of dead people like my brother and grandmother. Voices of people who live in my yesterday like Abigail and John and David and Molly. Voices of people who live in my today like those professors who tell me I am not good enough to be a thinker and a writer. Voices of my ancestors whose words I cannot make out, only hearing their screams and their joy and their rage and their sweet whispering about revolution.

One of those voices is little Marcos. I don't know what he is saying. It's garbled, he's speaking in tongues, he's not saying anything in any known language. What is it? I try to hear through the vacuum of time and space. He's so far away. What does he need? What does he want me to know? In memory, in my thoughts and flesh, in the writing yet to come is where he is.

My father tells me he wishes he knew how to write so he could jot down his thoughts for me. I think his brain works like mine. He has his own chaos, his own choir of voices. He sees the contemplative calm writing has given me. Seeing me in the passenger's seat of his truck jotting something down as he drives me home from the train station. Being there with him on the couch typing away as he watches boxing or the news in Spanish. He wants to write because he wants me to know what he thinks and how he thinks when the thoughts come to him. He believes in spontaneity, that memory and ideas come to you in flashes, brief and fleeting. He tells me this aspiration to one day write because he wants me to recognize him. Recognizing him on terms his son has come to cherish. Recognizing he has a story to tell. Recognizing that he, this man who cannot read and write, this dark brown man who hails from the center of the hemisphere, is a thinking and feeling being.

My desire to write—no, my need to write—is the one thing in my life my parents understand profoundly. They think of me as a writer and I feel, for the first time in my life, they get me. Their baby boy, their little Pedro, a writer. Our being together, at last, through these words on the page, these forms of our love the writing takes.

13

TO PEDRO WITH LOVE

You're the modern-day romance. Picture precisely cropped, filtered, and angled to enamor the onlookers at the other end of a dating app or social media account. More a smirk than a smile is what you give us, presenting impudent coolness, what you believe is sexy suavity. Who are you trying to fool? I know your type. The boaster, the gloater, the rambler. Your pictures present a carefully curated display of who you want us to think you are. The Pedro who sometimes we fantasize you being, the Pedro we would like you to be. I know the game, Pedro, and I fall for it. Fall for it hard, as all of us do, all caught up in this most modern-day game.

Pageantry is what it is. The meticulous composing and showcasing of a fictionalized self. The light falling so perfectly on the skin. The body angled to slimmest proportionality. The blemish-free face. We are many selves these days, real and unreal. To different people and groups, in our different compositions of self, we mean various things. The digital age allows us this freedom. No more essences, as if there ever were.

I've scrolled through your photos on apps and social media

for years now, Pedro. Dark-skinned, and light-skinned. Radiant Afro on your scalp, long straight hair past the shoulders. Third-generation, and newly arrived. The skinniest of musculatures, the thickest of frames, the mightiest of bulks. Cisgender, transgender, and nonbinary. Islander and highlander and forester and city dweller. Your image is many, Pedro.

I come to know these many images of you in New York City. The small town of the first eighteen years of my life does not house this diversity of bodies who possess some relationship to the histories and cultures of Latin America. I understand Puerto Ricans to look like my uncles, light-skinned, and I understand Mexican men to look like my father and aunt, darker-skinned. I am told to believe in ethnic and racial essentialisms that erase and negate the histories and realities of many, particularly Black Latin American peoples. Going to New York for college, these ideas of ethnic fixity are challenged. I meet Black Puerto Ricans. I meet white Mexicans. The earlier understandings that I inherit from my family of what it means to be Puerto Rican, Mexican, Latinx, and Latin American are revised once I start dating and hooking up with the many Pedros like you.

There is no one way to be you, Pedro, but we are made to believe the illusion. Though we are shaped by this most accelerated digital information age, we are no different from our forebears. After all, they are the ones who have passed down what it should mean to be Pedro. Pedros are masculine. Pedros are skinny or buff. Pedros are light-skinned or white. Pedros speak with an accent. Particular ways of being Pedro are made to be universal. One type of Pedro becomes the stand-in for us all.

Engaging with Pedros like and unlike me, being confronted and challenged by our differences, differences that do not need to be overcome or transcended but appreciated and negotiated and discussed, is the only way in which I come to see how these universalities and generalizations work against us. For years, I do not know how to date or hook up with men who look like my father. It's not that I find darker-skinned Mexican or Central American men who are of indigenous descent ugly. It's that I find them too close to home. To grind up against such a Pedro on the dance floor is to brush up against my own history of internalized hatred, my own desire to be proximate to whiteness and the same as white people. To touch such a Pedro, to hold and to be held by him, is to expose my search for commonality and incorporation and sameness that drives me to feel how I do about my father, family, and myself for so many years. To put my lips on such a Pedro's lips is to reveal how whiteness operates in the Americas, shaping our thoughts and desires and fantasies, posing itself as *the* universal we should all aspire after, as universality itself that we will die in the pursuit of.

Pedro, dancing and kissing and fucking and being with your multitude, articulates all this. Your plenty puts into words what I have always known to be true but did not know how to express. Words, Pedro, which become my refuge.

YOU ARE NO photo. No selfie or shirtless pic. No two-dimensional body by which to assess you. Sometimes you roam about online faceless and disembodied, a profile of sparse words dictating what it is you want and are looking for. When you present yourself like this, it is ofttimes for a specific reason. You might not be out or have yet to identify to others as being gay, bisexual, or queer. You might identify as heterosexual and do not want people to know you are attracted to men or the masculine body. You might not fit the normative beauty standards of a community that shames the bodies of fat, femme, disabled, trans, or racialized peoples. You have your reasons for what you do, I'm sure.

Many abhor when you do not disclose your image, Pedro. Many claim you are being dishonest, living a false life, deceiving those you come in contact with. Our most modern-day age demands for our genders and sexualities to be expressed and expressible, clearly and easily and definitively. I do not believe you go about dishonestly because you choose to be faceless. In a world demanding hypervisibility, demanding everyone fit the script of a particular identity or way of thinking and living, you offer something else. I can meet you at the written word. We can be worded intimacy.

I enjoy engaging with you when you compose your self in this way. Asking what your name is knowing the answer might be an anagram of your name, some version of your name, or another name entirely. Messaging that can be just about our day, the humdrum of work or the plans for the weekend, or messaging that explores our erotic and sensuous desires, two entities of language precision trying to know the other. Taking note of how you phrase why you are on a hookup app, how you describe the particularities of your erotic sensibilities, and how you use exclamation marks, irony, capitalization, and other elements of writing to stylize who you want to be to me. I like the allure of not knowing fully who you are. Not exactly knowing this Pedro who, on the street or the subway or the world, is so limiting and delimiting of who and what we can be together.

Who am I kidding? I, too, Pedro, present another self to you, to all Pedros. Flirty here, sappy there. The wordy intellectual in this or that message, the grandiose descriptions of what my body wants and how it wants it. I am an elaborate show equally as imagined as yours. How revolutionary, is it not, Pedro? To choose who you want to be and who to be it with. I have many selves because that is what it means to be with others unlike you. To be in the wondrousness of difference, to share words and space across differences. Each person, each Pedro, drawing from me a different self, a different way of being, and I, in turn, draw it from him. Our messaging to each other becomes our own creation made of language. Our history and past and embodied realities ever present in this mutual construction of ourselves, but there is more room for us to be who we need to be, who we want to be.

But you know better than me, Pedro, all of this is not always sunshine and roses. There is conflict, or awkwardness. There is the wrong comment said, the rubbing-up of contrary attitudes and dispositions. Sometimes, we just plain old don't get along so well. And that's ok. We learn to coexist, or must try to, because that is how we live together better, Pedro to Pedro, how we forge networks and communities together through our differences and disagreements and dissensus.

LONG BEARDS, AND rounded cheeks. Belly laughs, and stooped postures. Drug dealers, therapists, construction workers, and chefs. Acquaintances on social media, one-night stands in dorm rooms, friends, seasonal flings, subway cuties who will forever be nameless strangers, and long-term boyfriends. The years of my life will tack on, Pedro, and your image will only proliferate. You become faces, messages, bodies, and stories blurring together to form a collage of lives. Lives interconnected through time and space, through distances real and imagined, through a memory that will make some of you unforgettable and forgettable. I will think upon this collage in my mind and it is how I will carry you with me. How I will keep you close even if you don't remember me, even if you have never even known me, even if you, once upon a time, loved me.

Maybe this is what it means to date and love and laugh and cry and fuck and hurt in the twenty-first century, Pedro. Maybe this is what it means to compose a life. Nothing more than this collaged intimacy, this messy tangle of love and letdown and longing.

14

BORDER THEORIES

With the projector light across his face and reds, whites, and greys splashing his skin dark, he asks, *"Can you take a picture of me?"* I look behind me hoping no one heard. There's no one around, just me and him, this boy, this boy I call mine, this boy mine for now. I want to tell him it's inappropriate, possibly even disrespectful because this is an exhibition in a gallery space in an institution of higher learning. Does he not get Museum Etiquette 101?

In the spring of 2017, *State of Exception/Estado de Excepción*, an exhibition housed at the Parsons School of Design at the New School in New York City, puts on display objects like backpacks, wallets, and water bottles left behind in the desert by migrants. The exhibit's website notes how it "presents traces of the human experience—objects left behind in the desert by undocumented migrants on their journey into the U.S. and other forms of data." The gallery space for *State of Exception/Estado de Excepción* contains special-effects video installations, found items, audio testimony by migrants, photography, and other object installations. The materials for the exhibition have been collected by University of Michigan anthropologist Jason De León, whose Undocumented Migration Project has been working to highlight the migrant experience through archival construction, testimonies, and other forms of data collection.

There, in the gallery space, his face is serious. Smile stern, taut cheeks, posture narrowed. I have always found him so photogenic. To explain to him why I feel it is inappropriate to take a picture in this setting is to flout my "white-boy English," the eloquent speech imposed upon me as a child, the elaborate words I mastered in order to get good grades in my undergraduate courses, the vocal tones and hand gestures of a PhD candidate—necessary for any dream of upward mobility. He doesn't feel the structure around me as I do. Our loving is at the border of our oppositions.

I take the picture.

ON NOVEMBER 18, 2013, Cruz Marcelino Velazquez Acevedo, a sixteen-year-old from Tijuana, Mexico, dies on the border. He does not drown in a ditch, canal, or the Rio Grande like so many migrants trying to cross over into the United States. He does not dehydrate in the deserts of Texas or Arizona or California. He is not even trying to cross over to, as so many call it, "illegally migrate." In San Ysidro at the border crossing of United States and Mexico, he dies from an overdose, from too many sips of the liquid methamphetamine he is trying to smuggle over.

MOST OF THE pictures come out too dark because of the low lighting in this part of the exhibition. In this section, an installation projects footage onto two walls. The camera views are in the first person, making the viewer feel immersed in the footage's movements. The first perspective is undoubtedly a moving vehicle driving straight ahead. It's dark out, those awkward minutes when the sun is nearly set but not fully, with light lingering in engulfing darkness. Clouds like the oncoming clouds of a rainstorm, a rainstorm fussy and scattered, are on the immediate horizon. The second perspective is of a camera moving forward recording a sideways view: daytime, a light grey sky, an encroaching dark mass of cloud breaking through the frame. The footage is an endless loop depicting a red fence with desert brush and desert mountains beyond it. The impression is of movement, steady and concentrated progression, but the camera's angle does not change, the scenery appears no different, as if the viewer is moving in place, moving nowhere, stuck in movement. Overheard are everyday sounds: rocks crushed by car tires, wind against metal, light rain on the windshield.

The visitor experiences all of this footage simultaneously. Weather and gravel and angles and clouds and fences. No humans, no words, no rhetoric. Fables of migration and better lives and US exceptionalism and cartels and Latin American backwardness and bad hombres are nowhere to be found. Narrative, if the viewer's aim is narrative, requires further research. The footage resembles the ordinary, that is, movement across terrains, temperamental weather, rocks sounding out, the flash of lightning, the headlights of a truck. The ordinary: an experiment in the extraordinary that is the everyday in these Americas.

***20/20* DEDICATES AN** episode to Acevedo. The episode's title is "Life and Death at the Border." As is the genre of the program, *20/20* conducts an investigation into what happened. They provide a minute-by-minute rundown of Acevedo's time in the border checkpoint according to the footage made public by US Customs and Border Protection. The program includes the testimonies of the two border officers who—accused but never convicted, never reprimanded in any way—coerced Acevedo to drink the liquid in order to prove it was not drugs as the teen had said. They bring in a toxicologist to give expert analysis on what overdoses do to the body, and a former commissioner of the agency who deems the actions of the officers "inappropriate" and "misconduct." The television program highlights the ruthlessness of the cartels, the lucrative market of methamphetamines, and the violence that happens on the border. The program fits into an hour time slot where the baggage of the border—hundreds of years of conflicts, insurrections, and civil wars—is condensed. As in the title "Life and Death at the Border," the border, like anytime we say the words *the border*, becomes yet another theory of what the border is supposed to mean, another theory we can agree to disagree on.

MINUTES PASS IN this trancelike state until New York City interjects: a truck horn from the street. I remember: E— is sitting next to me. He is looking up, around him, around at the video installation. On his face are the lines from the fence. He once told me he believes his great-grandmother was from Haiti. She had a French-sounding name. He thinks she crossed the border between the Dominican Republic and Haiti, on foot, and with the utmost casualness started another life in a country but a few miles away from what she had been calling home. One can only speculate she was in search of, as the cliché goes, "a better life." He does not know if she ever found it.

I AM TWELVE years old when my brother dies. My mother and sister ask the coroner, "Was he in a lot of pain when it happened?" He felt nothing, according to the coroner.

But if the coroner is telling the truth, how can he know what my dead brother experienced? Where is the evidence for the existence of this nonpain? My mother and sister feel it is a justice if he felt pain. It corroborates their theories. For if he felt pain, much like if Acevedo felt pain, we can project all our anger and torment onto the ones responsible for creating the pain: the drunk driver, the United States government. But if there is no pain? If the coroner is right and life, in an instant, in a flash, extinguishes into nothingness, without those human things we call suffering, pain, torture, violence, what then? How do we justify a life? How do we prove to others that my brother or Acevedo mattered in the world?

For those who loved Acevedo, or, those like me, who stumbled upon him in a Twitter post, who did not know him but who see something familiar in him, something distant yet so near, there is proof of pain: video footage. Millions have seen it. His loved ones can watch it over and over again if they want, if they need it. The footage gives us a minute-by-minute narration of how his body reacts after drinking the drugs:

7:11 p.m.: Acevedo wipes his forehead.

7:36 p.m.: He starts sweating heavily, the body shaking.

7:48 p.m.: Handcuffed and standing up, Acevedo screams "mi prima," "mi hermana," "mi corazon." He rocks back and forth, several officers witnessing. The one officer who told him to drink the liquid drugs wipes the sweat from his forehead.

7:51 p.m.: He is strapped into a gurney, eyes rolling into the back of his head, the limbs in a frenzy, the head convulsing.

8:24 p.m.: In the hospital, he is unresponsive, pupils fixed, fixed on the beyond.

8:39 p.m.: Acevedo is put on a respirator.

8:57 p.m.: Acevedo dies from acute methamphetamine intoxication.

In the court of law, in the break rooms of Customs and Immigration, on the big-screen TV of some John and Joanne's home in the Upper West Side or Springfield or Malibu or Main Street, does this footage prove anything? Can this tell the millions of viewers why he risked it all to traffic drugs into the United States? What dire poverty compelled him to drink these toxic liquids? What hundreds and hundreds of years of history in these many Americas brought him to the border the day he died? But any pursuit of a why presupposes there is one reason, one cause, one deciding factor that urges bodies to risk everything, to risk death in order to live. The *20/20* footage produces more than a why; the footage documents the story of torment and NAFTA and the cry for loved ones, "mi hermana" and "mi prima" and generational poverty and revolutions and dispossession and assimilation and United States investment/divestment and the body breaching its limits, "mi corazon."

AN INSTALLATION: A wall of backpacks. All sizes, all colors, all varieties. Each one is considerably dirty, and many are blanched by constant exposure to the sun. What are we looking at? Scratch that: What are we being made to see or not see?

After more than ten minutes of suspension, one backpack in particular catches the eye. The backpack is a pink that pops, the plastic-looking pink you see in the Walmart back-to-school section. It is small, its smallness making it stand out amongst so many larger backpacks, standing out against the landscape of faded browns and blacks. Plastered on the front of the backpack is Dora la Exploradora. This backpack must have belonged to a little girl who, for one reason or another, had to abandon her backpack along the border of the United States and Mexico. Any other details of her life are unknown.

Unable to move from standing in front of the Dora backpack, I take a picture. I concentrate on the backpack. I tell myself to think beyond this blankness I am feeling right now. I do everything I can standing in place, as if some sentence from the void will pull through, some word or clause or syllable will whisper to me, shout at me, tell me what to think.

The backpack does not open itself up to interpretation.

VISUAL WITHOUT AUDIO. What is on trial is not verbal language but body language. One of the officers makes the gesture to drink by bringing hand to mouth. The other officer places the liquid substance before Acevedo and nods his head, encouraging, commanding, enforcing. Acevedo swallows from the bottle of the liquid drug four times, hoping to convince them it is not a drug, so he can cross through, deliver it, and return home without any backlash from the cartels. The incident report filed the same night notes Acevedo "voluntarily" drinks the substance. Protocol, according to the report, is followed.

This report is a document of the United States of America. *20/20*'s report is an intervention into the federal report's status as fact and proof. The program attempts to counter the report's Truth with their own, analyzing (but never overanalyzing, given the time constraints and commercial breaks) the facts of the matter, the body language, expert opinions, and eyewitness accounts. There is no doubt the viewer will notice the program's sympathies are with Acevedo. It is on the side of Truth, Justice, Awareness, Freedom of Speech. Its aims are the aims of exposing the wrong, putting wrongdoing on trial. A stalemate occurs, nevertheless, because under the eyes of the law, the language of the body is not proof. Under the eyes of journalism, government corruption sells. The nation on trial is a scandal with the highest of ratings. Oversights and misconduct and infringement of rights and cover-ups are wonderful premises for an hour-long special, an ad on Twitter, an award-worthy program. Exposure is profitable as long as more instances of exposure can be created, as long as more bodies are made violable and disposable, as long as the eradication of all violence is never realized. The issue is one of getting rid of a few bad apples, nothing less, making sure they hire no more bad apples, nothing more.

E— TELLS ME it was for the best I did not bring my dad. A paraphrase of his objection: Why bring him to this exhibition when he has already lived through this, when he might have to live through this again? The border, and the many meanings of the border, are not meant to be relived. The border is to be tucked away safely in a memory box, dusted off on occasion for a brief recollection, but it is never to be reexperienced. The border is a trauma, living in the body, triggering and affecting, passed on to other bodies. The border, as E— seems to be suggesting, can manifest even here downtown in New York City, so far from the US–Mexico border, so far from my undocumented father who now lives in rural New Jersey.

***20/20* CITES OTHER** deaths along the border. A family picnicking on the Mexican side is shot at by border patrol on a boat, killing the father. A teenage boy, accused of throwing rocks across the border, is shot ten times. A man is Tasered over and over again by a mob of border patrol agents for being, apparently, belligerent and on drugs. In all cases, no charges are brought upon these officers, no protocols against violence are implemented. These flashpoints of life and of death are innumerable. They define the border as we know it.

The reporter for *20/20*, sitting with the former commissioner of Customs and Border Protection under the Obama administration, waves a stack of complaints, a stack of evidence, against the agency. The former commissioner emphasizes it is but a few officers who engage in this behavior, and that the means of investigating are getting better. These officers are rare, the exceptions not the norm, just a few bad apples.

ON DISPLAY: A SPIRAL-BOUND notebook. The pages are warped by water damage, the effect producing an accordion-like swerving of its papery body. The paper near the metallic binding appears to be eaten away, lined with holes and tears. The front cover, made of plastic, looks to be melted, the colors a faded swirl of blue, tan, and black—no doubt the result of a ruthless exposure to sunlight. Though unopened (perhaps even unopenable?), the pages appear blank, no pencil or pen bleeding out of them. One can only surmise that the waves of a river or the soaking in a ditch washed away whatever stories, fragments, or ramblings were contained within them. Or maybe, just maybe, there was nothing yet written down on those pages. Blank pages of journal entries yet to be, poems in process, theories waiting for the right words to explain themselves.

ACEVEDO'S FAMILY'S LAWYER asks one of the officers, *"At some point did you hear Cruz screaming?"*

"Yes, I could hear Cruz."

"You could hear him in pain?"

She hesitates, an "ummm" trips on her lips, she nods her head slightly, her facial features formulating the appropriate sentence, the appropriate language, the appropriate face for the camera watching her: "I can't . . . I heard him screaming." She looks down at the table before her, wringing out her wrists, eyes red, biting her lip. The scene changes.

"I heard him screaming" is an objective statement. Fact of the matter. Because to admit Acevedo is in pain is to admit he is a body capable of experiencing suffering, is to admit guilt, is to admit wrongdoing, is to admit she or the organization she works for killed Acevedo.

ON DISPLAY IS an empty gallon of water with these words written in black marker: "Buena suarte amig@s!"

WITHOUT THE BORDER officer admitting to killing Acevedo, the investigation tries to find guilt in the visual cues given by the body. The footage of the officer's testimony in the *20/20* special is masterfully edited to account for her frequent pauses, eyes downward-cast, intelligible language breaking down into unintelligible sounds, a sniffle here and a clearing of the throat there. We are being directed by the camera to find the crime, as well as the regret of the crime, in the body of the individual. We are searching for the wrongdoing in the visual and audio clues of a human body. We are asked to see in her personal motives or human shortcomings: vendettas, hate crimes, ignorance, negligence, and so on and so forth. We are made to believe some humans are just naturally born evil, corruptions of humanity, exceptions to some unspecified norm, a backwardness to be transcended.

Yet we see over and over again killings of Black people on video, helicopters broadcasting live on the border men beaten to death by a mob, a bystander recording a man dying from a chokehold screaming out "I CAN'T BREATHE! I CAN'T BREATHE!" and we cannot imagine governments or mindsets or corporations at work, enabling individuals to commit such violence, allowing them to perpetuate such killings. If the logic of the camera in the *20/20* special is followed, that wrongdoing and guilt can be detected in direct statements or visual cues, then nations, organizations, corporations, ideologies, and systems of power and oppression are incapable of guilt or wrongdoing. Their immaterial bodies cannot be recorded, edited, and represented like the bodily testimonies of a human. If there are no directly stated admissions of guilt, or visual cues to work from, then there is no evidence of wrongdoing. We try to penalize and punish individuals, "bad apples," in the pursuit of some sense of justice, some sense of doing right by the violated and killed, but what justice is it when the systems in place go unscrutinized, maintain themselves dutifully without question? We become cogs in the machine of violence by the virtue of not knowing another form of justice.

We must work to think beyond punitive justice for our visions of liberation from racial violence, exploitation, and death. We must reevaluate the faith that if we are tax-paying, law-abiding, respectable citizens who civilly protest when the time is right, then in return the nation will defend and protect and honor our lives. We must break the belief that ignorant humans, who think in certain kinds of ways, who live their lives in certain kinds of ways, will, eventually, in due time, be phased out. The bad apples emerge again in twenty, in forty, in a hundred years chanting different rhetoric, rhetoric updated for the times and conducive to the systems of power, presenting arguments we thought we had transcended years ago. We wonder, yet again, yet always, why history is repeating itself, as we forget history is meant to repeat itself.

Progress and advancement and enlightenment and civilizational improvement are our history, or at least how history is written in the United States, the Americas, and any land shaped by the touch of empire and colonization. In the name of progress and civilization came the devastation of communities, the forced removals and extractions of labor, the mass suffering and death. And, in our most modern age, in the name of progress and civilization we search to prosecute individual police and border patrol in the hopes this will finally be the last straw—only to find ourselves grasping, once again, at nothing.

E— CALLS ME over to where he is. "*Mira . . .*" he says, directing his finger to an object I had overlooked earlier. The object is one sheet of lined paper with writing on it. The sheet appears to have been water-damaged, the tint of the page a dark brown as if exposed to muddy waters, the edges of it curled as if fried by the sun. A letter? An essay? Spoken-word poetry?

The letters are blocky, as if the writer was pressing down on the pen hard, belabored. The words are in English. Full sentences cannot be deciphered but the beginnings of some are as follows: "TheRE GOES my . . ." "LET THE Good . . ." "My BRown eye . . ." One word that reads as "VASANOVA" has the words "we on the," above it, as if the writer is amending a thought, being more precise with their meaning. Given the free use of uppercase and lowercase letters in these words, I hypothesize the writer is an English-language learner, teaching themselves, though imperiled, though endangered, though risking life, a foreign language on the border. Beyond this, I cannot make any more educated guesses as to the identity of the author. Interpretation has its limits.

I want to ask E— why he directed me to see this, why this moved him in some way, but it soon hits me: he directs my attention to it because he knows it will have this impact on me. He knows I love studying penmanship, analyzing how a loop, a space between letters, an illegible word can tell us about a life we do not know. He knows writing in all its forms is important to me.

"Who do you think wrote it, E—?"

"I'm not sure but if you look at the writing maybe it was . . ."

The loose leaf leaves us to our theories.

THEY SAY MY brother died instantly. He felt nothing, apparently, nothing besides his lungs bursting as the ribs caved in on them, his large body frame compressed to half its size as the metal of the car found itself wedged against a tree. Physics killed my brother.

The toxicology expert *20/20* hires gives the viewer a rundown of what Acevedo is experiencing: blood pressure raising exponentially, a fever spiking, the body unable to cool, delirium, the body working double-time. Chemistry kills Acevedo. The toxicologist needs to emphasize to the reporter interviewing him that *"Cruz was in an immense amount of pain." Immense*: an adjective describing quantity, intensity, degrees. *Immense* as syllables as an adjective as a word as language tries to describe the indescribable. Futile as it may be, the toxicologist uses the word in efforts to describe to us, as best as he can, how the body is bound by laws, how the body is testimony, how the body testifies.

ABOUT TO LEAVE. E— and I are staring at photographs of the Arizona desert where many of the objects in the exhibit were acquired. Though beautiful, though sublime, photographs have a harder time of catching my attention. Too still, possibly, too bounded, maybe.

I turn around from the photographs, and from E—. There are four women looking at a tire I had glossed over earlier, a tire once employed by border agents to help hunt down migrants crossing the US–Mexico border, a tire turned museum object. I didn't see them enter the exhibition. They look like my tías and primas. One appears to be in her late thirties and the three others look to be no older than fifteen. The women are huddled around the tire. Bodies poised in attention. Their brown eyes the eyes of concentration. What do they contemplate there before the tire? How do they do this combined effort of thought?

I look at them looking at the tire until E— asks me, again, *"Can you take a picture of me, please?"*

15

PEDRO OF THE AMERICAS

It takes twenty-five years for me to leave the country of my birth. It takes twenty-five years to save up enough money to leave the country of my birth. It takes twenty-five years to convince myself the United States is not enough.

E— and I go to Mexico. To the land of my father, to the land of my ancestors. I don't tell E— this but one of the main reasons (maybe even *the* main reason) I wanted to go to Mexico so badly is for atonement. I go to Mexico not as the boy in college, or in high school, the boy worried so much about his proximity to whiteness. I go as the adult in graduate school, studying literature by and teaching courses to people of color, as the person who will be the first one in the family to hold a doctorate, as the writer who finds pride in the histories that have created him. I go to Mexico with the oh-so-corny and oh-so-cliché hope of finding myself. Mexico: the Promised Land.

Mexico. Here a Frida Kahlo painting, there a mariachi serenading a tourist. We drink pulque and don't really like it. We ascend the volcano Popocatépetl with a tour group and take well over two hundred photos. Tortillas and eggs for breakfast.

The dark-skinned servant entering a barbed-wire fenced home. A dog without an owner eating garbage on the street. The child playing a guitar to earn money. The tamales.

This is the first time E— has gone to any country besides the United States and the Dominican Republic. Both of us have the magic of newness in our eyes. Every detail, whether large or small, dazzles us. Is this what it feels like to be a tourist? Am I a tourist? As much as I would like to say no, as much as I would like to say these are my people and this is my homeland, they are not. This is not mine to lay claim to. Foreigner in a strange land.

D. H. LAWRENCE, having published several books in England, as well as having some books banned, flees his beloved Europe for the Americas in the 1920s. He first finds his way to New Mexico, and then to Mexico the country. The American landscape promises Lawrence something. The promise of yesterday, society unspoiled by modernity's technologies, a landscape uncorrupted by the industrialism of European ingenuity. He is in search of the American spirit, whatever that means, something along the lines of a land premodern, primordial, sensuous.

Lawrence writes a little travel book about his experience in the Americas, *Mornings in Mexico.* Several of the essays feature Rosalino, the indigenous mozo or male servant Lawrence hires in Mexico to help with the everyday chores of the house. One essay is dedicated entirely to the mozo. He writes of the mozo derisively, as if he is in a relationship with him Lawrence would much rather not be in: "He hated us and gave off a black steam of hate, that filled the patio and made one feel sick. He did not come to the kitchen, he did not carry the water. Leave him alone." Or how Lawrence describes Rosalino's moodiness and indifference as objects and animals: his "black, reptilian gloom, and a sense of hatred"; "his heart was an obsidian knife"; and this telling account of a duty done: "he sweeps the whole of the patio, gathers up the leaves and refuse, fills the pannier-basket, hitches it up on to his shoulders and holds it by a band across his forehead, and thus, a beast of burden, goes out to deposit the garbage at the side of one of the little roads leading out of the city."

Lawrence writes degradingly of the mozo but the mozo does not budge for Lawrence. There is an impasse between the two, an impasse Lawrence tries to overcome by theorizing on what the mozo knows and how the mozo lives, the way the mozo learns language, how the mozo uses language, how the mozo subverts language to get what he wants. Lawrence hypothesizes Rosalino is merely mimicking the white man when he uses language, trying to copy him "exactly like a parrot," as the writer says, reaffirming to him and those men like him that their ways of using language, their ways of thinking, are the best, are the norm.

But Rosalino's tricksterish ways disprove Lawrence's hypothesis. The mozo refuses tasks outright, he gets moody, he plays dumb. He rains on Lawrence's picky and demanding European parade at every turn. Lawrence may write prose exuding control and mastery and aggression but the writer is at the mercy of his most American muse, the mozo.

What does Rosalino think of Lawrence? A question that cannot be answered because there is no history for Rosalino. If we were to speculate upon what Rosalino thought of Lawrence, of how the mozo viewed the jefe, trying to assemble some account of Rosalino's days with Lawrence, of how Lawrence spoke to him and demanded of him, of how Lawrence gazed at Rosalino like a muse with pen in hand, writing the mozo into existence at his desk as the mozo swept, dusted, poured, and labored, then we would have to read between the lines of Lawrence's prose. His story is in Lawrence's hands.

IN MEXICO, I am a tourist. No shame to my game. Selfie stick? Check. Cheesy smile? Check. Fanny pack? Check. A large part of me has to admit to the fact I want to be a tourist. I have never had the experience of going someplace and knowing I am there with some money to spend, of being able to revel in this not-belonging, to be in a new landscape for but a joyful moment. Tourists growing up were the adorably white boys and girls in the Disney ads mailed to our home. My mother would subscribe to get brochures and promo VHS tapes and other such items in the hopes someday, somehow, we, too, would find ourselves on the front of a brochure, smiling bright and happy. The first time I ever get on a flight to experience what it is like to be a tourist I am sixteen. We go to Florida and to Disney. We take pictures with Mickey and Minnie. We visit Cinderella's castle. We melt in the Florida heat. I do all these touristy things knowing in the back of my mind this all came with a price, this was all possible with a sacrifice. The settlement for my brother's death gives us a nice chunk of money. Enough to go on a flight together, go to Disney, enough so I can know there is a world beyond our small town, enough though it is never enough to replace a brother, to take away the hurt of a brother's loss. It's a small world, after all.

THERE'S SOMETHING ALL-AMERICAN about the trailer park. The unpaved roadways, the American flags waving loud and proud, the junker car forever immobile in the patch of grass. The trailer park is the allotted space where the white people who could not live up to the norms of middle-class white America, those white people who fail at one form of whiteness, go.

We were always one bounced check away from the trailer park. My mother's pride, her uncompromising insistence we were not trailer-park trash, is what kept us out of one, is what kept us in the shack of a house on the outskirts of town. For my mother, the trailer park put on display, unabashedly and flagrantly, one's poverty. If you said to someone that you live on Meany Road or Mary Street, then they would know your condition, know you are down and out. My father did not want to live in a trailer park for very practical reasons. The trailer parks nearby were slowly being occupied by Mexican and Central American folks, folks who were hounded by immigration, every other week a raid upon their little mobile homes. My undocumented father would rather stay in our shack.

Lana del Rey sings of the trailer park, her voice a trailer-park aesthetic, a voice slumming it up for us loyal fans. "You have to take me right now / from this dark trailer-park life now," she sings in her song "Yayo," her voice sultry, a bit dazed and nasally. The lyric is but a fiction, for Lana, Lana the singer, Lana the person, has never lived in a trailer park. The biography of her on Wikipedia states she comes from a well-to-do family who lived in upstate New York. Why then the lyric about living in a trailer park, why the kind of low-down whiteness Lana embodies?

There she is in the video of her song "Ride," donning a feather headdress in the worst form of Native appropriation, jean short-shorts, American flag draped around her neck. Be in awe as she rides on the back of a motorcycle, a cadre of men in leather surrounding her on their bikes, a spectacle of white bodies riding down the open road somewhere in the desert. Canyons and cliffs and plateaus are in the backdrop as she arches her back, arms extended, reaching out in pursuit of the American spirit, like those days when Kerouac and Ginsberg and those other white American writers went in search of the American spirit, their America a fantasy of what they wanted

America to be. I dig this song—hard. I dig the way the music flows through me and I, too, feel the Arizona wind against my face, and the highways cutting through the desert, the freeing sensation of the body.

Yet the song must meet its end. Like any good high, there is a crash, a returning to reality. I am not Lana and in no way shape or form near her experience as Lana nor want to be like her. That fantasy that is the fantasy of Americanness, of feeling oneself as belonging to the category of American, is just that: a fantasy. The fantasy of an authentic "American" spirit. The essence of which is constituted by the perpetual erasure of living indigenous peoples and lands, and off the insistent dismissal that these settler lands were made bountiful and economically productive off the labor of African peoples. But I can't help but think how well she pulls off whatever this is she is pulling off. I believe in her whiteness, I want to believe in her whiteness so American, so authentically American and white. Let it be so, I plead to myself, so I can believe there is an American identity out there we can all aspire to. And it might in fact be so but in the back of my mind I can't help but think of her own upbringing and her masterful ability to create an aesthetic around a version of whiteness so deplored. By camouflaging herself as something she is not, she makes cool what is so frequently the butt end of jokes: the trailer park ethos. This is the magic in her all-American video, in her all-American aesthetic, what makes Lana so uniquely American and why we want her to be so.

THERE'S NO WAY if you are a tourist in Mexico you are not stopping at the house of Frida Kahlo. E— and I walk through Frida's house in awe of everything. The little bed on which she slept. The collection of books she read for inspiration. The striking blue of the house. The tiled countertops in the kitchen. The many self-portraits of her.

The first time I encounter Kahlo is in a graduate course on modernist literature and culture. The professor, to put it lightly, is eccentric, and as Maggie Nelson puts it about this professor we shared, "It's like she's pulling Post-it notes out of her hair and lecturing from them." We hurtle through three to four writers and artists a day, as if we are sprinting with no finish line in mind, the professor favoring surrealism, that movement of dreams and the unconscious, where writers and artists were creating from the depths of their consciousness. Favoring her PowerPoint slideshows, the professor presents a slide with Kahlo's *What the Water Gave Me*. The painting is of Frida in her bathtub, pudgy toes and red-painted nails, imagery in the water from former paintings: a skyscraper, a conch shell, her parents, a dress, two women holding one another. In the water of Frida's bathtub is the Americas, its brown women, its skyscrapers, its plants, all there in this topsy-turvy dreamscape painting.

Frida is a portal to Mexico, one portal into the history of Mexico, to its people and its rhythms, and Frida is a portal to myself. I am a different person than I was during my high school or college years. I let everyone know in my graduate program who and what I am. I am out and proud on social media. I put up pictures of my father and of my Mexican family. I no longer pass as anything other than the person I want to be, authentically and truthfully.

A year before this trip E— and I go to an exhibit at the Botanical Gardens in the Bronx displaying the plants Frida used to cultivate and was inspired by, and some of her paintings. There's the *Flower of Life*, a poinsettia-looking plant, what looks to be the sex organs of a male and female, the duality of life and its origins. There's the *Still Life with Parrot and Fruit*, a watermelon and orange bitten into, other fruits ripe and full of life, a green parrot perched on top of them. There's the *Portrait of Luther Burbank*, the American botanist who created many hybrids of plants, a man transformed into a tree whose roots sap the energy from a lifeless corpse, life and death.

A day after we visit the exhibition my Puerto Rican grandmother, a woman who was a mother to me, dies. All I can think of is the little exhibition in the Bronx, the plants wilting and blooming, the paintings vibrant, so alive, and to what Frida gave to me: where there is sorrow, there is joy; where there is death, there will always be life.

MY MOTHER ASKS me when I will go to Puerto Rico. Soon, I say, saying soon every time she asks, not knowing why this trip never seems to happen. Soon becomes not quite soon because

Hurricane Maria strikes the island, leveling so much of it and leaving the island in a precarious position. I'm upset at myself for not going because now the town my grandmother was born and raised in, Salinas, will not be the Salinas my grandmother knew. There will not be the roadways that she walked, the buildings that she went into, the house she inhabited. I'm afraid I will return to the land I have never been to with no history, no point of reference, no way in which to access this part of my story, this part of the returning.

THAT THING CALLED the tourist. The surveyors of lands and their pleasures. The tourist demands a landscape that will accommodate their every whim and fancy. The tourist wants a landscape fit to be consumed with little or no resistance from the environment, the people. The tourist requests a certain kind of experience of a place. The tourist is so needy for a particular kind of experience.

I try to deny this impulse while in Mexico. This impulse to demand, to use the money I am spending as a weapon against the people and their land I am visiting. I let myself wander, observing the activity around me, the footfalls of tourists and the pandering of vendors, men and their looks and women and their hurried steps, the life and the masses of life moving. I see people on the streets I want to photograph working or interacting or what have you but I resist. I instead turn to my notebook to jot down these characters in my drama, characterizing them and emplotting them and giving them purpose in ways funneled through my outsider lens, my Mexican self in the diaspora. I try to make sure I do not interfere or intrude upon events that are in no way shape or form meant for my inclusion, opting instead to be a bystander, to be a presence when I can, when I have to be, when I ought to be.

I am a tourist in Mexico. But I want to think I am a different kind. One rooted, one whose roots can reattach to the land, one who makes sure not to put roots where his roots do not belong. I am a stranger in Mexico, a land where nobody knows my name, and where nobody might know how to say my name. This boy who is too Mexican and Puerto Rican in some places, with some kinds of people, and in other places and with other people not Mexican and Puerto Rican enough. How can I be a tourist in a land some deem mine, a land I should know, a land I should find familiar? Mexico is nothing familiar to me. It is a terrain I want to continue knowing, continuing exploring, continue experiencing. I want to do all this further exploration not in the way most tourists do, most tourists whose quest to experience and know mimics far too closely the conquerors of yesterday, replicating too easily the power dynamics which gave shape to this unequal, this suffering, Americas. I want to be in the world, with others, those I know and those who are strangers, gently, with attention to their lives and differences. I want to belong not to a land or a national identity, not the belonging that is wanting to possess, to have, to lay claim to. I want the belonging that is the shared desire for caring better for the lives of those we don't know. The belonging to the shared goal of wanting the well-being and thriving of the neighbor I do not know, the familiar face of the stranger seen every day in town or the subway ride to work, or the masses of people in far-flung places we will never know. The belonging to the commitment to unlearn what we have come to understand as normal ways of being and living together on this planet. The normality of possessive individualism, monetary accumulation at all costs, and lawful exploitation of others which colonialism and capitalism has wrought across this Americas, and this planet. This is the Americas I want to be a part of. This is the Americas I imagine in my head as I undertake the role of the tourist. Another kind, another way.

"AN OCTOPUS OF ice. Deceptively reserved and flat / it lies 'in grandeur and in mass' / beneath a sea of shifting snow-dunes," begins Marianne Moore's poem "An Octopus," a poem about her experience visiting Mount Rainier and traveling through the northwest United States in 1922. The poem describes the mountain and the landscape, its "twenty-eight ice-fields from fifty to five hundred feet thick / of unimagined delicacy," and "the fir-trees, in 'the magnitude of their root systems,'" interspersed with snatches of prose taken from guidebooks on the mountain and travel literature. Moore adapts the ordinary description of the mountains and landscapes for poetic effect, a cut-and-paste job where the poem becomes a palimpsest, a text many-voiced, many-layered. The poem is all description and no action, landscapes "composed of calcium gems and alabaster pillars, / topaz, tourmaline crystals and amethyst quartz," where describing is the means through which a plot, or a desire for a plot, a demand for conflict and narrative and conclusions, appears. The American landscape in Moore's collage-like description is vivid interconnection. This coordinate on the map of the Americas becomes irresistible through Moore's pen.

Far less poetic than Moore's account, Christopher Columbus describes his first time seeing the island of Hispaniola through contrast to Europe and in descriptive terms that will ignite the imagination of centuries of other men bent on changing the composition of the planet.

> All these islands are extremely fertile and this one particularly so. It has many large harbors finer than any I know in Christian lands, and many large rivers. All this is marvelous. The land is high and has many ranges of hills, and mountains incomparably finer than Tenerife. All are most beautiful and various in shape, and all are accessible. They are covered with tall trees of different kinds which seem to reach the sky. I have heard that they never lose their leaves, which I can well believe, for I saw them as green and

> lovely as they are in Spain in May; some were flowering, some bore fruit and others were at different stages according to their nature . . .
>
> There are many kinds of birds and varieties of fruit. In the interior are mines and a very large population. Hispaniola is a wonder. The mountains and hills, the plains and meadowlands are both fertile and beautiful. They are most suitable for planting crops and for raising cattle of all kinds, and there are good sites for building towns and villages. The harbors are incredibly fine and there are many great rivers with broad channels and the majority contain gold.

A LAND SO richly described, so supple and giving in its composition, one can almost not blame Columbus for the history he will enact, for the disease and war and the depopulations he will bring about. King Ferdinand and Queen Isabella are convinced: these islands in the Americas are too beautiful, too picturesque to live without.

This inability to go without is so American. The western United States is opened up for white settlers to get a shot at the American dream, in the process corralling the original and rightful owners into reservations, a problem cast away to the edges of American society. The white populations in the cities across the settler nation known as the United States want more space and more to give their children, and less crime and less immigrants, so they go in their masses to the small towns, living out their lives in PTA meetings and minivans and the white picket fences. Now those migrations of white Americans who fled to the suburbs to escape those huddled masses in their darkness are returning, staking claims on what they did not earn, forcing out those who tirelessly and unendingly fought to call their city and their neighborhoods home.

W. E. B. Du Bois, while traveling on train through the southern United States, describes Georgia in this way:

> This is the Black Belt of Georgia. Dougherty County is the west end of the Black Belt, and men once called it the Egypt of the Confederacy. It is full of historic interest. First there is the Swamp, to the west, where the Chickasawhatchee flows sullenly southward. The shadow of an old plantation lies at its edge, forlorn and dark. Then comes the pool; pendant gray moss and brackish waters appear, and waters filled with wildfowl. In one place the wood is on fire, smoldering in dull red anger; but nobody minds. Then the swamp grows beautiful; a raised road, built by chained Negro convicts, dips down into it, and forms a way walled and almost covered in living green . . .
>
> And as I crossed, I seemed to see again that fierce tragedy of seventy years ago. Osceola, the Indian-Negro chieftain, had risen in the swamps of Flor-

> ida, vowing vengeance. His war-cry reached the red Creeks of Dougherty, and their war-cry rang from the Chattahoochee to the sea. Men and women and children fled and fell before them as they swept into Dougherty. In yonder shadows a dark and hideously painted warrior glided on,—another and another, until three hundred had crept into the treacherous swamp. Then the false slime closing about them called the white men from the east. Waist-deep, they fought beneath the tall trees, until the war-cry was hushed and the Indians glided back into the west. Small wonder the wood is red.

THEN FOLLOWS IN the timeline of history the clinking and clanking of the chains from those thousands upon thousands enslaved, the sound a feature of the landscape Du Bois experiences. Du Bois's American landscape is a landscape marred by history. The wood stained in blood, the war cries still echoing in the swamps, the convicts and their labor that made the road. Slavery's presence is not evidenced solely in the relics of a bygone time, the displaying of chains in a museum or the tours of plantations or slave shacks still standing. Every inch and detail of this United States landscape, as Du Bois shows, is itself the evidence of enslavement.

There is unfathomable power in the describer's hands. They can create landscapes, they can destroy landscapes, they can manipulate a landscape in their image. Perhaps we all do the latter in these Americas. Modifying and tweaking and adjusting a landscape to suit our needs, to accommodate us, to explain a theory. All just words we bend to our will.

I SEE MY deceased Mexican grandmother in every old woman I pass on these Mexico City streets. Long black hair? Check. Wide-set nose? Check. A largeness of body frame? Check. There is one woman I see on the way to get food who I am convinced is a reincarnation of her. She is seated on the ground. A pink shirt and a pink skirt billow out onto the sidewalk, the pink fabric creating space, an extension of the body. Her hair is in two tight plaits that drape across her big chest. Her face is lined with wrinkles in a radial pattern, circling out and out across the brown skin, as the black eyes twinkle starlike.

Beside her are muñequitas. They appear to be handmade. The muñequitas are little miniatures of the woman: plaited hair, a pink shirt and dress, the black eyes.

As I pass by I note how cute the muñequitas are out loud.

"Señor . . . ven aver las muñequitas . . . señor, por favor . . . señor . . ."

I want to stop and look. I want to ask her how she's doing. I want to know about her life here on the street in which she's perched, her pink-and-brown contrast. I want to gaze in the twinkling of her eyes and try to find an account of her life, her greatest joys, her greatest pains, her greatest triumphs. I want her to tell me about my grandmother, about the woman who raised my father, about the woman whose modes of being and modes of living continue to pass down to her kin, her grandchildren she has never met. I want there to be parallels between this stranger and the stranger that is my grandmother. This woman with the brown skin, the buxom body, the indigenous features of her face is a living portrait of the woman I know through photos. This woman sells her dolls on the street and my grandmother sold her candies on the street. These women strangers who share similar trajectories, who live out similar lives in Mexico, who I want to feel are kin and kind.

E— looks at me. He notices my hesitation, my thinking. He knows of my futile attempts at knowing my origins, of hoping someday a document will materialize, a diary, a letter, a birth certificate, detailing the life and times of the people who came before me. He knows I am staring at this woman because I want to know my history so desperately. He knows I am fighting against history. He knows the records and chronology of history were never meant to account for people like my grandmother and father. Our history is not the tick and the tock of the Gregorian calendar, this calendar imposed upon by men with their guns and their swords and their holy decrees, men who looked upon women like my grandmother and this stranger as bodies to be conquered, to be raped, to be put to work. Our history is a time out of joint, an oral record passed down and forgotten through time yet a memory alive in the ways our bodies hurt, grieve, love. Our history is a history of the body.

The woman is still on the ground.

"Señor . . . ven aver las muñequitas . . . señor, por favor . . . señor . . ."

E—'s waiting for me. He's hungry, as am I. I walk away and the woman keeps speaking, speaking in a chant-like way about her muñequitas and their craftmanship and about how far she has walked to get here in this place, this moment. Her words continue but I am out of earshot.

THE CUBAN INTELLECTUAL and writer José Martí in 1891 writes "Our America," a manifesto for the Americas. Martí is in pursuit of a distinctly American spirit, American ways of governing and thinking, trying to create a through-line through which the Americas can move forward in our divided continents. Martí casts the net wide by remembering the Black and the indigenous peoples who are in the Americas, and both are useful to Martí in order to draw distinctions from Europe. For in the darker races lie the secret of severing a European past, European modes of thinking, from an American one that will save these many nations in the Americas from their own ruin. Martí did not live long enough to see his Cuba turn into Fidel's Cuba, or Mexico into the corrupt state it is, or the

United States as a country changed and changing day by day by the bodies entering from Latin America.

Our America. Whose America? Universals are a particularly tricky thing to pull off in the Americas. There is no accord amongst our millions. My neighbors' America is not my America, my father's America is not my America, and E—'s America is not my America. How, then, to make an America, from sea to shining sea, for everyone? Édouard Glissant, philosopher and poet, writes about the common thread in American poetics.

> We have seen that the poetics of the American continent, which I characterize as being a search for temporal duration, is opposed in particular to European poetics, which are characterized by the inspiration or the sudden burst of a single moment. It seems that, when dealing with the anxiety of time, American writers are prey to a kind of future remembering. By that I mean that it is almost certain that we are writers in an embryonic phase and our public is yet to come . . .
>
> To confront time is, therefore, for us to deny its linear structure. All chronology is too immediately obvious, and in the works of the American novelist we must struggle against time in order to reconstitute the past, even when it concerns those parts of the Americas where historical memory has not been obliterated.

> It follows that, caught in the swirl of time, the American novelist dramatizes it in in order to deny it better or to reconstruct it; I will describe us, as far as this is concerned, as those who shatter the stone of time.

THE AMERICAN WRITER is a curious thing on our path toward any America where that plural possessive can exist. The American writer is a writer with, well, no real definition to it. Is she white or is she Black? Is he first-generation or second? Are they an immigrant to the Americas or not? The American writer is a generalization for a body of specificity. The American writer, according to Glissant, is a writer against time, who reconstructs time according to their needs, who is out of the linearity of time itself. In Junot Díaz's *The Brief Wondrous Life of Oscar Wao*, *fukú*, an indescribable curse that either came from the "screams of the enslaved," or the "death bane of the Tainos," or "a demon drawn into Creation through the nightmare door that was cracked open in the Antilles," is a thing that began in the past of the Americas and continues to plague its subjects. Oscar, the protagonist of the novel, must live with this curse upon his body, this curse so American, a curse working to strip him of a future, a curse of the past that will, by the end of the novel, end both his present and future life.

Then there is Henry David Thoreau, venturing into the wilderness of the Americas in pursuit of beauty, in pursuit of something distinct from the industrialization of the America yet to be, who writes of the disappearance of the indigenous peoples in his present, the entrance of the white man in the Americas creating time and futurity: "Their wares of stone, their arrowheads and hatchets, their pestles, and the mortars in which they pounded Indian corn before the white man had tasted it, lay concealed in the mud of the river bottom." The material objects of the past continue into the present because Thoreau remembers they are there. His present reaching back to the past in order to remember for a future reader.

Lest we forget Toni Morrison's *Beloved* and Sethe's rememory, that noun of a word that brings to the present the past, the unceasing past, forging a landscape of memories that continue on no matter how far one travels, how far one tries to escape.

Our America? Where is it? Columbus and his conquistador friends and the British pilgrims at Plymouth and the missionaries entering from every shore on the hemisphere arrive and they say this is the land of God. Holier than thou, they, in the name of God, march in search of gold, in search of freedom from the tyrannies of Europe, all the while stealing freedoms from others, displacing people, ravaging the earth, forcibly bringing people from another continent to work the stolen lands. This is all done with reasonable intentions, noble ones in fact, because the land is uncivilized, barbarities happening all across the Americas, these irrational people with their altars to their gods and their blood rituals proof of their degenerate minds. The land needs reason. These foreigners from Europe take it upon themselves to draft up laws and decrees and rationales that will bring order to the Americas, that will see an end to the chaos of irrationality. And their laws and reason carry into today, in the reasonable wars and deportations and police killings and incarceration, and into tomorrow, unless . . .

The American writer writing in the aftermath of 1492 must be a writer of irrationality. These are illogical and impossible and continuously exploited geographies we inhabit. The American writer must struggle against the reason imposed upon us, the rationales we are told we should abide by, the logic of the thoughts we should be thinking. The American writer must be unreasonable at every turn, irrational with the pen, dangerous with our thoughts. The Americas are exhausting, and they wear their subjects down into disjointed prose, the prose/poetry like Claudia Rankine's that equals no more than a drawn-out sigh.

> To live through the days sometimes you moan like deer. Sometimes you sigh. The world says stop that. Another sigh. Another stop that. Moaning elicits laughter, sighing upsets. Perhaps each sigh is drawn into existence to pull in, pull under, who knows; truth be told, you could no more control those sighs than that which brings the sighs about.

TAKE THE UNITED States South in Jean Toomer's *Cane*, vignettes of twentieth-century Southern life, people living Southern days of wonder and extraordinariness and realities unrecognizable:

> Rhobert wears a house, like a monstrous diver's helmet, on his head. His legs are banty-bowed and shaky because as a child he had rickets. He is way down. Rods of the house like antennae of a dead thing, stuffed, prop up in the air. He is way down. He is sinking. His house is a dead thing that weights him down. He is sinking as a diver would sink in mud should the water be drawn off. Life is a murky, wiggling, microscopic water that compresses him. Compresses his helmet and would crush it the minute that he pulled his head out. He has to keep it in. Life is water that is being drawn off.

OR THE UNREAL, the irrational, of Salvador Plascencia's novel taking place along the U.S.–Mexico border, *The People of Paper*, where entire passages are blacked out, holes are in the paper, and disturbances of all kinds interrupt the act of reading:

> That is what happens, the natural physics of the world. You fuck a white boy and my shingles loosen, the calcium in my bones depletes, my clothes begin to unstitch.

> Everything weakens. I lose control. The story goes astray. The trajectory of the novel altered because of him. They colonize everything: the Americas, our stories, our novels, our memories . . .

OUR AMERICA? OUR America, if it can be said to be shared, is this haunted landscape, this irrational geography, the bodies and the imaginings and the places and the memories existing in the today, the today where the spirits of yesterday carry forward into our tomorrow, our tomorrow into yesterday, this most history-riddled terrain. The arrowheads in the mud, the sighs, the *fukú* traveling across continents, the Rhoberts across the U.S. South, the weakenings, the rememories of yesterdays that are and are not ours insisting on being in the present, in the future, at all times. The Americas is a vortex of time, a time of precursors and a time of aftermaths, a time that makes little sense. The American writer or the writer writing in the Americas works with the universal that history and history's present and history's future must be reckoned with, that this chaos of rationality and logic and reasonings must be our muse at all times. Our America? Ours if we can imagine it.

NECK TURNED AT a 90-degree angle, forward-facing, a fixed mood in the face. The back is reclined as the weight of the body is balanced on the elbows, seductively, tantalizingly. A bowl in the hands above the stomach, an offering. The body is on an altar held up by two kneeling men. The color in black and white.

I can't look away. I am here alone in this dimly lit gallery gazing at the black-and-white picture of a man posing as Chacmool, a form of Mesoamerican sculpture. E— has wandered off to another part of this mausoleum-like space designed by the artist Diego Rivera, a museum dedicated to Mesoamerican artifacts and art. Obsidian knives, pottery adorned with imagery, statues of gods and men and animals in basalt and limestone abound. This picture with a man posing as Chacmool is undated, untitled, and without any kind of citation.

I search quickly on my phone to learn more info about this Chacmool. These stone statues are not representations of gods but are just a figure, a man in repose, possibly a slain warrior. The stone statues are depictions of people offering sacrifices to the gods.

I keep staring at the eyes of the man posing as Chacmool. Their darkness has allure. I have looked at men with eyes like this.. These are the men of the Americas whom I gaze upon. Men who have left islands behind for Washington Heights. Men whose families have spent generations in Harlem. Men who live out a diaspora in Brooklyn. These men of the Americas understand this sacrificial desire, this willingness to see the self obliterated for the sake of pleasure, our pleasure united. They know what must be done at all costs. We see the flame of the altar in each other's eyes.

Men of the Americas, hear my call, I at your altar willing and ready, let my body be—

"Marcos . . . come look at this."

E— is there in the frame of the door leading out of the room. He gives me his public smile. A smile disarmed, removed of the darkness I know it can contain when he and I are alone, in twilight, in bed.

"Coming . . ."

BEFORE I HEAD off to Mexico for the first time, I want some fun in the sun. A Latin lover to romance me for a night, maybe, a hunk of a man bronzed and six-packed to ogle over on the beach, perhaps. I want the cliché experience, whatever that means, of Miami. I used to play *Grand Theft Auto: Vice City*, which was a nice mash-up of every cliché you can imagine: neon lights, drinking on the beach, the Cuban gangsters. Miami is a cliché like many places are, because an everyday Pedro must piece together the world from the TV he watches and the video games he plays and the books he reads, his imagination assembling the world, there his Machu Picchu, there his Eiffel Tower, there his Timbuktu, all images salvaged from his day to day.

The beaches are unlike any I have ever seen. Tropical, the water so warm, the sky so blue, the foam on the sand so white. How many feet have traversed through these sands? How many boats have docked on these shores? On the horizon I can make out the outline of ships made of wood and their masts steering through time, the winds and the tides carrying empires across the oceans, the gold and the iron and the metal of conquests but detritus in the sand. There the bootprints of Columbus, hilt of a sword in his hand, eyes surveying the landscape ahead of him for the taking. There his men with their muskets, pointing the barrels of their guns toward the people they deem savages in the brush, shooting and shooting until they are no more, until their presence is but arrowheads lost amongst the sand. There the ships bringing men and women squished into ship decks, chained and dirtied with excrement, a human cargo ready to labor for centuries in the plantations of men who laid claim to land not theirs to claim.

The Miami of today does not reveal these histories. Then again, how can it with these metallic and sky-high buildings, the Jet Skis blazing through the waves, the men and women with their tans? There's no room for this history I see in the waves and beaches in the Miami landscape of 2017. That history so American is too ugly to remember, too much of a stain to let anyone remember. Better to forget, we are told, as the yacht in the distance glides down the waters, people with their wealth and plenty sipping champagne surveying the land from afar, surveying what can be gained and what can be lost, so alike to their ancestors who sailed those oceans so long ago, who sailed into the Americas ready to make a most grand entrance into the pages of history.

The Americas really do wonders for the imagination.

CORTÉS THE CONQUEROR of conquerors slashes and burns through the lower half of the continent convinced there is gold to be found, mountains and hills and caverns of it, destroying all that he so desires so his fantasy of gold can be satiated. Bartolomé de las Casas defends the rights of the indigenous peoples to be rid of slavery and, in turn, advocates that African bodies should be used as forced labor because he uses his mind to convince himself the Africans are more durable, more suited to working. Gabriel García Márquez conjures up the sweeping history of revolutions and tragedies in an imaginary country and writes one of the most-read books in the world.

The Americas were lands never meant to be yet, through the imagination, through the labors of minds coming together to issue mandates and decrees and rationales and reason, they are. The Americas, like and unlike many places, are an imagined space. It always has been because that is the history we have of the land, the history that we have inherited.

The Americas—that is, the imagination of the Americas—has its way of imagining us into existence. Particular histories produce particular results. Cause and effect span centuries. Audre Lorde in her biomythography writes of a woman who lives on One Hundred and Forty-Second Street in Harlem named Delois, a woman whose movements and body are so particular to the Americas, to its ebbs and flows, to its migrations and diasporas, to its flare and pomp, that she shapes Lorde into the woman she is:

> Her crispy hair twinkled in the summer sun as her big proud stomach moved her on down the block while I watched, not caring whether or not she was a poem. Even though I tied my shoes and tried to peep under her blouse as she passed by, I never spoke to Delois, because my mother didn't. But I loved her, because she moved like she felt she was somebody special, like she was somebody I'd like to know someday. She moved like how I thought god's mother must have moved, and my mother, once upon a time, and someday maybe me.

Observer describing her most American subject, dear Delois, these words to you because Lorde and I desire your unruliness and carefreeness and pride, your refusal to be but a subject objectified.

In Sandra Cisneros's poem "You Bring Out the Mexican in Me," the voice of the poem is as "arrogant as Manifest Destiny," assertive, forthcoming, demanding, a most American attitude though set in a different tenor, a feminine voraciousness: "You bring out the Mexican in me. / The hunkered thick dark spiral." The all-consuming voice, the feminine mystique Americana, the voice of illogic, unreasonable and unwilling to reason, a wild and untamed appetite to feel, to sense, to be without apology.

Toni Morrison's *Sula* gives us the character of Eva, a woman whose leg mysteriously disappears, disappearing into rumors of how and when and where it happened, Eva mythologizing her missing limb to explain away what a mother will do, what a mother must do, to provide for her children in a small town in the Americas:

> Unless Eva herself introduced the subject, no one ever spoke of her disability; they pretended to ignore it, unless, in some mood of fancy, she began some fearful story about it—generally to entertain children. How the leg got up by itself one day and walked on off. How she hobbled after it but it ran too fast. Or how she had a corn on her toe and it just grew and grew until her whole foot was a corn and then it traveled on up her leg and wouldn't stop growing until she put a red rag at the top but by that time it was already at her knee.
>
> Somebody said Eva stuck it under a train and made them pay off. Another said she sold it to a hospital for $10,000.

EVA DEAREST, THERE spinning yarns for the children, a leg and no leg, a now and then of the Americas, because all stories in the Americas are stories of loss, of what is missing in plain sight.

The Americas are continents of characters. Walking eccentricities, irregular and producing irregularities in types, the local and the national and the hemispheric and the global clashing, a big bang of identity.

This is the Americas. A mass of land with its history and specificities and differences and imaginings.

I'M MOCTEZUMA THERE upon the pyramid. Picture please, I ask a fellow traveler, photo-ready as I'm looking outward at an empire rising, an empire falling. Photo flash as the blue of the Mexican sky behind me reveals the omen Moctezuma sees signaling the arrival of the conquerors, a comet, a fire in the sky, the siege on a hemisphere. More pyramids in the distance of the photo and Moctezuma is calling for peace, a peace pierced by the iron blade of Cortés, the orbit of one world ending and another beginning. Five hundred years later and I am on the summit of my ancestors taking pictures for the scrapbook, Moctezuma and his people dispersed across a continent, living on as farmworkers, inventors of change, churro sellers, the writers of revolutions. The world turns in the days of cell phones and drones and tyrants, as it did in the days of Moctezuma and his gods, and as it will do in the undefinable tomorrow.

I REMEMBER LEARNING about the sublime in my undergraduate Introduction to Literary Studies course. The Romanticists, if memory serves correctly, were obsessed with the sublime. What is it? I think it has something to do with being in such awe in the face of something so great, so terrifyingly beautiful, that words are inadequate to document what is happening to you. The image in the textbook we had to use for class on the sublime (as well as the Wikipedia page on the subject, and other websites too) is Caspar David Friedrich's *Wanderer above the Sea of Fog.* The image is of a man in fine clothing standing at what appears to be the tip of some mountainous terrain. His back is turned toward the viewer as he looks on at the rocks breaking through the cloud cover, and in the near distance an outline of a mountain is visible. He is experiencing the sublime, one assumes, because before him is such natural grandeur, such heightened beauty he can only stare in awe.

We are on our way back from the town of Taxco. We are in the van of our small tour group. E— is in the seat in front of me, and I am in the back sprawled out, looking out the window of the Mexican countryside. There are mountains, there is fog, there are trees in mass. There a house on one of the hilltops, there a dog roaming for food. A cliffside like an oil-painted tableau on display at the Metropolitan Museum of Art.

Tears start coming out of my eyes. E— doesn't notice and I don't want him to. I need to be alone for whatever this is my body is doing. Is this the sublime? Is this what they talked about all those years ago in that introductory course? Is this what those explorers and missionaries and conquistadors saw when they first climbed Mount Everest, or saw the Grand Canyon, or ascended Machu Picchu, surveying the world from the tops of it, seeing the routes of commerce and capital and war opening up to them? Is this what the man in the portrait is experiencing?

I do not see some truth about myself in this Mexican landscape, I do not see the world opening up for the taking in this new terrain. I don't think this is the sublime because the sublime is a tradition bound to the bodies who coined the word, to the bodies who mapped the beauty of the world according to their interests, to the bodies who saw beauty in the world and then sought to monopolize on such beauty, to make beauty a thing in their image.

What this is, whatever I am feeling, is something else.

E— turns around. He smiles, the dimples in the cheeks, his toothy grin. I wipe the tears and smile back.

I'VE NEVER BEEN to Montana, never been anywhere near its state boundaries, but out of every state in these United States, this is the state I want to travel to most. Why Montana? a friend asks: Montana, it's the whitest state out there. I don't really have an answer besides the remoteness of it, the pictures online of mountains and prairies, the distinction it has from the New York I have lived in for nearly a decade.

But the whiteness of Montana has no allure to me, the fantasy of a hunky-dory white space nothing but a nightmare now. There is no longer the desire to use my lightness of skin to my advantage, to bleed into the background of white and forget, just forget for a moment what is, what was, what will eventually be in this hemisphere that has created me. Because white America, or the way whiteness operates in America, is about forgetting, or forcibly making yourself forget, about time and history and the events throughout the centuries. Forgetting how these are indigenous people's lands, now and always. Forgetting how these Americas were and are shaped by revolutions and massacres and enslavement and protest and uprisings. Forgetting the local contexts of resistance shaping every corner of this geography, no matter how white, cisgender, heterosexual, or patriarchal they may appear. Crisis in every region, tumult in every terrain that no longer, no more, can be denied. The working on behalf of another Americas, the imagining of an Americas rid of settler colonial white supremacy, is happening.

Places like we imagine Montana to be, overwhelmingly white, devoid of diversity, are no threat to me because I am no longer the sixteen-year-old boy who tries to deny with all his might who he is in that small town. I am no longer the eight-year-old boy who feels ashamed of who he calls family and where that family originates from. I am no longer the twenty-one-year-old boy who wanted to bleed into the whiteness of twenty-first-century New York City. I'm no longer *that* boy but I'm still a boy at the end of the day because I want to be, because I have been robbed of my boyhood, of my ability to just be a boy. I let myself throw tantrums on occasion, I overindulge in cartoons, I fantasize and strategize and theorize about the world much like a child would, a child full of enthusiasm, hope, and the profound need to keep on imagining more caring, more thoughtful, worlds.

Just an everyday Pedro in the Americas.

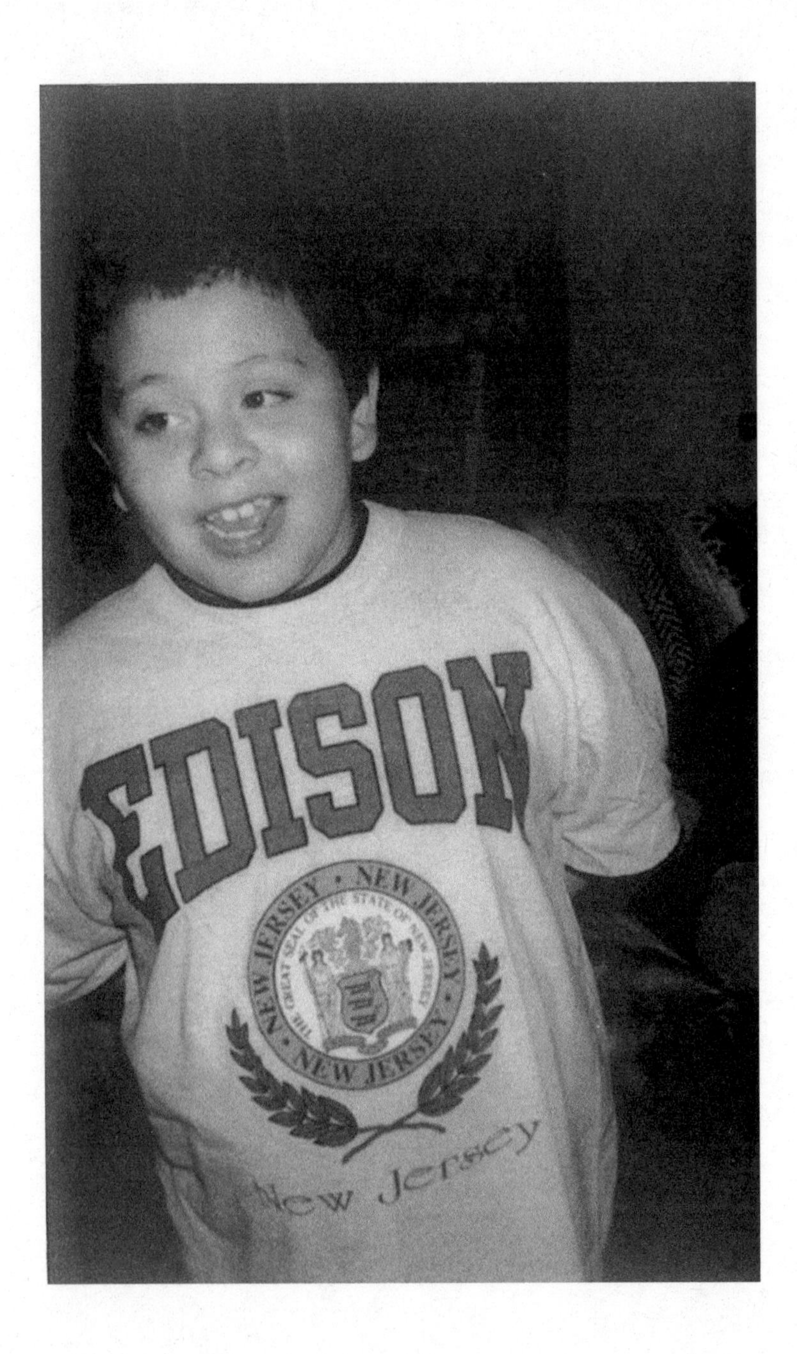
EDISON
NEW JERSEY · NEW JERSEY
THE GREAT SEAL OF THE STATE OF NEW JERSEY
NEW JERSEY
New Jersey

EPILOGUE

TO PEDRO

It's just you in the photograph. Your goofy smile, the two big front teeth, the gums and gaps. On some Monday night after school, or Saturday evening playing video games. Is your big brother telling a joke and it makes you laugh? Do you make a funny face and give theatrics because you know the camera is on you? Leaning over, the big and burly frame, swagger-full with the hands clasped behind as the camera's flash washes over your skin in an instant, a Polaroid memory, where there is joy.

Your first two decades of life you will come to memorialize as ones of great suffering. Far-too-memorable moments and events of compounded pain defining how you will understand childhood and young adult life. And all of this is true, all of it valid, and there is no doubt of that.

But do you feel that? The rush, the elation, the warm upsurge of life this little Pedro in this image is exuding? This photograph is no memory anymore. Your older self cannot remember the context, the date or time, who took it, because it is probably just an ordinary day in the nineties. Unremarkable, and forgettable, because it is not defined by a moment that scarred your psyche and body. It does not fit into the narrative you have had to compose for yourself for so long to make sense of those years. It is not a story others demanded of you. All of this everydayness is lost to you but this photo is yours, too. Fleeting though it may be, maybe even a happy-faced ruse, this photographic joy must be claimed, where claiming becomes an act of creation. Creations built from the fragments of memories suppressed, overlooked, or consumed by the proliferative sadness that defined this period of life. Creating another timeline of moments where joy, the mundane, pleasure, and encounters with the beautiful can exist. The perpetual losing to his father during a game of Jenga. The playing of his Game Boy to kill the boredom. Waking up during spring mornings to his grandmother outside tending to the garden, her careful attention to the growth of life. Holding a beetle in his hand dazzled by the form of the little creature's body. His mother vacuuming the living room dancing to salsa and merengue, dancing to La India, Tito Nieves, Elvis Crespo, Frankie Ruiz, dancing her liberation there before him.

Like a photo album, I insert these creations into what exists already. These differing portraits of people and places side by side with the ones well imprinted in the mind. These moments of laughter and contemplation and boredom and appreciation on the same pages during the era of doubt, confusion, and an existence in question. Why do I need to live anymore?

runs through the mind of this little boy who is you from the moment he can form sentences, the moment he can express himself, the moment he can create memory. He thinks and he can only think of the end.

Pedro, why so down? To explain it is to explain a centuries-old saga.

Pedro, why the frown? To answer it is to bear the burden of the story only ever being one of pain and suffering, over and over again.

But we need this image of you so desperately. This other form of Pedro, this Pedro existing elsewhere. Pedro with the goofy smile, the dorky swagger, on some Monday or Saturday, laughing at a joke or being theatrical.

Pedro, would you like to live again? Living anew, Pedro with the big grin, in your multitudes? Pedro laughing rapturously, in this moment all yours for the savoring, smile wide and say cheese.

ACKNOWLEDGMENTS

This book would not have been possible if not for my father, Santiago. To his many teachings, his many theories, who taught me knowledge and imagining does not come solely from degrees and universities. I am indebted to him, siempre.

Gratitude to my mother, Yasmin, for sharing her stories, and for teaching me how the past is always present, always living in us.

Lauren, my agent, whose continued support and belief in my writing has been nothing but nurturing, and sustaining.

Ryan, my editor at Melville House, for believing in this book and these words, for transforming it into what it has become.

All the thanks to Jess Row whose class was the first space in which I was able to talk through and draft pieces of what would later become this book. His generosity and kindness has extended beyond that class, and for that I am grateful.

For providing critical feedback on the first full draft, for sitting with me through all the many conversations and venting sessions and tears related to this book, I give my fullest gratitude to my dear friend, Alex.

Finally, to my love, Emmanuel, whose intellect and care carried me to the end.